THE SPLINTERED EYE

THE SPLINTERED EYE

Beth S. Patric

NEW HORIZON PRESS
Far Hills, New Jersey

Distributed by
MACMILLAN PUBLISHING COMPANY
New York

Copyright © 1987 by New Horizon Press
All rights reserved. No part of this work may be reproduced or transmitted in any form or by any means, electronic or mechanical, including photocopy and recording, or by any information or retrieval system, except as may be expressly permitted by the 1976 Copyright Act or in writing from the publisher.

Library of Congress Cataloging-in-Publication Data

Patric, Beth S., 1949–
  The splintered eye.

  I. Title.
  PS3566.A777S7   1987   813'.54   87-12192
  ISBN 0-88282-031-1

New Horizon Press

*Dedicated to
My parents who encouraged
my dreams,
My husband who believed
in their reality*

Each man is in his Spectre's power
    Until the arrival of that hour
When his Humanity awake,
And cast his Spectre into the Lake.

> —William Blake
> Jerusalem

PART ONE

Someone had scrawled "Happy Reentry Jesus" in fat, uneven letters across the steel door. The annual countdown for Easter had begun. Gray-crusted snow freckled the street. Through the wire-skeined windows she could see dingy furrowed borders pushed back by the huge snow machines. She sat on one of the initial-scarred benches which lined the hall corridor—a fragile, wren-like creature, trembling.

    Was it yesterday I was brought here? she thought, her head aching as though it had felt the impact of shatterproof glass. The time on the large luminous clock suspended on the opposite wall was hard to distinguish. Running her tongue over dry, cracked lips, she sighed wistfully. "Tired, I must be too tired." Long, dark hair fell over her eyes as she squinted, trying to see through the strands. The

THE SPLINTERED EYE

rooms in which row after row of cots lay in neatly symmetrical lines were locked each day right after breakfast. She nervously darted toward the closest door and turned the knob.

"No luck," she said aloud in a child's whispery voice, peering into the dank collection of brooms, mops, and pails. "No luck." Visiting hours came twice a day but had not yet begun. Slowly, as she shuffled down the hall and drew nearer to the recreation room described in the pamphlet given to each patient, figures could be perceived—squirming forms which clenched and unclenched hands that did not remain still. A few inmates continuously popped plastic bubble sheets given them by uniformed aides. Most of the other facilities advertised in the pamphlet were nonexistent anyway, and no one read the booklets. The patients narrowed their eyes into slits in response to nurses who asked wearily that the hospital's written instructions be followed. Kristen wanted to obey. She wanted to be good. In the past, rules had been important, but now the words in the pamphlet appeared covered with a shimmery haze like that seen when the sun glistens, caught on a winter drift. Marks moved spasmodically before she could catch them and guess their meaning. "Please stop," she said. "You bloody fucking idiots, stop." She tossed the booklet to the floor.

Muffled sounds seemed to speak from other benches to each other, to themselves, to no one. One quivering voice said to her, "My name is Barbara Nored." The introduction was murmured by a high-cheek boned Nordic-looking girl. "I'm so happy here!"

"Here?" Kristen looked up. *Here* was Brookhaven State Asylum.

"You don't know what it's like. My husband's been married four times. He never works, just comes home, beats me and the baby, and leaves." The girl's pale-gold locks were pinned up in a chignon held with a tiny orange ribbon. She looked so clean that Kristen was afraid to stare too hard.

"What's your name?" the blonde spectre shyly asked, edging closer. "Mine's Barbara Nored. This is the third time I've tried to kill myself. They have to send you here after the third time. He doesn't give me any money. It's all right for me, but the baby has to eat." She held her wrists up. There were deep gashes stained in red across each one. They matched Kristen's own. "It never works, though."

I know, thought Kristen.

"It never works," the girl said with a smile. Leaning her head toward Kristen, she repeated, "What's your name? Mine's Barbara Nored." Each time, she confided her secret amiably and then added sweetly, "I'll have to try something else next time." Kristen smiled in return. The voice began fading in and out of her ear like a car radio passing beneath a series of bridges. What was screaming? A siren, a human voice, the sound of herself? Kristen Blakely was never quite sure. On the loudspeaker sounds wailed. She put two hands up to her ears to make the noise stop, could not, and began to moan.

THE SPLINTERED EYE

The-makeup-room-is-now-open. The-makeup-room-is-now-open-for-the-next-ten-minutes. Several shapes rose, maneuvering their way toward the windowless cubicle where everyone kept her toilet articles under the watchful eye of attendants who made sure no one would abuse the privilege of being alone to comb her hair and try suicide instead.

Another announcement blared: *It-is-5:30. The-phone-will-be-open-until-5:45.* One call per person was allowed each night. There were fifty patients. Long lines formed. Some never made a call. Some didn't want to.

A thing within her was holding its breath, and Kristen felt her heart pound as she made her way into the room with metal doorless stalls in which were the communal toilets. Shitting in the sight of others implied a camaraderie she hated.

Halfway into the bathroom she heard something pant behind her. "Hey, you're one of those narcissists," a husky, flirtatious voice said. "You like looking at yourself. Come here, sweetie, I'll make you feel better." The woman who walked toward the stall reached out with stubby nail-bitten fingers to squeeze Kristen's breast hard—harder—then bleakly she laughed. Cries welled up in Kristen's throat, choking her. Half-jumping across the toilet, she became entangled in her underpants. The sight of the gaunt girl within the metal mirrors which lined the far wall made her gasp. Tension rose within her and a tremor of repugnance. "Twenty-four, am I still twenty-four?"

THE SPLINTERED EYE

People had always spoken of her as "that golden girl." Now huge dark rings outlined her ghost-like eyes. Near them a small patch of hair was newly white and matted. "When did I comb it last?" Bending her head, she inhaled the pungent odor beneath her arm. The woman's deep-throated laughter carried across the room. Still, Kristen was captive to the sight of herself and moved closer to the mirrors. The stubble on her legs and under her arms as she lifted them cast a blurred, dark shadow whose reflection could be seen across the room. How ugly she was.

"What the hell is the matter with you staring like that, you crazy bitch? I'm made the same as you. See my cunt?" Spreading the hospital kimono wide, the angular middle-aged woman revealed her dark, thick pubic hair. Kristen swallowed, trying to speak. The woman moved closer. "Whatsamatter, need a fuck?"

Kristen opened her mouth wide, but no sound came. Screaming, she thought, I saw you screaming. For the first time she looked at the other figure. "This morning you were screaming."

As the woman laughed again, she revealed a gaping hole where two teeth should have been. Attendants had carried her into the ward right after breakfast. Dress wet, plastered above veined thighs. That same dark patch uncovered when she kicked at the guards who held her, swinging her monkey-like through the air.

She'd yelled, "You mother-fuckers hate all blacks. Put me down, you assholes." The woman

THE SPLINTERED EYE

was white. Her red hair revealed dark roots. "Up yours," she'd gestured.

"You give me an Excedrin headache," Mrs. Kranz, the senior nurse, had called back. Just then a flailing leg caught Kristen's right temple. When the nurse on duty saw what had happened, she became very concerned, reassuring Kristen like one would a child and feeding her from a paper cup filled with gold liquid Thorazine.

Thorazine made her head very hot; the fingers of her hand blurred as she brought them close to her face.

"Here," she cried to no one in particular as she watched the black and white figures on the clock become one.

"Sleep," she said, a grimace on her face. She slid down and the cool glazed floor came to meet her. An attendant strode over and propped her up like a stuffed doll.

"Be a good girl, Kristen, or you won't sleep tonight."

The woman had been carried into one of the rooms. While Mrs. Kranz unlocked the door, the attendants tried to hold the woman. But she managed to work herself free, throwing herself into a series of violent teeth-jamming fits.

"She's so tough," Mrs. Kranz said gruffly. "You could slam her against the door and she'd bounce right back. Juanita, if you don't stop this nonsense, we'll have to put you in the quiet room."

The quiet room was a bare cell with only a mattress on the floor. Juanita seemed to stop for a moment. Then gathering spittle in her mouth, she spewed it into Mrs. Kranz's alligator-like face. Finally a crew-cut, slightly-built intern happened by. Taking the syringe from the attendant's hand, he plunged it into the woman's arm. Kristen smiled knowingly.

The nurse who had given Kristen the golden liquid spoke. "Now she'll be all right." One could see Juanita in the room through the open doorway. Her arms and legs stuck out rigidly. Like a zombie she repeated, "Ah, ah, ah, ah." Soon the sound stopped. The woman had apparently fallen asleep.

At eleven o'clock patients lined up in the hallways and divided into three clusters for group therapy meetings. Since attendance wasn't required, Kristen sat upon the hall bench trying to decide whether to get up. After a while it was too late; the meeting had ended and the only place available for escape was the bathroom.

The woman stood there.

Apparently enough time had passed that the sedation had worn off, for no one was with her.

Running out of the room, Kristen felt water trickle down her leg. There had been no opportunity to urinate, she thought, embarrassed. Quickly sitting down on a nearby bench, she saw the wet ring on her kimono and heard "Baa, baa," come from a room down the hall. An armed attendant blocked the inmates from danger.

"Come on, eat it up," she heard.

"Baa, baa," was the only answer.

"Don't throw it up again or I'll stuff it down

your throat," an attendant shouted. Tears ran down Barbara's face. She'd heard it too, thought Kristen, "I'm not crazy." A plump motherly woman with an Irish brogue began to talk, coffee-klatsch style.

"That girl's here all the time every time I come here. You should see her hair, kinky like a goat. Skinny, you wouldn't believe it. They feed her baby food. She's a retard, know what I mean? Can't speak or eat, just baa's all the time. Enough to drive you nuts." The woman's laughter convulsed her and she began to weep. "Bangs her head on the furniture. Bruises all over her, all over her, all over her."

Kristen sat up. "Keep quiet, you old bitch," she murmured, her fierce tenderness toward the vulnerable rising. "Shut up." Kristen's hands were wet and she washed her face with them. Kristen looked down, wondering if the woman noticed the blood Karl had left all over her body. She saw it spread over the tile floor and shielded her eyes. Kristen did not want to vomit. She covered her mouth. Her flushed face seemed like a mirage distorted in the glass of the overhead lights. The lights terrorized. All night they glared, seeing. She saw blood staring from the floor. Why had no one else seen it? Red splotches were on her hands. She decided to hide them in the pockets of the rumpled kimono and then she heard herself humming.

Almost before the tune ended, the loud-speaker boomed: *The-dinner-trays-are-here. Go-to-the-dining-room.* Everyone who could walked down the long corridor toward respectability. If one sat

THE SPLINTERED EYE

properly at a table, she was not really mad. Others could not walk. They reclined, heads wobbling, strapped in a combination chair-table like an infant feeder which was placed in the hall at mealtimes. Half-conscious from liquid tranquilizers fed to them in small white cups every four hours, they tried to coordinate their hands to eat. But unable to find their own gaping mouths, their spastic movements plunged endless trays to the floor. In the dark, cool state of anesthetized mindlessness, somehow they knew they had not met the qualifications for sanity. They could not eat properly.

"Honey, help me please," uttered one. Kristen slowly edged her way toward the recreation room, which became the dining room at mealtimes, and swiftly glanced up to see who had made the vast mistake of calling for help. No one who expected to return to the outside needed assistance. The woman had black coiled hair as short as any man's, and wore a standard white kimono issued to all who came without their own clothes. Food stains gave hers a tie-dyed effect. She stank. How could you want to help anyone who stank, Kristen thought. The woman's eyes rolled about in her head, unable to focus upon the form she had asked for assistance. Kristen automatically stopped, leaned over, and began to feed the gaping mouth. "Thank you, honey," the woman squirmed to the right. "I can't seem to . . ."

Kristen clutched her stomach; she wanted no food served here. Moving away from the dining room, she heard a nurse call, "What's the matter?"

THE SPLINTERED EYE

"I'm . . ." she tried to answer. Sick, she held herself tightly so that she would not flee; then she sat upon a cot rolled into the hall.

"You won't sleep tonight," someone said irritably. But Kristen saw only sanctuary and, surrendering to it, stretched out, staring into the past.

"Was I ever twelve?" she spoke aloud. Twelve, awaiting a miracle. Scanning the clouds each day, waiting, reviewing her catechism. Every Tuesday and Thursday the long bus ride to the convent near the outskirts of the village, encircled by thick stone walls interlaced with evergreens. The retreat house lies far back from the road. One cannot see even its faint outline until one enters the gate and walks almost a mile along the dirt path. Kristen always allows plenty of time for the stroll. She likes to climb the small hill within the grounds, eating the sandwich she usually carries and picking sweet juice-filled blackberries in the summer or swallowing snowcups in wintertime. The sisters at St. Francis de Sales call the hill *Hosanna* and have built a small chapel of stone near the top. Here Kristen rests, praying passionately to see—reciting rosaries and rereading the lesson she will soon be called upon to speak about. "The chapel in the sky," as she has renamed it, makes her feel the way her father looks after his Sunday walks along the beach. He no longer goes to church since her mother died. But each Sunday he walks the dunes near their home—a large, gray-haired man whose face has strong, stone-like fea-

THE SPLINTERED EYE

tures, the lines intensified by weather and time. She loves him very much although he will never approve her commitment to the Church.

Skipping down the hill, she thinks of herself dressed in the long black robes of the nuns. Kristen touches her own long hair; the picture of the nun she had seen seated at her desk one day when she had run into the private quarters flashes before her. The nun had looked so strange without her mantle, her head bare-skinned, that Kristen smiles as she remembers. Somewhat breathless, she runs up the steps, almost crashing into Sister Margaret Rose.

"Hello, Kristen, slow down. Have you reviewed your catechism?" asks the stocky sister as she ushers the girl out the back door into the small tranquil garden that lies at the rear of the house. It is early spring. Flowers have been planted about the statue of St. Francis. But no real birds make their homes on the shoulders of that stone figure. The roof of the church shades the garden, protecting the site from direct sunlight, so that many species of flowers have difficulty growing. Plastic blooms are placed in between the sparse real colors. They look almost real and few people detect the difference. To Kristen, who cannot take her eyes from Sister Margaret Rose, the gold at the nose of the nun's unrimmed glasses seems to catch the light from the stained-glass windows of the church while the sister sits plump and rose-colored in a green lawn chair. A few beads of sweat challenge the serenity of what Kristen perceives is an ageless demeanor; but the girl hardly notices this human failing. "Kristen, all these lines across the margins, between nearly every line of your catechism. Are you sure you still gain the true meaning?"

"Oh, yes, Sister. Please ask me the questions."

One of the prisms of artificial light catches the naked wonder in the girl's face and, in answer to the sister's first question, she begins to recite excitedly the rhythmic phrases. Sister leans back in the easy chair and listens to the humming sound, relaxes. Almost to herself she mumbles, "The girl will be all right. She asks too many questions sometimes, but she can be counted upon to do the work correctly if prodded."

"Sister, I love to read of our Lord. It is my dream to be just like you."

"Like me, child? I am no one. I have given myself to Him. You must search yourself to know if you are worthy to know His joy. But I have discussed your case with Monsignor Gray. I have told him how joyful you are, how you love God, and of your desire to join the sisterhood. Monsignor is acquainted with your father, Kristen. He says your father will not be happy if you forsake the world."

"But I shall be happy, Sister. I shall be so happy, and he will be glad for my sake."

"All right, child. You must pray for the Lord to help and guide you to Him and He surely will. Now Kristen, back to today's lesson. Let me answer all your questions now. I must not be late for vespers."

The sister turns to the day's lesson and be-

THE SPLINTERED EYE

gins to read. "Sin is a rejection of God's love, a refusal of an opportunity to accept His love and pass it on to others. It is as if God says 'Here is an opportunity to spread love in the world, to grow yourself in love and happiness,' and we refuse, we reject His loving guidance. Ultimately, sin is a personal rebuff to our loving Father, to Christ our Brother and Savior, to the Spirit who is love within us.

"Incredibly, the infinite God is concerned with our rejection of His love. Christ tells us in Matthew 25:40, 'As you did it to one of these, the least of my brethren, you did it to me.' Kristen, what is mortal sin?"

Kristen gazes at the nun raptly. "Mortal sin is a fundamental rejection of God's love. By it we drive His grace and presence from us, Sister. But God forgives every sin if we are sorry. Why does it say in the next paragraph that a person in mortal sin cuts himself off from God's love?"

Margaret Rose loves questions like this. She answers reciting, "God's love—actual graces—still surround him, but he is a lonely, self-centered, spiritually-starving individual. Remember, one judging himself to be in mortal sin must confess his sin and be reconciled to Christ and the Church before he can take part in the Eucharist."

"You mean that a person can do the same thing over and over again—even murder—and God will make him clean?"

"Kristen, it says, 'God will forgive any sin again and again and again—even the most serious—as long as we are truly sorry . . . 'If your sins be as scarlet, they shall be made white as snow; and if they be red as crimson, they shall be white as wool.' Isaiah 1:18."

"Wouldn't the best way to show Christ one is sorry be not to commit the sin again?" whispers Kristen, her voice trembling as it always does when she perceives herself doubting.

"Kristen, do you not see the answer to that question in the text?" Sister grows impatient. Sometimes the girl's endless questions can be annoying, especially when the obvious answers are so clearly recorded in black and white. "Kristen, you must ask that your faith be strengthened, 'For by grace you have been saved through faith and this is not your own doing, it is the gift of God—not because of works, lest any man should boast.' You remember those words in Ephesians?"

Kristen looks at the sister who seems so knowledgeable, so much at peace. "I will pray more often, Sister," she says devoutly.

"Good, Kristen, and your prayers will be answered. I am sure of it. Do you know the gospel of St. Mark?"

"Which part, Sister?"

"When St. Mark recounts the story of the father who brought his boy who was possessed with convulsions to Jesus and said with tears, 'I believe; help my unbelief.' Jesus then cured the boy, showing us that a sincere plea for faith will not go unanswered. You must ask God for complete faith, Kristen. Christ said, 'Ask and ye shall receive.' You will see one day that what I have been telling you is the truth. Study your catechism. Say your Rosary whenever you falter."

"Then I will be like you, Sister. I will be just like you."

Sister smiles. "Kristen, you are a dear girl. You will become a faithful part of God's flock." Almost to herself she adds, "One needs only patience with the young to teach them the way." She nods. "Now, Kristen, I will ask the questions and you give the answers. We shall see how well you do." Continuing, Margaret Rose's voice has a systolic beat. "What is mortal sin? . . ."

Visiting-hour-has-begun. The loudspeaker interrupted Kristen's reverie. Visitors came off the main elevator and passed through the iron gate. A uniformed attendant stood near the open doorway checking passes. Karl's panther-like walk was easily distinguishable. As he moved toward her he smiled nervously, glancing quickly around as if expecting to see someone else. Tight, flared pants accented his short muscular frame.

"Hello, Kitten," he said affably. "How was today?"

For a moment, gazing at him, she forgot where they were and responded to the sound. He possessed her like a tract of land to which he had laid claim.

Then she remembered again. "Please, Karl,

get me out." She clung to him. Anger mounted inside Kristen, made her wish for death.

He patted her head. "I told you before, you're here for a purpose."

"What do you mean?" Her wispy voice rose despite her efforts to remain calm. "You don't know what it's like—what have I done to you?"

"Done?" he broke in. "Nothing. Now you're going to do something. Listen, Kris, just relax. You're sick. You'd better eat, you look like hell . . ."

Looking up at him, her eyes flooded with tears and she choked on them, unable to speak. Something was wrong. This couldn't be Karl. Someone had put him up to it. Her head pounded with rage. Who was it?

"Don't worry," he hissed. "Everything is going fine I've talked to Burt Cald—you remember him?"

Kristen's eyes widened.

"We're going to get you into a nice place. It's like a country club—wall-to-wall carpets, tennis courts—my sister was there once. She loved it."

"Karl, Burt's not a real psychologist. He doesn't even have a diploma. He runs that place for rich nuts whose families want to get rid of them."

"He's better than these damn quacks. They don't listen."

"Then why did you put me here?"

"Are you crazy? You were hearing voices again. Don't you remember calling me at work to ask, 'How do you want me to kill myself?' I had to put you somewhere quick before—"

"But I didn't try to kill myself...."
"Then why are you here?" Karl mocked.
"They said I . . . Burt swore out a statement that I'd tried to kill myself twice before. They had to take me. The doctors here couldn't take the chance. They pumped my stomach and I'm asthmatic—I couldn't breathe, but I didn't try to kill myself—you know that."
"What's the difference? You're here now and we're going to take care of you."
"The doctors say I can go home if I call my family. I haven't even got any money to call."
"I'm your family. I've been taking care of you all this time. We're married."
"What are you talking about, Karl?"
"In the eyes of the law, you've been holding yourself out as my wife. We're married by common law, so don't try to get out of it."
She tried to control herself so that the nurses wouldn't give her another dose of Thorazine. She didn't want to become a robot as did so many of the other patients. "Please, Karl," she whimpered.
"Baby, stop this whining shit. Stop bothering the doctors with your crap also. You're not going to have your way anymore. I'll take care of everything now. Listen, I have an appointment for dinner. Try to relax and behave yourself."
"Clothes, Karl," she cried numbly. "I can't wear this," fingering the rumpled kimono.
"Jesus, Kristen, you take the cake. Even in the looney bin you're the princess royal, huh? All right, what do you want?"

She tried to think but couldn't remember what clothes she had. "Anything," she said. "My makeup kit, some slacks, a shirt."

"Tomorrow." Turning, he motioned to the guard to let him out. Then he placed his hands at either side of Kristen's cheeks, stared at her a moment, and brushed her forehead with his lips.

As she leaned back on the cot, she heard, *Visiting-hour-is-over-now. Visiting-hour-is-over-now. Please-leave-one-at-a-time.* Kristen grimaced. They were afraid a patient might sneak through unrecognized. She thought how funny it would be if the chief nurse discovered locked inside the cage a supposedly sane visitor who'd been imprisoned. An idea for a future book, she thought, hearing herself laugh aloud. Then she became self-conscious. "I must stop this or they won't believe me when I say I'm sane." A few moments later she saw Barbara Nored, who sat on a nearby bench, hold out a piece of bread saved from her dinner tray. Fascinated, she watched as the girl broke the bread into small pieces, rolled them into small pill-like pellets in her hand, and then popped them one-by-one into her mouth. Hot tears filled Kristen's eyes.

Attendants began to give out evening medication. Everyone seemed to get the same thing. Thorazine mixed with pineapple juice so you couldn't tongue it, followed by a chaser of pink mouthwash. Grasping the cup Kristen gulped. Going down the medication gave a comfortable floating sensation as if one lived in several gauzed

THE SPLINTERED EYE

layers of reality, all cloaked by an impenetrable haze.

Time turned backward.

The afternoons come early. It is October. Winter pulses. The ice cream wind flavors her pursed lips, accents her rising euphoria. She hurries to the hotel at which she vacations. For the first time unchaperoned, alone in New York, not confined to a dormitory room at NYU studying the night away—free. She dashes into the Regency, waits nervously, eyeing the clock. Stands near the mahogany Directoire armoire, then sits on the pale-gold settee. Carefully pulls a strand of dark auburn hair across her forehead, a moment later pushes it back behind her ear, which is small and curved and pink like a shell. Martine, her best friend in graduate school, has become a systems analyst for IBM. She has arranged a blind date. Kristen's heart beats quickly like the fading daylight. She is waiting . . . for some very real thing to pick her up like the wind at the backs of the pedestrians on the streets, a force which will push her in the direction for which she is destined. It is that time of her life: she is twenty-three. Kristen feels very strangely animated, not at all like the Kristen Blakely who sits nunlike in her graduate seminars, pulling her skirt down to cover her knees. This new person beating within her has been riffled by the wind which has torn something else loose, a thing which waits excitedly beating . . .

THE SPLINTERED EYE

He bursts through the revolving doors and rushes toward her. Let down, she perceives that her fantasies were mistaken. He is too short, almost stocky, old, his hair tinged by gray. Disenchantment grips her. Martine has promised someone fascinating. Apparently he recognizes her, immediately comes toward her, and grasps her hand.

"I'm Karl West," he says forcefully.

"Kristen Blakely," she softly answers and finds herself gazed upon by penetrating blue eyes, which fasten upon her with such intensity that she runs her fingers across her paisley blouse to see if any buttons are undone.

The military-type blazer he wears is quite high styled. The dark blue color of the jacket complements the mauve shirt and further amplifies his unusual eyes.

"A friend of mine is sponsoring an op art exhibit near here. I told him we'd stop by, if that's okay." Not waiting for an answer, he strides ahead while she, a trifle nonplussed but amused, follows. The weather has gotten colder, she shivers. He takes the plaid woolen coat slung over her arm and wraps her in it. His gaze wanders over her slowly, almost possessively.

"Someone should take care of you," he says.

Further up the street, he darts into a boutique and returns to wrap a cream-colored cashmere scarf about her throat.

"As soon as I saw it in the window I thought of you." Her words of appreciation are silenced, so she smiles. They rush on. Just as she thinks she has adapted to his pace, he changes it unexpectedly, and slips into a flower shop. This time he brings her one white rose edged in deep pink.

"It is a mutation," he explains seriously, "grown by delicate grafting." She touches the petals, runs her lips across their silken texture.

"How beautiful," she murmurs. In and out of the streets they wind—he like an accomplished equestrian, she the wary novice—not sure where they are or how long it has taken, until he signals that they have reached their destination. Directly in front of them is a long flight of salmon-colored marble stairs which lead to a Madison Avenue townhouse. By this time Kristen tiredly begs him to slow down.

"Come on, slowpoke," he joshes. "The whole show is passing before you even get to the theater."

"Perhaps," she says, "but I am not sure I want to see it, or am even interested."

"How can you be certain if you never arrive?" he asks. "If you keep your eyes averted and stay at home, before you know it all the lights dim, the whole panorama ceases."

"And that you could not stand."

"Of course not; there is so much to see."

"Could we wait about five minutes to see it while I try to breathe normally?" she laughs huskily.

"Of course," he answers, sitting down on the step above her. She notices his feet tap continuously as if he is unable to stop the nervous energy within him from idling. As she watches him, her own responses quicken. Her face takes on a glow. Flushed with new energy, she rubs his foot.

"Let's go," she says laughing. "I think I can make it now."

He grins back, luminous eyes twinkling, and bounds up the stairs two at a time.

The art studio is at the top of the landing. A large rose crystal chandelier shimmers, highlights people who stand compressed in small glistening bunches like expensive flowers in a too-slender silver vase. They are talking very loudly as Kristen enters. She wants to withdraw. Cocktail parties frighten her; she hates being attentive to stick figures who respond with animated motions or sounds to comments they cannot possibly hear. Yet this time Karl West's protective arm causes her to view the party-goers differently. They are not just open mouths outlined in red or glasses with slim, tapered fingers curled about them, but forms which scintillate as she scrutinizes them. Although he drinks little, Karl is exhilarated as he moves restlessly about, introducing her first to the host—a tall, lean man who Karl explains has recently resigned as head of Drake Press to ski and play his clarinet in Aspen fulltime. Before she can respond to their introduction, Karl moves her ahead, pointing to a strange, dark, blue-and-white optical illusion on the velvet-covered wall; moments later he rushes them over to greet an old friend. "He's a leftover from my airline days." It is the first time he has mentioned his profession. It suits him, she thinks admiringly. She reaches out to touch his arm, but he has disengaged himself and sprinted across the room to speak to a silver-blonde woman with incredible eyebrows to match. Kristen's excitement fades. She feels alone again, her discomfort rising. She waits, arms weighted at her sides, wishing she could look in a mirror to be sure her hair is in place. The other people around the room all seem to know one another. Cautiously Kristen recedes to a corner and half leans against the wall. Someone reprimands her: "Please be careful not to touch the paintings." Other than this, no one notices her. Moving to the outskirts of a group she tries to nod at all the right places as if she is a participant instead of an outsider. Suddenly, a deep gentle voice with an unmistakable British accent calls her name. She squints, the lighting making a clear identification impossible, and sees a distinguished-looking youngish man come toward her. His curly brown hair looks copper-colored in the lights of the studio.

"David Hetherington," she cries as the distance between them lessens. He eases forward, his dark-brown pinstriped-suited elegance almost too formal in this funky chic atmosphere.

"How are you, Kris?" he asks, gazing attentively at her.

"David, I've met someone," she says. He glances around, a look of sadness on his lean, attractive face.

"I'm happy for you; do I know him?"

"His name is Karl West. There he is." She points proudly to Karl, and doesn't notice that Hetherington, who follows her gaze, winces.

Abruptly he changes the subject. He points at the Vassilary painting on the wall above them. "This isn't really my idea of art. Perhaps I'm too old-fashioned, but it is too mathematically precise. The essence of art for me is neither nemesis nor precision, but imagination expanding reality both in terms of color and form."

"I feel the same way," Kristen nods, studying the painting. "I cannot call what can be duplicated by photograph or machine art. Art must be," she pauses, "more than that. It must present a vision, an order never perceived before."

Hetherington picks up her thought, "Or the individuality which marks real creativity is absent." They smile at each other, at their shared interchange. Karl, meanwhile, has overheard their comments and joined them.

"Hello, Hetherington," he says almost formally. "I trust you've been well."

David stiffens almost imperceptibly. "I'm fine. Nice to see you again." His face is dark and quizzical. He glances up at the picture on the wall.

"The emperor's new clothes," Karl observes with a slight grin, "but then so is most avant garde art."

"I can't accept that," Hetherington interjects.

"Real art," Karl hurries on without pausing,

THE SPLINTERED EYE

"was produced by Da Vinci, Rubens, Rembrandt, Michelangelo. When you enter the Metropolitan or the Louvre, isn't it these masters' works to which you're irresistibly drawn? If you could magnify every inch of their canvasses a hundredfold, you would know what art is."

"Yes, but that would only suffice as a definition of traditional excellence. It would be an inadequate criteria by which to judge artistic innovation," Hetherington counters.

"Old forms are inadequate to illustrate contemporary reality," Kristen adds.

"Perhaps," continues Karl, "but great art is technically conservative. Rubens spent eight years copying the works of the old Italian masters—how long do you think it took to develop Michelangelo's instinct for glyphic, for Rembrandt's use of light? Today's artists think they can learn to paint through a crash course by the art guild." Hetherington stares wonderingly at Karl.

"You seem to be quite well schooled on the technical aspects of traditional art," Hetherington says, not without a touch of snobbery.

Karl replies, "We street guys pick up a swish of culture here and there." He glares at Hetherington. "My roommate in the Navy, you remember *him*," he smiles secretively, "majored in art history. I took advantage of the opportunity to see how you of the leisure class amuse yourselves while my group cleans up after you—I believe it's what you call token equality."

Hetherington flushes. "West, I hadn't meant to sound so patronizing," he says. "Please don't be offended at my lack of sensitivity." He offers his hand to Karl, who accepts it grudgingly.

"Obviously your taste is impeccable." Hetherington smiles first at Karl, then at Kristen. "I envy you your good fortune." Karl grins. "I must be going now. Goodbye, Kris. My regards to your father. Again, my apologies, West."

As Hetherington walks away, Karl says accusingly to Kristen, "How do you know him?"

"David is Daddy's attorney, that is, his *law firm* is. I used to have quite a crush on him, but he was married then and paid little attention."

"Both those events have changed," Karl relates. "Unfortunately for Hetherington, though, fate has intervened." Kristen feels vaguely apprehensive. Karl obviously relishes Hetherington's distress, but she shrugs it off as Karl slides his arm around her shoulders.

"Do you know David long?" she asks.

"We've had occasion to meet," Karl answers. "He used to be in the Navy and then he was a public defender, one of those new society reformers."

Kristen giggled, "I'll bet my dad isn't aware of that tidbit."

Karl's attention has already wandered. "Come on," he says, "I want to introduce you to that woman on the far side of the room." They cross the studio together and approach the elegant lady with silver-blonde hair and eyebrows to match who, Kristen, relieved, notices at closer range, is aging.

"Lydia Carstin, editor of *Paris Marches*, this is a rather lovely girl with whom I am about to fall in love—Kristen Blakely."

Kristen, caught off guard, laughs guardedly. She hopes he will not notice her discomfort and fumbles to acknowledge the introduction.

I am too gauche, she thinks, too unworldly amid this graceful, attractive throng, especially compared to women like Lydia, about whom a society columnist could spin a lavish tale of the beautiful people. I'm probably going to ruin tonight by dropping a glass on the floor or stammering my answers amidst polished mahogany phrases. Kristen grimaces, her own smile feels stilted to her, but she can't seem to ease out of it. Lydia Carstin is obviously amused but kind as she and Karl trade retorts while Kristen awkwardly stands nearby, silent, wishing she might add just the right phrase to the conversation. Finally, a voice from another group hails Lydia, who kisses Karl on his cheek, entreats that he call her the next time he is in Paris, and waves goodbye.

Karl and Kristen return to each other. Karl whispers, "Let's go somewhere to talk." She finally relaxes as he concentrates upon her.

"I'm starving," she admits guiltily, and laughs. He nods. Outside, night has fallen. Around them people glisten, white-black people with somewhere to go hurry across the streets, whose lights turn green then red as if cued by autumn. Karl

THE SPLINTERED EYE

hails a cab which stops to let them in. He sits very close to her and does not speak until they reach a building which has multi-colored stone jockeys astride painted black iron horses. The headwaiter at "21" apparently knows Karl. He welcomes them with a grin, all white teeth and lowered shrewd eyes. Then he shows them to a side table for two near the bar. Waiters hover, expecting larger tips than necessary from these two whom they judge prematurely to be lovers. Kristen and Karl sit holding hands, oblivious. Kristen stares raptly at Karl; at the throat of his mauve shirt is a pale blue and white silk ascot which gives him a Byronic air. She wonders what had made her think at first glance he was not her type. He looks much younger in this atmosphere with his broad muscular build and intelligent alert face. Within her that distinct fluttering which had begun in the hotel lobby appears again.

 The astute waiter bends solicitously over them and suggests caviar as an appetizer. Kristen has never tried it, but Karl nods his approval and asks to see the wine list. Authoritatively, he orders Mumm's Cordon Rouge. She bites into the translucent ochre bubbles, sips the vintage champagne, and feels reckless and heady. An unfamiliar reflection, her own features caught in the polished surfaces, accosts her. Her glazed, excited eyes glow back at her. She is tantalized by this new image. She reaches out to touch Karl where the silver in his hair glistens, and says softly, "You are quite incredible."

THE SPLINTERED EYE

He answers in the limber French of a dancer, *"Dans le monde entier, je n'ais jamais rencontré une personne comme toi."* He smiles at her, places his hand beneath her chin—a claim—and brushes her lips with his own. His personality, she realizes, cannot be catalogued. He is multi-dimensional, like spires of stained glass reflecting different moments of light from morning until nightfall. It is clear to Kristen as she sits beside him that he projects messages of love with his body; his gestures are more potent than actual speech, and she acknowledges to herself as they sip the champagne that she, too, is falling in love.

Hours pass; they sit close and say very little, united by the pressure of their hands, which must be wiped dry of perspiration every once in a while. And then, the place is about to close. Waiters who a short time before were attentive to their every wish begin to jangle silverware noisily and extract linen cloths from nearby tables.

Karl looks at her. "I think they want us to leave," he says, and they are given their check immediately. He precedes her into the lobby, hands a ticket to the hat-check girl, and wraps Kristen in the wool plaid coat, fastening the purple velvet collar carefully to protect her from the cold. Outside the night is more balmy than raw. Not wanting to perturb him, she leaves the coat buttoned, though she feels suffocated. The uniformed doorman whistles, a Checker answers, and soon they are at the Regency Hotel. Karl strides to the desk to get her key. He returns and takes her arm.

THE SPLINTERED EYE

"It's late; I'll take you upstairs."

The elevator swallows them, muffling her reply. The door to her room opens easily. "May I come in for a few minutes?" he asks. The night maid has turned the sheets down. A small gold lamp, its sconce crowned by angels, casts a soft incarnadine luster. As if the scene were occurring in a novel or a movie, Kristen excuses herself, then returns quickly from the bathroom clad in a filmy coral lounging gown. He doesn't laugh at her attempt at sophisticated seduction. Instead, his words are soothing, hypnotic as he sits beside the bed. Then he lies on the bed, swiftly undressing. A passageway inside her opens and she glides through it toward him. Within her there is a letting go—a powerlessness as his arms close about her. He undresses her, she hears her heartbeat grow louder, threatening to explode and, when it does, he says, "Hello, Kristen," quietly relinquishing her, only to bring her back to him deftly on a second wave of excitement. She wants to merge with him, to intermingle with his skin and bone . . . but the moment ends. This time she clutches wildly at him and he drives hungrily into her for what seems forever but ends as she hears him scream her name. Afterward, as he sleeps, she gently untangles herself and goes into the bathroom to bathe. She stands dreamily before the mirror, views the red teethmarks on her shoulder, touches them with wonder, bewilderment, surprise. Still in a trance, she steps into the shower; warm water splashes over her body. As she comes out, he is framed in the doorway.

"What are you doing?" he asks.

"Making myself beautiful for you."

"Come back to bed. You're beautiful enough. I don't want you bathing all night. You'll wear off your skin by tomorrow," he jokes. His arms, which seem to Kristen very strong, make her dizzy with happiness. He runs his fingers up and down her body while the sensations centered within her spread until her whole self—limbs, belly, womb—twitches in anticipation. He is, she sees, ready himself.

"Am I good for you?" she asks seriously.

"You shouldn't have to ask that."

"But it means so much to me."

"Of course you are." He nibbles her cheek and enters her again.

Afterward she floats into the sweet inertia of unconsciousness, but wakes to find him alert and sleepless, filled with nervous energy.

"I must have dozed off," she says apologetically, "I'm sorry."

He sighs. "Don't be silly. I never sleep more than a few hours a night. You looked so lovely there, so small and perfect, I didn't want to wake you. At any rate, I have an early appointment. I have to shave and change and there isn't much time," he speaks rapidly. She closes her eyes, embarrassed, about to cry, feeling she has done something wrong or he would not be leaving like this.

THE SPLINTERED EYE

He rises, quickly dresses, and comes back to sit on the edge of the bed, his eyes dark with fatigue. Gently, he touches her hair. She does not want him to leave.

"Walk me to the door," he says and smiles. Her voice is thick and unnatural as she whispers goodbye and opens the door. He kisses her chastely on the forehead, a fatherly kiss.

"I'll call you."

Then he is gone. She returns to the bed, but unable to sleep, she thinks of his fascinating face. She lies tossing in the damp, disheveled bed, not able to close out his image until morning. Then she pushes herself up, showers, changes into dark blue denim slacks and a shirt, pulls her ponytail back with a small, pale silk ribbon, and calls the hairdresser Martine had recommended.

The day is chilly as she walks toward Madison Avenue. Pictures of sleek, short-haired women fill the windows of the beauty salon. She goes in and places herself in the hands of the French coiffeur who looks disdainfully at her ponytail. A few hours later she emerges, hair cut so that it feels like raw silk against her cheek as she turns her head. At the Regency, the desk clerk hands her a pink slip with a message that Karl has called. She races to her room.

An hour passes; finally the call comes. On the phone Karl sounds distant, hardly recognizable. She swallows and covers her nervousness with an embarrassed greeting and a few remarks about the hairdresser.

He cuts her off. "Your hair, you changed your hair—without asking me." His angry tone shocks her, makes her twitch involuntarily. She feels bewildered, hurt, but tries to soothe him.

"It grows very quickly," she says. "I thought you would like it this way."

"Of course," he replies. "It's just that your hair is what I liked best about you."

"Don't worry, in a few months I'll be the same," she comforts him again, imagining herself gluing on the cut pieces one at a time. She is suddenly aware that in so short a time his opinion is so meaningful. The subject changes to their next date.

"Tomorrow night?" he asks. "I'm stuck in Danbury and won't be back till then."

"I've a date," she answers. "My brother's fixed me up with a friend."

"Kristen," he interrupts, "I must see you."

"As soon as we get off the phone I'll call—"

She hears herself offer to break the other date and realizes how desperately she wants to see him again.

"Good, Kristen. 'Til tomorrow then."

He hangs up while she stares at her hand, which still holds the telephone. Within her the sound of his voice continues to ring like music which one keeps hearing even when the lyrics end. She feels that she cannot go out until she sees him again.

She spends the next day locked in her room, reading. As she brushes her hair, gets in the tub,

THE SPLINTERED EYE

eats, she hears Karl's voice, sees him press against her, remembers how he felt.

By five she has picked up the phone numerous times to make sure it is operative. At six she is sure he has forgotten; tears spill from her eyes. When seven comes, she begins to dress anyway, just in case. An hour later he rings from the lobby, entreating her to hurry. Her heart pounds, she recombs her hair, moves to the door fast, faster, in order to be with him again.

Beneath the gold ormolu clock in the lobby he waits, restlessly shifting his weight from one leg to another with almost feline grace. Even from across the room, where she can only dimly perceive his outline, the intense energy with which he moves is apparent. She reaches him. He smiles and holds out his arms to welcome her.

"Let's go," he says and, without asking where, with no need to ask, she follows.

They go to a posh Italian restaurant where sleek people like those she glimpsed at the art exhibit dine. The restaurant, Orsini's, is very dark. One can only perceive glossy silhouettes nibbling at the rich, splendid food. Karl orders Noodles Alfredo for two and Pouilly Fuisse, which the waiter chills in a silver ice bucket. The sweet, creamy pasta taste drifts through her, punctuated by his touch as he runs his fingers through her hair or feeds her from his fork. Mostly they are silent, but strangely close; between the pattern of hunger felt and quenched, her dizzying need for him returns. And she waits for him to say the right words so that she can answer yes. Before coffee is served, they leave. They rush out into the autumn night exhilarated, the wind roaming through their hair.

"Let's walk back," he says.

Obedient, she nods. Patches of people on the street appear to part as she and Karl make their way across town. Because of his brisk energetic pace she falls behind, breathless.

Finally he notices. "Are you okay?" he asks, pausing under a streetlight to stare at her.

Gulping air she answers, "I think we dropped my breathing apparatus three blocks ago." He laughs in staccato bursts, loudly, like a clock striking midnight.

"Christ, I'm sorry," he says. "You're such a little thing. I wasn't thinking. Let's get a cab."

When they return to the hotel he looks at her hesitantly. She hands him the key, her heart hammers, and her face tells him everything he wants to know.

This time he stays for breakfast, flings back the drapes so that the misty, dreamlike morning breaks into the bedroom. But the outside world is merely an addendum as they lie side by side. In the shower he scrubs her skin until it tingles, then rubs her with a warm towel.

He grins and says, "First let's call room service. Then let's go back to bed for the rest of the day."

At three they emerge glowing, pick up a picnic lunch at the Brasserie, and then take it to Central Park where, wrapped in blankets smuggled from the hotel, they talk. First one then the other. Everything they say proves how little they have in common. But it intrigues her that he was born in a ghetto, even more than he is a Jew. Her revelations, however, make him combative. Her ambitions to be a social worker, cause him to make bitter jokes about Sunday liberals. Of course, he holds her as they argue so that his criticisms are easier to withstand. She tells herself they are meaningless, part of his insecurity. He tells her he had been married and has a daughter he seldom sees.

"My wife was a bitch," he adds, his eyes becoming dark and distant, "a crazy bitch."

She presses her hand to his cheek to convey her sympathy and he visibly relaxes. They are quiet, then he speaks again.

"Kristen, I'm sorry I have to be away for a few days—a client with business in the West. I have a small air transport company," and adds almost as an afterthought, "I want you to think about coming to stay with me when I return, to move into my apartment."

"Karl, I don't think—"

"Please," he presses his fingers to her lips, "just think about it. I want you so desperately."

Minutes pass.

"I need time," she whispers. They leave the park, their arms encircling each other. In the lobby of the hotel he slowly kisses her goodbye.

"I would be very good for you," he says, his confident face focusing upon her.

"A few days, Karl, give me a few days."

"Of course, darling," he answers in a hurt tone, "I understand."

Darling—she hugs the word as she goes to her room, explores, dismantles, adds binding implications to Karl's word and then, content with the significance she assigns to it, falls into a rose-tinged sleep.

She supposes he will call the next day. She is surprised, then annoyed, when he does not. Wending her way through East Side streets, she moves languidly, a dreamwalker. The things she sees seem blurred and indistinct; a throbbing begins within her. Back at the hotel, a man calls. They go out for a drink but in the middle of the evening she feigns a headache, excuses herself, and returns to the hotel. There are no messages. The next morning, her eyes red and haunted, she goes to the library to take out some books which will serve as background for her thesis. All around her people read or quietly take notes. She is unable to concentrate on anything. Picking up the newspaper from the mahogany table on which it lies, she scans the headlines. She feels vaguely irritated but cannot raise her interest level. Finally, her number flashes on the overhead board in the reference room and she claims the books, sits back down, this time at a desk, trying to look busy. The afternoon slowly passes, minutes at a time.

There are still no messages when she returns to her hotel. Feeling sickish, dazed, she lies on the bed and flips on the radio. She turns the music up higher and higher in order to still her thoughts, but the memory of Karl's touch returns. Later she drifts into a troubled sleep in which his image expands, then contracts.

In the morning her head aches and she orders tea and toast from room service. The thought of him has become a rhythm within her. It vibrates. Things continue. She spends the next day back in the library.

And then, unable to control herself any longer, she goes to Karl's apartment. She has gotten the address from Martine, from whose questions she turns away. The cab takes only fifteen minutes to reach the right street, almost as though fate has decreed the meeting, she perceives. She stands on the corner and watches the well-kept brownstone, but does not see Karl. Finally she leaves, only to be drawn back a few hours later. This time she strolls past the building, a noisy rumbling inside of her, a surge of excitement. And there he is standing in the doorway, talking to an attractive, dark-haired woman who looks vaguely familiar.

"Kristen," the woman calls.

Kristen stops, paralyzed. The woman with Karl is Roslyn Gorky, one of her professors from NYU. Swiftly through her mind flashes the desire to be invisible or to run, but she does neither—merely stands, eyes closed, barely breathing. Suddenly he is beside her, enfolding her so tightly she cannot move away.

Roslyn Gorky's laugh floats toward them. "I guess I don't have to introduce you," she says, disappearing into the house with a wave.

Without further communication they make their way up the stairs to his apartment. Once inside, he leads her by the hand to the bedroom. He begins to kiss her eyelids, her hair, until she reaches out for him feverishly.

"I'm so glad you have come," he says as he undresses her. Pressing her back onto the bed, he strokes her, caresses her. Soon she moves with him, their flesh one. Then he covers her with himself and becomes her center, filling her again and again so that she will never be empty of him. Toward morning they fall into a dark, succulent sleep.

The next day she moves from her hotel into the brownstone in the West Village.

A white apparition glided by. Moments or years had intervened—she couldn't be sure which.

"You have another visitor." Kristen stared at the nurse dazedly. "He's come a long way, so we've allowed him in after visiting hours. Five minutes, Mr. Blakely."

Kristen turned and focused mistily upon her tall blonde brother who stood before her.

"Hey, baby," he said, and she began to gasp, feeling she could not breathe. His words, so casual, made the incongruity of the scene more pronounced. "Easy, baby," he said softly.

"Oh, Jamie," she spoke in a hoarse whisper.

"I'm getting you out of here, Sis, tonight," he said as he held her against his chest gently.

"How did you—"

"You gave Dr. Wicklin my number, remember?" Jamie quickly surveyed the surroundings.

"He called me this morning. I threw some things together. Look, we can talk about all this later. I've got to meet Karl for dinner. He doesn't know I found out where you are. The little bastard has been trying to suck money from Dad—" Jamie muttered angrily.

"Something is wrong with Karl," Kristen responded, her voice lower. "He's ill, I know it. You'll see there is some reason... Karl wouldn't do this. Someone must have put him up to it. Try to talk to him, Jamie. If he's in trouble—"

"Good Christ, Sis," Jamie frowned, "Karl *is* trouble. He's the slime of the earth. There isn't a decent bone in his body and there never was. You're lucky he didn't push you out the door of his plane. If you had married him, you can bet that would have been the next step. He wants money, Kris, any way he can get it. When are you going to stop these fantasies?"

"I love Karl," she protested.

"What is there to love?" Jamie asked sharply.

"You don't know him. When he's gentle, there is no one in the world—"

"You *are* crazy!" Jamie glanced toward the doorway. "Karl put you here, remember?"

"My head hurts," Kristen murmured urgently, "you don't understand. People are nice here. They are more sensitive to life than people outside. Some hide, some fantasize, some pretend, some splinter, and pieces are lost. They try to find them here but never can."

Jamie scrutinized her face more closely. "I'm taking you home, Krissy."

"I don't want to leave," she said softly.

"You'll need some good food. Dorothy will take care of you. We'll all take care of you," Jamie said decisively.

"Karl said that," she said half to herself, her mind pivoting to the past.

Wincing, she shook her head, "It's so hard to figure out."

"What did you say, Kristen?" Jamie asked. His dark, brooding eyes slowly fixed upon her.

She looked away. "Nothing, Jamie, my head aches." She pressed both hands to her temples. Jumbled scenes sprang up within her tangled thoughts. An ambulance clanged in the night, a tunnel, white-garbed figures lifting her strapped to a stretcher, someone speaking, *We'll be there soon.* A cabin in the woods, Karl's friends, laughter, bruises around her face, screams mincing the silence. What had happened? How had she gotten into the ambulance? Questions revolved and became half threats as she tried to think back. Karl, she thought searchingly, will help me remember.

Placing his hands on her shoulders, Jamie tilted her chin toward him. "Listen, Sis. Forget what I said. Try to rest. I'll pick you up at midnight. I've explained it all to the administrators. Let's get you out of here. That's the first step." He paused. "I'll bring some clothes from Karl's place. Gorky still has an extra key, doesn't she?"

"But I want to pack myself."

"No way," he announced firmly. "I don't want you near that place until I find out what the little kike has up his sleeve."

"Please don't use that expression," she protested.

"All right, St. Theresa," he laughed. "Try to get some sleep. Reform my prejudices on the way home. You'll be safe there. The nurses will tell you when it's time. Meanwhile, don't speak to anyone. Your friend's probably paid off a few of them. Although he's such a cheap bastard, that's probably interfered with the success of this little venture."

A young, red-haired nurse walked toward them. "Mr. Blakely, your time is up. Does Kristen know you'll be picking her up later?"

"Yes, baby, and I'll see you later, too," Jamie said, winking at the nurse who flushed in return. Kristen turned to look at Jamie's firm jaw and sharp Scottish features, and felt intense pride.

Then reaching for the nurse's arm, she allowed herself to be led back to the ward. She slipped into the bed as wriggling thoughts made their way through darkness. Overhead ceiling lights cast streaks which shone on the dust balls gathering in the corners of the room. Shadows formed intricate webbed designs on the bars and fraying window screens streaked with dirt. Kristen lay down with eyes wide open. She did not pray.

"Good night, Karl," she said reverently.

3

Just as he was about to step into the elevator, Karl West felt a tap on his shoulder. Instantly whirling around, fists clenched, he found one of the staff psychiatrists, Harold Wicklin, gazing quizzically at him.

"I'm sorry to have startled you, Mr. West, but would you mind coming with me?" the young bespectacled intern asked quietly. Karl nodded, annoyance plain on his face, and followed Wicklin down the long corridor.

Now, what the fuck does this sonofabitch want, he muttered to himself. I've got a goddamned appointment with Kristen's brother—which will take hours probably—and here's another delay. He shook his head. How am I going to make my flight tonight with this fucking idiot going to pablum-feed me that Freudian drivel and hold me up for God knows how long describing Kristen's childhood dreams? I'd like to know how the hell I got into this when all I wanted to do was get laid. . . .

A rather large, windowless alcove served Wicklin as an office, and indicating the more comfortable of two Salvation Army mock-leather chairs, he motioned to Karl to be seated. He himself sat down at a rickety wooden desk. "You seem very angry at me," Wicklin began in a matter-of-fact tone.

Here we go, thought Karl. "Not at all, just worried about Kris," Karl retorted shrewdly. Already squeezing my balls, he warily noted. This could only happen to me. This is probably his third day here and he psychoanalyzes everyone he meets for practice. If I run, he'll think I'm cracking up and bring out the nets.

Karl watched the shrink settle back in his swivel chair. Probably a gift from Portnoy's mother, Karl cracked to himself. Wicklin casually lit a cigarette and blew the smoke out slowly. And now a few tricks from television's favorite shrink, Bob Newhart, Karl groaned inwardly. As he watched the patterns formed by the dissipating smoke, his thoughts drifted. He tried his usual prescription for relaxation: he imagined himself drifting down a snow-drenched mountain on which he alone was skiing powder. It didn't work. He squirmed on the chair, his left leg quivering. At forty-three years old, Karl West was no more able to sit in one place than he had been as a small boy.

His eyes would dart around the room as if they sought a way out. Indeed, being anywhere for any length of time made him feel imprisoned. His skin was browned by the wind. Deep lines etched his face. He had the hard, flat belly of youth and a certain thrill-seeking air which captivated some and frightened off others.

There had been only one long-standing love affair in Karl West's life and that was with aviation. He had eaten, drunk, and slept with more planes than he could remember. And he had loved them all—from the grasshoppers flown by the old needleball-and-airspeed techniques to the four-engine jets.

At eighteen he'd escaped Hunts Point in the Bronx, having been beaten up more times than he cared to remember, and went to live with his Uncle Max on Long Island. Max West was a pioneer pilot who had never married, since he didn't want to be tied to anything or anyone who could possibly bitch about the fact that every moment of his waking time was spent in the air. He had immediately taken a shine to the brooding, complex boy begging to learn to fly. Karl idolized his uncle, whose blue language blasted through the non-pressurized cockpit. Max had sent him to a nearby aeronautics college to be rubbed down with a little culture because, as he explained, "flying was fucking different these days."

"Fuck," Max used to say, "is the best-feelin' word in airline lingo, and it's a damn sight better to say it instead of chewin' it over and over again like everybody else with a bellyache does." Karl knew just what Max meant. Pressure had been building inside him since he was born.

"I've probably got a fuckin' loose valve," he said one dawn, taking off his cap to run his fingers through his hair. He watched Max, his goggles securely fastened, get into the small, squat plane, sit on the seat, and buckle himself in. The old guy always wore the same leather jacket split down the back with its lamb's wool lining oozing out. That was Max's good-luck charm. He kidded that it warded off evil spirits which could attack some musty cub rattling its valves or shaking with a weak shock absorber. Karl and Max were comfortable with each other. Max didn't try to manipulate him, crowd him, or tell him what to do with his life. Together they coasted, not worrying about the next day or week or month, stimulated by the excitement and freedom every time the control tower announced *Cleared for take-off* and the nosewheel lifted. Each time the excitement made Karl's body and senses tingle, like a child on the morning of a much-awaited birthday. The sky—timeless and mysterious—awaited him and he knew it lay there, silently breathing, waiting to be touched.

Four years later he was ready to move on. He joined the Navy, ready to be a gung-ho fighter pilot, itching to get into the Korean fracas. He had flown every mission he could for three years, collecting the distinguished Flying Cross without, as he commented later, getting his ass slung. Early on, Karl had learned that those who were careless got their brains knocked out and to count on no one but himself. He didn't count on the flight mechanics any more than he had trusted the police officers in his old neighborhood to save him. He remembered in detail being jumped by guys while the cop walking by yawned, "That's just too bad." Before every flight he checked out every inch of the plane himself and then double-checked it. He'd hung in with the Navy for a few years after the war. The pay wasn't bad and the restrictions were livable, but a Navy career was "out of the question for a little Jewboy from Hunts Point," as he put it. More than anything, though, he wanted to continue to fly. He watched carefully for his opportunity and one summer morning taxied his silver Corssair straight up to the Manorville office of Leighton Steel.

Bounding out of the plane, he demanded the chief pilot. The stunt apparently impressed Tim Lane, a rugged individualist, because he reported it to Leighton's chairman of the board. Two weeks later, having left the Navy, Karl had his first job in civilian aviation. His restlessness, however, played havoc with his opportunities. Over and over again just as he was about to be promoted or as he was about to clinch some important deal, he'd be out flying to some unknown destination. Yet ideas sizzled within him. He wanted the members of the board at Leighton to grasp, as he did, how planes could give one mobility in the military logistics sense. A company could use them to move equipment or personnel where they were needed, when they were needed. In fact, Karl West was ruthless and brilliant, but he was also restless and greedy and had a strong desire to have money in his pocket immediately—a lot of money. The combination proved explosive, and Karl was a street fighter, not a methodical planner. When a door closed, he would kick it until the thing caved in. Within three years he had risen to senior captain but found his job frozen there. The corporate bureaucracy had decided he was not a team player, had no loyalty to the company, was insubordinate to the passengers if he felt like it and, moreover, was Jewish.

The bottom line had been written almost four years after he had joined Leighton on one red-eye flight from Montreal. Karl had been staying with the rest of the crew partying like crazy at the Queen Elizabeth Hotel, and had stopped drinking just in time to make the twelve-hour grace period. Departure time came and went; the field was socked in by fog and rain, and the crew was cranked up. Karl paced up and down. Finally, calling it a day and going to the bar, he ordered a Horse's Neck, but got a particularly unappetizing flat Tab. Throwing the drink to the ground, he sauntered to his room to grab some shut-eye, only to find he had misplaced the key. All hell broke loose by the time the night clerk arrived with the message that the vice president of Leighton was fuming at having missed an important meeting. Karl's temper was boiling over. Grabbing the poor quivering clerk by the arm, he had thrown him over his left shoulder King-Kong-style while the poor sonofabitch screeched, "Please, Captain West, if you'll just wait a minute."

"You fuckin' idiot. If I wanted to wait, I'd tell you," Karl shouted. The clerk shivered. His teeth chattered. While Karl hit him with a load of abuse, he kept nodding his agreement. Finally, the manager appeared with a master key and calmed Karl down. But the scene left him bitched and vituperative, and he was dutifully reported to those higher up the corporate ladder. When the vice president of Leighton rang at 8:00 A.M., impatient at the delay, Karl agreed to leave, even though early weather reports indicated a hundred-mile-wide, north-south line of thunderstorms all the way up the coast.

Okay, buddy boy, he thought, this is one ride you'll never forget. The first few bumps hadn't disturbed the passengers very much. The vice president's roost was in the first seat of the airplane. The three other passengers were grouped around him, briefcases open, papers spread about. Karl watched them over his right shoulder from the Gulfstream's cockpit. Suddenly the plane slammed into a wall of water. The airplane appeared to stop momentarily, then was carried up at a terrific rate of speed. The vertical wind speed indicator hit maximum. Driving rain, hail, and violent wind buffeted the plane, tossing it about like a confirmed insomniac. Karl became instantly clear-headed and calm. He turned his full attention to controlling the Gulfstream. Carefully, he guided the plane through the storm. But there had been no time to prepare the passengers, whose papers and highballs had been tossed all around the aircraft. The vice president sat upright, both hands clamped on the armrests in a death grip. In the midst of the turmoil, as the aircraft slammed about, he bellowed: "West, you did that on purpose, you kike prick! We've had enough of your antics! You're fuckin' fired!"

For twenty minutes the plane slammed up, down, and sideways. When Karl looked back, one of the passengers who had been calmly smoking had bits of the cigarette in the corner of his mouth. He appeared to have swallowed the rest of it. Another was retching into a paper bag. Managing to break out of the heavy turbulence, Karl breathed a heavy sigh of relief and made the bumpy approach to the runway. No one was talking. Walking back to the terminal, the inevitable was apparent. He had blown the job, and, soon after that, his marriage to a jet-setter he'd met at a Leighton Company party. He was on the toboggan.

The next five or six years were tough sledding. Leighton's staff and their minions had made him a leper. Even though Leighton was small cheese and the giant corporations like Chrysler and Ford had fleets of planes, more than many commercial airlines, no one would hire him. And even if they had, such employment was destined to be short-lived. The corporate pace affected Karl like a numbing death. It made him feel like a servile private carrying out the orders of the brass, most of whom, he believed, were comatose shitheads.

For a while after leaving Leighton, Karl flew the second seat with STA, an overseas carrier. He'd found the job through the help-wanted ads of the *International Times*. But that soon ended when one of the stewardesses joined him in the first-class toilet to become a member of what Karl called the mile-high club, and some other member of the crew ratted, sticking the shaft in deeply.

After that, Karl West bounced around the country ferrying cargo in anything that would fly. Often he slept near his aircraft in a sleeping blanket to save the price of a motel room in order to get a stake together. The scope of the country amazed him. His early life had been spent in a suffocating tenement. The rest of his neighborhood stank from cast-off garbage. It remained in his nostrils the rest of his life, poisoning the taste of what was to come. The fact that he was small and Jewish had been an added disadvantage. Even as a child he'd learned to keep his eyes open and his fists up in order to survive. That instinct gained momentum as the world laid on its licks.

Yet, as he roamed sporadically, Karl caught glimpses of a different world. Places existed which weren't filled with rats and holes and dark buildings falling apart. Places where junkies and drunks didn't sleep on the sidewalks where kids played stickball, and where rape wasn't an everyday occurrence which only mattered if it happened to your mother or sister. And he was goddamned well going to find one of those places for himself, no matter who he had to push out or on.

And sometimes as he slid out of his sleeping blanket and gathered dry sage and wood to build a fire for his morning coffee, he would glimpse a stillness he had never known existed and realize that there were spots in which he could rest when the itch to move was not upon him.

Finally getting a few bucks together, plus a small cash settlement from his ex-wife, which included a clause to stay away from his small daughter, he had gone to his Uncle Max with an idea for a small air carrier which would ferry business executives or important documents to out-of-the-way places which the commercial airlines couldn't feasibly reach. Max and a few old cronies put together enough scratch to begin, and they bought a three-year-old Beach Baron, a small Cessna, and two slicked-up B-24's. They called themselves "Pioneer Aviation." But soon the name changed to "Air Scape," which had, Karl felt, a better sound.

A sad-looking World War II hangar, on top of which was a shredded wind sock, served as their operations building and control tower. A second-hand rotating beacon was on top of the diner next door. Still, Karl felt euphoric. He owned a piece of the dreary dump and was sure he could make it pay off.

By the end of one year they were moving ahead and, for the first time, Karl seemed to be on the verge of crashing the success barrier. Then a recession changed his paper wealth to just plain toilet paper. That was thirty-eight months back. His sporting chance had since turned to horse piss. His enthusiasm hadn't paid off. Murphy's Law prevailed. One goddamned thing got fucked up after the other: malfunctioning engines, non-precise fuel gauges, propellers that wouldn't feather for some unknown reason. In the middle of it all, he felt as if the devil had given him an extra-cheap shot—his disastrous affair with Kristen. Yet he was still leading with his fists. There had to be a way to come out on top, to grab his rightful piece of the action. Then he could buy a ranch somewhere in the mountains where a man could hear the sound of himself and the nearest town was sixty miles away. Old Max, who had become increasingly deaf from years of flying, would be able to live with him. When that itchy feeling came upon him, he could fly his plane up and down the mountain gorges hunting wild horses.

Maybe tonight would be it, if he ever got out of here and collected his passengers. He had made the acquaintance of the two businessmen he was meeting. They had agreed to put up five thousand for the trip if he would fly where they wanted despite the weather. The report suggested hazardous conditions might prevail. He shrugged. Nothing would stand in his way, not this time. It was going to all add up exactly as he wanted.

Karl tried to force his mind back on the present but staring across the desk at Wicklin, obviously another smug over-bred college kid who had never hustled a buck and was trying to stick it to him, a torrent of anger rushed through him. He thought of the tennis games he'd played over the years, the pleasure of moving cat-like in the sun. He wondered about the thin, pale-skinned doctor: had he ever sucked a woman's cunt or sweated; had he ever wondered where his next meal was coming from or how the rent was going to get paid? Or bled gas with his mouth out of the tanks of a closed service station? How much did the creep know? What had he guessed? Nothing, probably. Karl breathed in deeply. He had handled the groundwork well, and Kris had really come unglued anyway. Of course, he was concerned about her. She had gentled his days with her quiet humor and warm body. But there were other broads who could do it, that was for sure. Candy Shelton was one of them, and she was stashed in Burt Cald's apartment right now. The thought excited Karl. He couldn't let his feelings for Kris stand in his way. Women were all the same and he wasn't going to develop a craving for any one of them. That was a feeling that would lead to disaster. He cared for Kris, but she was whacked-out, with her highfalutin' education and crazy ideas about the future and him. He glanced down at his fly. The pleasure he got sure wasn't worth the trouble it got him into. He had to keep his thinking straight. He sighed. All he'd ever wanted was to be free. This was his big opportunity, and he'd be damned if that love crap was going to fuck him up.

Tuning in on Wicklin, who had been rambling for a few minutes, Karl tried to focus on what the shrink was saying.

"You know, of course," Wicklin continued, "that Kris is a very sick young lady. She is a twenty-four-year-old married—" he drew the word out, "—woman who had threatened and attempted suicide and feels she is losing control of herself."

Very good, doctor, thought Karl, holding his hands steady upon the sides of the chair and wishing he could take a leak. He's probably practicing for next week's patient presentation.

"Did she mention to you, Mr. West, that last night she went into my superior's office and began taking books off the shelf, one by one, and dropping them to the floor?" Wicklin paused, shaking his head. "She threw down one hundred thirty-three books."

Karl's eyes narrowed. "No," he said, restraining his impulse to laugh. He'd wanted to add "No shit," but controlled himself. "I told you when I brought Kris here that she had problems."

"One hundred thirty-three books," Wicklin repeated grimly. "Dropped them one by one. Naturally, knowing she is a passive-dependent, passive-aggressive case, I tried to explain to her that people need to let off steam once in a while to escape from unpleasant situations while trying to get their bearings, but they must do so in socially acceptable ways."

"That seemed wise advice, Doc," Karl said flippantly.

"But Mr. West," Wicklin went on, "Band-

Aids are no substitute for having Mrs. West—" He stared searchingly at Karl, drawing out his words, as he watched Karl's reaction, "—work through her problems so that she is more in touch with the outside world as it really is and not as she imagines it to be. She has, as you probably know, severe emotional blind spots and several phobic reactions. The question is, just how depressive do you think she is?"

"I don't know," Karl said irritably. "How depressive do *you* think she is?"

"I'm looking for important clues to her feelings. Can you tell me anything which might be helpful?" the doctor fingered the pipe on his desk as he leaned forward attentively.

"Well, you know," Karl fumbled for the exact words which would trigger the response he wanted, "she's got one hell of an Oedipus complex."

"Explain what you mean, Mr. West."

Karl stared straight into Wicklin's eyes and paused. He had picked up this trick for unnerving people at Leighton's corporate headquarters. "Well, when I met Kris she worked part-time at her father's office in Portland and commuted a few times a week to night classes at NYU. That was about a year ago. At twenty-three Kristen had never lived away from home except in a college dorm and still snuck her sex in cars. You might say I liberated her."

"In what way, Mr. West?" Wicklin inquired politely.

Karl looked at him sharply. "She grew up wanting to be a nun, but her old man nixed the idea. There was a huge fracas about her commitment to what her father apparently believed was a bunch of crap . . ."

"Do you remember the details, Mr. West?"

Karl resisted the impulse to smile. He had him going now. "Kris doesn't like to talk about the past. Claims it's boring to her. But once when she was pretty high on some acid a friend gave her, she got completely shook up, began to cry hysterically, and turned the apartment upside-down looking for some little packet of medals she usually had pinned to her bra. She started to scream about having thwarted God's plan for her, and when I asked her what she meant, she said, 'We are all going to hell. There is no absolution.' Then she folded up crying, 'My father took them.'

" 'Took what?' I asked.

" 'My books, my medals. Don't you understand? I disappointed him, and more than anything I want to please him. He told me I can't go. I'm all he has. He grabbed my sacred books, ripped their pages out, and slapped me hard across my face! She fingered her cheek saying, 'He wasn't going to have anyone in our family fall for that crap. He screamed at me until I gave in. He said if I didn't stay, he would die just as my mother had and this time it would really be my fault.' "

Once more there was an uneasy silence.

"You have an incredible memory, Mr. West." Wicklin's voice held a touch of sharpness.

"So I've been told," Karl answered, wondering if the shrink was being facetious.

"Do you think she accurately recounted the events?" Wicklin leaned forward in his chair.

"How the hell would I know?" said Karl, growing exasperated.

"Were you able to calm her down?" Wicklin asked.

"I tried but couldn't. I had to slap her around a bit. Then I told her she wasn't the nun type anyway, and we made a lot of love."

"Were you aware, Mr. West, that when Kristen entered the hospital she had bruises all over her body and one significant hematoma on the right temple," Wicklin said quietly.

Instantly, Karl was on his feet. "How the hell would I remember that? Do you remember what she was like when I brought her in? We had to subdue her some way."

"*We*, Mr. West?" His eyes met Karl's.

Karl sat down again. "Dr. Cald and a few of my buddies. She wouldn't get into the car. She seemed barely conscious, and I didn't want her to die on me before I could get her here, did I?"

Wicklin frowned. "Had she taken a lot of medication?"

"I'm not a doctor," Karl coughed nervously. "She said she'd taken enough to fix me and looked like it. When a person tells you she wants to die and has been acting like a damn nut for as long as you can remember and you care about them, you get concerned. Hell, terrified is more like it! Kristen's been pulling this shit for a long time—long walks to the seashore in winter, driving into the mountains till her car runs out of gas, gulping sleeping pills. What the hell would you do? I've tried to whip her into shape."

"I'm sure you have, Mr. West," Wicklin said somberly.

Karl nodded, "Damn right. I've tried, but her family has ruined her."

Again there was an awkward silence.

"Is there anything else you can tell us which might be of help?" Wicklin looked at Karl strangely.

"This isn't the first OD bit she's pulled," Karl said sharply.

Wicklin nodded.

"And," Karl continued, "I doubt it's the last."

"She'd be an excellent candidate for long-term therapy," Wicklin mused. "Bright, young, and not psychotic. She has such a powerful need to be taken care of that she fools herself into believing she *is* being cared for. She has to learn that she has more control over her life than she thinks."

"That's just what I think, Doc," said Karl nodding his head. He'd been right all the time about Kris. She was nuts. What he was doing was best for both of them. "That's why I'm relying on the advice of one of the most respected men in your profession, Dr. Burton Cald." Karl paused. "With his help, I'm going to move Kristen somewhere where she can get the long-term help she needs."

Wicklin sucked on his pipe thoughtfully. "There are several places I can suggest, Mr. West."

Karl smiled faintly, "Why don't you write

them down for me. Cald and I are going to discuss Kris later tonight." Karl relaxed. It had all been so easy. Cald was wrong to suggest bribes. Doctors like Wicklin were too straight for that. Anyway, no payoff was necessary to gain what he wanted. Why resort to dirty money when a little Freudian bullshit worked a lot better?

Wicklin handed the list to Karl hesitantly.

"You don't know how much I appreciate the attention you're giving Kris." Karl's voice grew stronger. "She means a lot to me." He stood up and reached for the doctor's hand. "Why don't we get together again in the next few days to discuss this in more detail?"

"Of course, Mr. West," Wicklin replied, while Karl, relieved and excited, moved briskly toward the door.

Wicklin, his eyes filled with thought, stared down at the file lying open on the desk before him. He did not see Karl West, restlessly waiting at the elevator. Nor did he see him pause to stare with fanatical intensity at the grilled gate before shooting down the back stairs.

4

Walking from the hospital, Jamie felt the biting wind stiffen his face and he thrust his cold hands into the pockets of his mackintosh. He wished he had brought a heavy overcoat. As he tried to collect his thoughts for his meeting with Karl West, he found himself distracted by the noise of thickening rush-hour traffic. Around him the city edged into night. Neon scintillated, posters revolved, and people whispered furtively to each other while eight-hundred-foot buildings encircled by glass threw shadows which distorted the faces of passersby outlined by the streetlights' white glare. Jamie wished he were on his cruiser where the smell of the sea was a greeting. From the day he was born he had loved it, or so it seemed—the cold stars over the harbor, the vast sky taller than these somber buildings. He had joined the Navy at twenty-one and would have been a career man had it not been for his father, who insisted Jamie return home ostensibly to take over the fishing fleet, but really to remain under his tutelage until some unknown future date. He had wanted to sail beyond his family boundaries in dark ships of war where papers were still speared on sharp steel points and the captain's Victorian-like cabin was filled with polished oak. He thought himself cut out to run a carrier or destroyer; he who from childhood had kept his toy soldiers in top-notch condition, neatly lined up facing forward. He had carefully mapped out his plans. He charted his imaginary course in various far-off oceans, where he would be always ready to fight some new enemy. He often fantasized how his family would watch his numerous gallant departures with resignation. But now it was hopeless. He could never return to the Navy. His father had made that clear and he had to agree. There was no one else to take over. No one to look out for Kristen. His father was getting old and had already suffered two heart attacks. There was never a day in which Jamie did not think of the future he could have had and the injustice of it all. But that's the way it was and he couldn't fight it. Simply didn't have the balls to tell them all to go to hell. You couldn't do that kind of thing to your own family. No, he would have to bear his misfortune with equanimity. Most of the time, anyway, he enjoyed his job at the dry dock, even if the men were still calling him "Master Jamie," like some boy who had taken to long pants too soon. Christ, he was thirty-two this past November and they still thought of him as his father's boy, the one they had lifted on their shoulders to see the smithy hammering one-of-a-kind iron fittings. One of the wise guys had told Jamie the sparks were fireflies. Like a fool he had tried to gather them up, scorching his fingertips as he fell against the smithy's floor-length leather apron. Well, they'd had their last laugh. One of these days it would all be his and he could run it and them his way instead of the old man's way. Until then, he would bear it all and admit it was his father, not he, who owned the fishing fleet. Eben Blakely had been the pride of his immigrant Scottish family, and still was. Everyone relied on his counsel—sisters, aunts, nephews, brothers. Whenever anyone lied, stole, hit, got in trouble, or fell for the wrong kind of girl, he was called in to settle the fracas. He was huge in stature and reputation: a throwback to some old feudal lord who had been the master of a village of respectful vassals. Unfortunately, he had poisoned his only son with the bitter taste of total authority.

For Jamie, the aftereffects had crippled his spirit. But he was going to hang on until his reward came, if it came. Defensively, he ran his fingers through his blonde sun-streaked hair. His strong, classic chin rose.

"Christ, I need a drink," he thought, going through a mental checklist of things he would have to secure in order to get Kristen safely away.

He took the address Karl had given him out of his pocket and caught sight of the street sign. It was only another block and a half. Keeping his head down and his lips pressed together to keep the wind off, he quickened his pace.

Entering the dimly-lighted cocktail lounge, Jamie momentarily lost his balance. Adjusting his vision, he scanned the faces at the bar. There were several tables clustered behind a white plastic fence at the rear of the room. He strode a few steps closer to complete the search. Karl West had not yet arrived. Suddenly Jamie felt a tight, rigid feeling at his temples. He wondered if this was the sensation Kristen felt: the one that made the doctors call her neurotic. He forced a more relaxed pose, then strode back to the bar. The bartender came to his rescue.

"What'll it be?" he sleepily asked, half-shut eyes barely viewing the nervous man before him.

"Whiskey and soda," Jamie answered gratefully. "A double." The bartender poured slowly.

"Waiting for someone?" he asked disinterestedly.

"Karl West. Do you know him?" Jamie inquired, drawing deeply on the whiskey.

"Ain't been in tonight," muttered the man behind the counter.

"I'll wait," Jamie said. He wondered why Karl had chosen this dingy spot instead of the "Wings Club" or "21," where he usually took those he wanted to impress. He had only met Karl three or four times but he had gotten a pretty good picture of the egotistical little bastard.

Jamie watched the tawny-skinned girl at the

piano. She was a little shorter than he would have liked but had beautiful breasts. She began singing softly, her voice sort of warm and cool at the same time, like smooth scotch flowing into your mind and coating your senses. Gayle, he thought, as he watched her more closely. The thought of Gayle made him uncomfortable. He remembered the way Gayle had looked two nights before as she stood near the window in her apartment wearing the creamy satin minislip he had bought her, tears glistening, nipples hard and straining against the smooth cloth. He felt his cock begin to harden. It seemed impossible to him that he would be thinking so much about Gayle. Always it had been the sea which occupied his dreams. But now it was Gayle. He was caught short by his hunger and was beginning to wonder if . . . but that was impossible. He shook his head. He couldn't marry her. Still he could not help thinking about her. Each time he thrust it out of his mind, the thought returned in moments.

 His mind drifted back to the beginning. Gayle sang at a small club near the harbor. They had met last April at the Harbor Club when he had come to New York to talk to the head of some new fleet of ice trucks that had set up a branch office in Portland. The man had been polite enough as he made small talk about the current and the depths he drifted his lines at, but Jamie knew what he was thinking. The real business decisions were still made by Eben Blakely, and the words "Executive Vice President" on the cards Jamie had recently had imprinted were meaningless. Jamie felt frustration again rise within him, cover his natural pride with despair. The Harbor Club wasn't far from this one. The first time he'd seen Gayle strumming her guitar he wanted her. She was coffee-colored, with long shiny hair which hung down her back caressing her tight buttocks. He felt his breath come harder as he noticed her staring at him, her huge hazel eyes fastened on him with an expression of deep curiosity. He had walked very deliberately over to her. "Hi," her throaty voice beckoned. He followed her to a table at a back corner of the bar and they sat for quite a long time without speaking.

The glow of her face, the excitement in her eyes warmed him, and as she began talking to him he forgot the racial thing and felt an ease he had never before known. He rented a small room near the club, telling his father he wanted Kristen to have a place to retreat to, and began dropping in to see Gayle on a regular basis—two, even three times a week. Her audiences at the club had begun to respond to her electricity and the place quickly became crowded. Her voice and gestures seemed to hypnotize the audience, yet she didn't appear to care, provoking this response almost unconsciously. Always she seemed impatient with people's attention and anxious to be alone with him. At the beginning, neither seemed to think about the problems which could crop up in their relationship. During their first few dates he kissed her only as the evening ended, acting as though they were two innocent kids. At the end of their fourth date she said, "I want you to stay," and led him into her apartment, through the living room and into her bedroom. As he bent his head toward her, a little surprised at the force of her passion, he felt his own desire rise. Sensations grew in him and, clasping her, he heard her excited voice urging him on.

"Don't stop, darling," she crooned.

"I won't, I won't," he replied, his mouth dreamy and soft as he undid the zipper of her dress and brushed his tongue slowly past her shoulders, kneading and licking her nipples. He felt them rise beneath his lips.

Quickly they both undressed, scattering their clothes around the bed. They seemed to melt into each other without strain or self-consciousness.

"I think I love you," he said wonderingly.

"You don't have to say that," she said. "Please don't make me into a cause. I couldn't stand that."

"I'm not much on flags," he grinned.

As time passed he found himself able to talk to Gayle in a way he had never spoken before. She seemed to understand his agitation and depression. She, too, had learned to camouflage pain, but where and under what circumstances she would never tell him.

"Not to worry," she always said. "I've come out of it and found you."

"But I want to know all about you. What you were like as a little girl. Were you ever lonely? Were you ever in love?"

"Today is where my head is."

"But we spend all our time talking about me," Jamie protested.

"You're prettier," she said, lightly reaching up to tickle him.

For the first time since he could remember, someone put him first. How good it felt, a kind of reassurance that he had some special worth still to be salvaged. And more and more he wanted to spend the rest of his life in the calm of her arms.

"I never want to leave you," he said, amazed at his own forceful disclosure.

"Then don't go back. Stay here with me." She gently covered his hands with hers.

"I can't," he grimly replied.

During the weeks that followed their love grew. A warm haze surrounded them. Often they would take her small red Triumph and drive without destination into the surrounding countryside. Spring filled the soft, moist air. When they found a spot that suited them, they would jump from the car, holding each other and laughing.

"We ought to be together forever," he had told her one day as they walked along a beach picking up tiny snail shells which had turned radiant shades of purple in the sun. "We like the same things. In a few years, no one will give the racial thing a second thought."

"What about your family, Jamie?" Gayle asked quietly.

"We'll move away, maybe Australia. Somewhere new. I can do it, Gayle. Let me try," he said emphatically.

She interrupted, "What will happen the first time they need you?"

"Don't you want me to get out?" he asked sharply.

"It seems so impossible. I don't want you to end up hating me." Gayle moved away from him and looked searchingly into his eyes. "I just don't think you could handle the feelings which would come afterwards. Maybe not right away, but next year or the one after that when your father dies and you aren't there because of me," her voice quivered. "Let's stay the way we are." Her eyes were misty.

"No one can do that," Jamie said wearily, sinking down in the sand. He reached hungrily for her and in his mind's eye tried to recapture his vision of the future they could have if only things were different. "We'll wait," he told her, but the reason why escaped him. Soon he found himself noticing that the club was filled with young girls who, having seen him with Gayle, began to make overtures which he suddenly found attractive. More than once he felt himself respond to them even when he and Gayle were together. At first he excused his distractions by blaming them on Gayle's indecision, but later he became aware that he shared her mixed feelings.

All through that long, hot summer he vacillated between wanting to see Gayle and his intoxication with the exciting girls who had begun to notice him.

"I don't know why I took so long to call," he usually said.

"You couldn't sleep," she replied, "and I'm better than a sleeping pill."

"Don't be silly. You know what you mean to me," he protested.

More than once he tried either to end it or make some final decision. But he couldn't seem to stop needing her nor to break with his father for whose promises he had sacrificed so much. It was strange. He was unable to move and yet guilty not to. His body grew taut with the strain of being stretched in diverse directions, but by this time Gayle's understanding, her mute compassion for his predicament, only made him want to escape from her more often than he wanted to see her.

"What's happening to us?" she asked, beginning to mourn the inevitable.

"Don't cry," Jamie answered, unable to meet her eyes. "I don't want to make you cry." He felt exhausted, unable to cope. In Gayle's off-hours he frequented the club, going out with whomever was available. It was inevitable that he and Gayle would collide. Two nights ago he had found her in his room. He had forgotten she still had the key. She had wanted to surprise him. One of the barmaids was with him. Gayle had been standing there near the door, those huge eyes filled with tears. He had gotten rid of the other girl immediately. "It means nothing," he had said, walking toward Gayle. "Nobody's perfect." Shame contradicted him but he shook off the feelings. He embraced her. This time it was he who wanted to cry. "Do you still want me?" he asked.

"Of course," Gayle answered. "Nothing has changed." But her eyes grew more ghost-like and distant. And it was not the same. They both knew it.

He was sick of thinking of the past year and about to order another round when he spied Karl West, who advanced rapidly toward him.

"Hey kid, glad you called," he said, rapping Jamie's shoulder enthusiastically. "When did you get into town? Do you need a place to stay?" Jamie was incredulous. The sonofabitch is too much, he thought, but held his tongue. He matched Karl's senseless bantering with his own.

"I'm on a buying trip. We're looking at a new kind of gaff and harpoon."

"Don't tell me the old guy's goin' to change the historical approach. I don't believe it. Too bad you missed Kris."

"I hoped to see her." Jamie spoke quietly, forcing himself to face Karl. "How long ago did she leave?"

"Flew the coop two or three days ago, I guess. I flew a cargo in from Granger. Got home to find one of her sick-joke notes—'Need time to seek peace. See you in a few days.' The usual shit. Sometimes I think that sister of yours is bananas. No wonder she can't finish her Ph.D. I keep telling her she'll get her degree with Social Security. Every time the urge hits her she's off, literally and figuratively."

Jamie pushed back the urge to smash Karl's mouth. Calming himself he said, "She always was a little restless."

"You mean spoiled," Karl interjected.

"Maybe that, too. Since our mother died, she's been the only bright spot in Dad's life. He babies Kris."

Karl cut in, "And therein hangs her tale of woe. What she wants is another father."

Staring at Karl's gray hair, Jamie couldn't resist the opening. "Well, you almost fill the requirements. At least you've conquered the generation gap."

Karl reddened. "I just took my flight physical and the doctor says I've got the body of a thirty-year-old." Tightening his muscles, which quivered as he flexed them, he glared at Jamie's tall, lean form. "Whipped some smart-assed young New England tennis champ today 6-2, 6-2," he said, his condescension gone and obvious dislike surfacing.

"Great, Karl, great. You always were quite a sport."

His good humor returning, Karl entreated, "How 'bout some food? This place isn't much to look at, but everyone in the know bums it for the pasta."

"Sure, why not, Karl. Then I've got a date," said Jamie, smiling quietly.

"Sure, I know, kid. I remember my salad

days." Throwing one arm around Jamie's shoulder, Karl waved to the owner who showed them to a table.

"Is this all right, Mr. West?" the proprietor asked solicitously.

Karl looked around, surveyed where the other customers had been placed. "I'd rather have that booth in the back corner," he said, striding toward it.

"Sure, sure, Mr. West, whatever you want," the man fawned.

Karl slid in the booth's right corner where he could watch whoever came in and motioned to Jamie to slide in the other side. Then he called to the waiter. "Bring me a Horse's Neck—I'm flying later—and plenty of Chianti for my friend."

5

"Sorry to eat and run, Karl."

"Don't be an ass, kid. If I had a hot prospect waiting, I'd hurry, too," Karl winked. "Look, are you sure you don't need the apartment? I'm taking some joker to Keene late tonight and won't be back 'til mid-morning."

Jamie paused and then picked up the cue, "Maybe you're right. I'll take the key just in case."

"What do you mean," Karl said, amused, " 'in case.' It's a sure thing," Karl laughed, passing the key to Jamie.

"This is really nice of you," Jamie said apologetically.

"Forget it, Jay. Have some fun. Your father keeps that leash too tight."

Jamie flushed and moved the table in order to get up. Karl waved him on saying, "Next time you're here let me know and we'll set up something."

"Sure, Karl, see you then. Take care of yourself," Jamie said and could not help the brittle tone creeping into his voice.

Striding out of the restaurant, Jamie glanced back to see a small, pinch-faced girl with a long blonde braid down her back being led to the table where Karl sat. She looks vaguely familiar, thought Jamie. On Karl's face was a look of annoyance which made Jamie wish he could hear their conversation. But anxious to get Kristen's things, he hastened to hail a cab and called out Karl's address to the driver.

Within minutes the shrill sounds of the Mardi-gras bacchanalian swarm of MacDougal Street accosted him. More single nubile women ran around per square foot than Jamie would have guessed could be found in any other spot on earth. During the winter they clustered together in small apartments to await something they couldn't quite put their fingers on, and when summer came they fled, dressed in bright swirling skirts, to beach houses at Fire Island to avoid the housewife syndrome their mothers had chosen. Many of the men who roamed about wore this season's high-camp skin-tight chino pants instead of Levis with their black leather jackets and engineering boots. Their hair was carefully layered. Jamie found it hard to tell who was queer by staring, but couldn't resist trying. Mostly the residents were just semi-Bohemians or pseudo ones, trying to appear relaxed and casual despite the frenzied outbursts of the neighborhood around them. Karl's converted brownstone gave little respite from the constant noise. Reaching the floor where Gorky lived, he heard high-pitched laughter and acid rock. Gorky's door stood slightly ajar. He went in.

Gorky lounged upon her beige suede sofa surrounded by four or five student-disciples who sat cross-legged on the hemp rug. While she spoke, tendrils of brown hair which she had attempted to restrain with a tortoise comb bobbed about her face as she gestured, her long graceful arms illustrating her images, and deftly fingered the delicate gold *Chai* which hung just below the neckline of her blouse. Positioned on either side of her, two lean young men opted for twindom. Both had long hair and tank shirts and were shoeless. Jamie made his way to the sofa while Gorky disengaged herself and scattered her followers, who immediately began to mingle with the other guests. Gorky had gained a modest amount of fame as the author of such tragi-comic novels as *Finders Keepers*, but though her books were critically praised, none sold well. To make a living she taught at NYU, where both Jamie and Kristen had studied. She was a kind of legend on campus, having sided with the students in several uprisings. However, it was her very real charisma which brought her into contact with activist students—Chicanos, street hippies, black militants, and apostate WASPS—who gathered near her. Gorky's office at the university had the appearance of an Eastern commune. The door remained opened and the coffee hot, and inside, slumped upon the desks or posturing on the floors and chairs, were assertive women's libbers, springy blonde afros, the shirtless and the barefooted, as well as those more conventionally dressed. Amidst this tumult of strewn books and bodies Gorky would sit, stallion-like legs tucked under her, as she read or discussed various theories on Vonnegut, Hesse, Brautigan, and Kesey, obviously quite content. Early in her career she had found that equal parts of chaos and tranquility suited her. She thought it quite marvelous that the world had adapted to her style and could not imagine why she should want to change either the world or herself. She had long since become convinced that despite the fact that life was suspended between two utterly immovable events—birth and death—and was frequently filled with a crock of shit in between, individuals still had the power to create meaning. Fortified now and then by what she considered to be a sufficient amount of alcohol, and not withstanding her periods of angst, she had deliberately set out to find out how and where. Oddly enough, she seldom travelled—even on sabbaticals—preferring to vary the characters who populated her quarters on a semester basis, and she seldom changed her uniform winter or summer, wearing an endless series of rumpled plaid blouses and blue denim skirts. It was rumored around campus that early in her career she had had an affair with a young talented female student who later committed suicide. If this was true, she never spoke of it, and at the age of forty-four or thereabouts Roslyn Gorky seemed to have smothered any desire for a personal relationship.

She enjoyed her own raucous parties, where she would stay up all night drinking undiluted scotch and talking to her friends about "Lima" (life, its meaning and purpose), while about her various forms of communion—sexual and otherwise—were taking place. Still it seemed to her that being alone was the most vital part of life, and she didn't hesitate to eject visitors who interfered with that tenet and overstayed their welcome.

Jamie, glad to see that Gorky seemed in one of her more convivial moods, found himself responding with affection to the bearlike hug with which the professor greeted him.

"What brings you to this den of iniquity?" Gorky exclaimed warmly. "Have you had dinner?"

"Yes to the second, trouble to the first," Jamie said grimly.

"No doubt the name of this game is Karl West," Gorky said mockingly.

"Exactly. Could we talk?" Jamie mustered his strength and thoughts.

"Come with me, friend. My inner sanctum is at your disposal."

They made their way out of the clamor, strode down the hall, and unlatched the door to the alcove which served as her combination den and retreat.

Jamie loved the soft amber quiet of the room. Today, however, he felt too nervous to appreciate it.

"Look at this," he exclaimed, taking a folded sheet from his wallet and passing it to Gorky who glanced at the message briefly.

"Son of a bitch," she murmured disgustedly and gave the paper back to Jamie. "Son of a bitch," she repeated.

"Exactly," Jamie replied.

"Where is she?"

"Brookhaven."

Gorky shook her head. "Good Christ. She must be terrified. Kristen has such a frail way of coping, like a hurt and pleading child—"

"I don't think she is," Jamie said quietly.

"What?"

"Coping," Jamie passed a hand across his head, "or even facing what has happened. She seems to be drifting as if where and what she is can be obscured by not looking."

"Very poetic."

"She is that, but also goddamned stupid," Jamie said angrily.

"If one is filled with ideals about love and reformation, one shouldn't try them out on a rabid dog," Gorky interjected sharply. She paused, "Brookhaven isn't the wisest place to have stashed her. He should have gotten her out of the state."

Jamie nodded, "That obviously was his next move after he removed the hassle of a kidnapping rap. He's been telling the officials at the hospital they're married."

"That's cute." Gorky paused before continuing. "How much did the note say he wants? Two hundred fifty thousand dollars? That's chicken shit. Wonder why he didn't ask for more."

"Our name's not Onassis you know," Jamie said tersely. "Anyway, I'm getting her out tonight."

"In what condition?" Gorky asked deliberately and carefully.

"I'm not sure, but it's too dangerous to leave her where she is." Jamie's voice was troubled.

"From the way she's been acting lately, I'd say taking her out isn't a reliable solution either."

"I can see that," Jamie made an impatient gesture, "but she'll be better off at home."

"With the family brand of chicken soup, New England Conch Chowder?" Gorky quipped.

"Come off it, Gork," Jamie added ruefully.

Gorky looked at him. "Kristen doesn't need more care. She's already an emotional twelve-year-old. She needs to get off her ass, quit hiding in her room reading, reciting poetry, and wishing she'd taken the veil. She has to face the fact that although there are plenty of people who want to care for her for one reason or another, she can't depend on that kind of commitment being a lifelong occupation. Sure, she feels lonely, but so does everyone who isn't numb and grabbing someone who will dominate her and make all the decisions. We all have to make a bedmate of loneliness in order to get to know and like ourselves. And sooner or later Kris has to come to terms with that."

"Gorky, that's easier for some of us to accept than others."

Gorky declared decisively, "We all have to

ante up life's initiation fee. It's a one-time phenomenon. You have to shit or get off the pot."

"That's what my dad and I are afraid of. Kris isn't like other people."

Gorky threw up her hands. "None of us are. That's what loneliness is—finding that out."

The room grew silent as each fled to his own thoughts.

Gorky broke the soundless pause.
"Where's West?" she asked softly.

"We just had dinner at Gino's. He gave me the key for upstairs in case I get some action tonight."

"Not much chance of his coming back here, then?"

"Anyway, he's got Candice Shelton in tow."

"His half-sister?" Gorky asked sharply.

"I thought I knew her," Jamie hesitated then went on, "He tried fixing me up with her once, but it didn't work out. No wonder she looked familiar."

Gorky nodded, "They're doing a Byron-Augusta. Incest is in, you know—"

"Christ, he's too much." Jamie snorted.

"You don't say." Gorky's laugh was hollow.

Together they left Gorky's apartment and climbed up the next two flights of stairs. Quickly, Gorky grew winded.

"Time sucks," she said bitterly.

Jamie quickly retorted, "And that's not all."

THE SPLINTERED EYE

They laughed as they entered Karl's tiny apartment, and flipped on a light switch.

"The only thing that made this place habitable was Kristen," Gorky said distastefully.

"Who was it said a house is not a home?" Jamie asked, looking around at the meticulous, sterile surroundings. Nothing was out of place. Even the cigarette labels in the glass upon the coffee table faced forward. None were higher than the others: equality reigned. It was difficult to discover anything about Karl West from his living quarters.

Nervously Jamie opened the bedroom door and crossed over to the closet. Karl's clothes hung in fastidious order. First pullover sports shirts, then button-downs, sports jackets, and suits. The entire wardrobe took up less than half the closet. Toward the back Jamie spied Kristen's Gucci suitcase. He had given it to her when she graduated from college. Reaching for it, he unzipped the case and saw her things placed neatly inside. Jamie shook his head.

"Obviously Karl's arranged everything," he said, looking over at Gorky.

"How do you know that?" Gorky inquired.

"Well, neatness was never one of Kristen's virtues," Jamie quipped, pulling out a pair of slacks and a shirt. "Let me just see if her makeup case is here." Jamie fingered the inside pocket. "Yeah, it is. I guess that's all."

He picked up the suitcase. "Let's get out of

here. I thought we'd be able to talk, but this place is like the catacombs."

"We can go back to my apartment," Gorky offered, "if you've got a few minutes."

"What about the party-goers?"

"They're used to my periodic absences. They'll survive."

They walked down the stairs silently and returned to Gorky's tiny den. Gorky settled into the huge leather easy chair, pulling up her favorite mohair afghan. "What do you propose to do when West finds out?" she asked, fingering the well-worn fringe.

Jamie slumped into a nearby chair and considered the remark, wondering how much to involve her.

"My father's taken care of that. One doesn't work around the waterfront without connections," he shrugged.

"When you use shit like that, you're right on Karl's level," Gorky objected.

"They'll just shake him up a bit and wish him *bon voyage* to a warmer climate," Jamie answered tersely.

Gorky grimaced. "What do you think Kristen's going to say about that?"

"By the time she knows, he'll be long gone," Jamie said quietly.

"When?" Gorky asked thoughtfully.

Jamie Blakely watched Gorky's face with a taut expression. "Tonight, he'll get the message. He should be gone by tomorrow." Then, as if he had read her mind, he said, "Look, there's no choice here. Something had to be done quickly." Again he paused before continuing.

"There are always choices," Gorky interjected irritably.

"Not if she's your sister," Jamie said accusingly.

Gorky waved him to silence. "I didn't mean that. I meant the *gunnif* way you're handling this. Why don't you call the police?"

Jamie considered. "That would involve Kristen in a crock of shit and you know it. Mentally she couldn't take it, logically it would ruin her future, and emotionally she just might let him commit her to expiate some unknown guilt."

"Your plan could throw her over the edge." Abruptly Gorky sat up in her chair. "Moreover, it puts you on a par with West. Have you ever considered that with a little insight Kris might find the similarities appalling?"

Silence again. Then Jamie glanced at his watch, "I've got to get her now, Gork."

Gorky shook her head, "Okay, Jay. You're probably right."

"Hell, I hope so," Jamie said nervously, passing his fingers through his hair. "I damn well hope so." He walked over and patted her shoulder affectionately and without another word left the room. Slowly Gorky got up and strode to the file cabinet. Without deliberating, she reached to get a glass of her favorite scotch. Then she headed for the party across the hall from which the noise level remained loud and constant.

It was almost a quarter after eleven when Jamie stepped wearily into the hospital lobby. He sighed. Wicklin should have gotten the go-ahead from one of the administrators and be ready to release Kristen. He hoped she was not going to oppose him and be pig-headed. What if she wanted to say goodbye to West? Jamie hesitated, marshalling his thoughts. Christ, West must be on his way to Keene, so that shouldn't cause any problem, although with Karl one could never count on easy solutions. His hand shaking, Jamie pushed hard on the elevator button. His emotions were whirling as he got off on the fifth floor. With a shock he saw Dr. Wicklin standing near the gate when the doors opened.

"Mr. Blakely, I need to see you for a few minutes before Kristen is released."

"I want to get her out as quickly as possible, Dr. Wicklin," Jamie said curtly, staring at his watch.

"I know that, Mr. Blakely. But it seems to me very important that I convey some things to you before you go."

Jamie drew a deep breath and stared at Wicklin's resolute face. "Okay, but let's make it fast," he muttered.

"Follow me, please."

The two men stepped into a small deserted

office nearby. Wicklin sat down at the desk and motioned Jamie to a slat chair pulled alongside it.

"Mr. Blakely, if you'll give me the clothes you've brought, I'll hand them to the attendant and Kristen can dress while we talk." Jamie passed them to him.

Wicklin handed back the boots. "You have to hold these until Kristen gets downstairs, Mr. Blakely."

"Jesus." Jamie's eyes widened. He became more nervous.

"It's merely a precaution," the doctor added quietly. He cleared his throat.

"Mr. Blakely, I would be remiss in my duties if I didn't tell you that I and the other attending physicians are against Kristen's being removed in this way."

For the second time that evening, Jamie took the folded sheet of paper from his wallet. His eyes glowed fiercely.

"Read this, Dr. Wicklin," he said. The words had been neatly typed.

Dear Mr. Blakely,

It will probably come as a surprise to you that your daughter and I have been living as man and wife for the past six months. During that time Kristen has been very troubled to the point where she has been cutting most of her classes and staying in bed a great deal of the time. Recently she's gotten deeply into dope. All of this has resulted in several suicide attempts. She has been ashamed to write to you. Because of her urging, I've taken her away and will need $250,000 within the next five days to place her in a suitable hospital, etc. If you wish to see her again, you will arrange for the money to be deposited in the Swiss account listed below. I strongly urge that you do not contact the authorities in regard to my requests, since I have conclusive proof that Kristen has not only been doing dope but dealing it and would then feel honor-bound to expose the information.

                                        Sincerely,
                                        Karl I. West

Union Bank of Switzerland
345994732
Zurich, Switzerland

    Visibly shaken, Harold Wicklin took out a worn pack of cigarettes and lit one, seeking to regain his composure. He shook his head thoughtfully. The case obviously puzzled him.

    "Mr. Blakely," he began slowly, his lips twitching. He seemed genuinely confused as to how best to phrase his thoughts. "Kristen is in a state of depression and helplessness. She seems to exist in a little shell. She is afraid of being abandoned by Mr. West and so accedes to his demands even though they may cause her self-destruction." A flicker of anxiety crossed his face; he paused a moment then went on. "She refuses to discuss her unresolved problems, nor can she handle them. After observing her with Mr. West, I have asked myself whether they might share a *folie a deux*, which is a rare paranoid psychosis participated in by two people in which the weaker adopts the delusional system of the stronger—"

Jamie sucked in his breath, "Look here, Wicklin," he snapped, "I think that's a lot of crap. Kristen's unhappy, has lost a lot weight, and has gotten herself involved with a goddamned nut who's convinced her that he's some Nietzschian superman when all he really is—is—" Jamie moistened his lips and stopped for a moment, searching for words, "—a kike bastard."

Wicklin flushed. "Regardless of Karl West's ethnic background or character and notwithstanding his possible paranoid personality, your sister is still a very disturbed young woman. Among her problems are cocaine, barbiturates, and amphetamines." He paused. "At this point, she's experiencing withdrawal symptoms. Moreover, she expresses suicidal feelings."

"Are you telling me she's having a nervous breakdown and might kill herself anytime?" Jamie asked, half-rising in his chair.

Wicklin sat behind the desk fiddling with the pack of cigarettes. "Only laymen use terms like nervous breakdown. I'm trying to say that Kristen is a delicate girl who has spent much of her life overly sheltered and now feels unable to cope with the stresses of her life." He leaned forward. "She needs therapy in order to focus on her strengths and do a great deal more for herself. I don't think she can get the kind of help she needs by returning to your family home where many of her early problems began."

For an instant Jamie felt an impulse to turn and run, but mastered it. He said, "That may be so, Dr. Wicklin, but unless she gets away from West, she may not live long enough to go anywhere." He shook his head. "I don't think my sister's crazy. I read the medical reports this afternoon. You doctors say her associations are logical and her reasoning is good. That means she understands what is real and isn't, doesn't it?" Jamie stared directly into Wicklin's watery gray eyes. "I think West was losing control of her so he labelled her 'sick' and sent her here to solve his problems. As for the drug part, who do you think introduced her to that stuff? . . . . West. If anyone ought to be here, it's him."

"Please, Mr. Blakely," Wicklin pointed out patiently, "I know this is a difficult situation, but we are trying to put Kristen's best interests first."

Jamie leaned forward, his fingers tightened visibly on the desk's edge. "Doctor, I don't have time to debate that point. What you're offering Kris, if what you say is true about her and I doubt it, is just another kind of crutch."

"Therapy is a method of helping the patient find the source of his unresolved feelings."

"And that makes the patient completely dependent on his therapist," Jamie snapped.

Wicklin shook his head decisively. "Not in the long run."

"How long is long in Krissy's case?" Jamie's face had become drawn, the anxiety showing.

"We can't be sure of that," Wicklin said earnestly. "Perhaps months, perhaps several years."

"Perhaps a lifetime. From what I've seen of the people in analysis, very few get cured," Jamie said slowly, his dark brooding eyes fixed upon Wicklin.

"But many function who could not previously do so," Wicklin answered firmly.

"Is that enough?" Jamie cut Wicklin's words short.

"Mr. Blakely, we are not miracle workers."

"More like soothsayers," Jamie protested.

Wicklin's voice was strained. "Mr. Blakely, I don't want to be involved in name-calling, but in helping Kristen . . ." He swallowed hard.

"I'm sure you mean that, Wicklin. It's your method I question. And I just don't have the time to debate this any longer." Jamie stopped, weighing his next words carefully. "We'll both have to rely on my family's judgment." He took a document from the inside pocket of his overcoat and handed it to Wicklin. His voice became surprisingly strong: "This is a power of attorney signed by Kristen. It was prepared by our legal firm, Bristel, Waring, and Hetherington. You'll remember, of course, that Judge Bristel is a former Associate Justice of the Supreme Court. Here is another document affirming that Kristen is not now nor ever has been the legal wife of Karl West. I must ask you now to immediately release her into my custody."

There was an uneasy silence.

"Mr. Blakely," Wicklin said slowly, "I have been told to comply with your wishes, but feel that I should attempt to acquaint you with the truth."

"As you see it," Jamie responded.

"As it is," Wicklin said emphatically. "Kristen is so sensitive and beaten. She has almost too much feeling. In a way, it is making her psychologically blind."

Jamie gazed searchingly at Wicklin. I'll be damned, he thought. Even here Kristen finds admirers.

His face troubled, Wicklin said, "Mr. Blakely, if Kristen should experience further hallucinatory episodes or severe distress, please get in touch with us."

Jamie tried to make his tone persuasive, "I will, of course, Doctor."

"If you will follow me, I'll take you to discharge quarters," Wicklin said tiredly.

Jamie nodded. The doctor moved ahead, passing through the admittance gate to a passageway and into a small room in which there were several straight-backed aluminum chairs and an elevator with a keyed triple lock near its operating panel.

"Here are the necessary papers for your signature." Jamie hesitated for only an instant, then leaned over and wrote his name. "If you will try to be patient, the nurses on duty will bring Kristen to you." Wicklin sighed. "I wish you good luck." Looking dismayed and very tired, he disappeared into one of the nearby passageways.

6

Glistening with perspiration, Kristen spun in slow motion through dense, flaccid woolen fantasies; one held her captive, bobbing weightless in air, a prisoner sentenced to perpetual motion. She tried to twist around, afraid she would smother. Sounds became elongated, distorted. Plaid patterns hemorrhaged, colors bled into each other, fused, then metamorphosed into vibrations again. She tried to crawl between midnight and dawn the way a child wedges through a picket fence, but found herself stuck between down-filled spaces which covered the ground beneath her, cushioned her head, and muffled her words. Suddenly a thick cloud bank loomed ahead. She was heaved toward it. Vapors of ice splayed cold fragments, then an arctic coffin opened, sucking her in. A scream formed in her throat but no sound came. The wet fluff in her mouth turned to steel wool and she choked. Someone took the gag from her mouth and Kristen heard the electric shock treatment pronounced a success.

Bent over her, a white ghost mumbled. From the bottom of viscous sleep, Kristen rose. The fluttering room took a hazy shape. She felt a clammy rubber hand upon her shoulder. Another nurse held a plastic cup to Kristen's lips.

"Drink this," the woman said. "Drink this, you'll feel better."

Stunned, still in a trance-like state, Kristen shook her head to disagree, but the sweet liquid dribbled down her throat.

Wrenching herself free, she tried to sit up. "Are you crazy?" she mumbled, "you'll drown me."

No one seemed to hear her.

Darkness seeped through the window bars. It was still night. Colorless rain fell.

The nurse set the slacks and shirt Jamie had brought on the drab blanket. He had forgotten underwear, Kristen noticed. "Please, Kristen, I know you're tired but you must get dressed. Your brother's come to take you home."

"But I like it here," the girl cried.

A second starched white uniform quickly appeared.

"Kristen, be still," she said crisply. "You'll wake everyone and spoil my ward." Kristen wanted to lie back and turn off the incessant babbling. Why should I get up, she wondered. Why doesn't everyone let me alone? She considered hiding, but it would do no good. They would find her, seek out the place. Beg, cajole, or order her to desist. Easier, much easier to give in. To hear, 'good girl, Kristen, that's better, Kristen.' All her life, no matter how tired or bruised she felt, it was always the same game in which she made the necessary moves to receive the obligatory reward.

"Kristen, are you listening?" the first nurse spoke loudly, jabbing at Kristen's shoulder with a red-painted nail. Anger flashed through Kristen. Head throbbing, she tried to get up. Time slipped away and when she awoke another white ghost chanted.

"That's fine," the nurse spoke in a nursery rhyme sing-song, holding up a hairbrush which Kristen grasped she was to use.

She looked around her. In the other beds were women who cursed, wept, peed, or wrapped themselves in gray cocoons of drugged sleep as she had. Ceiling lights seethed. Old-timers covered their heads with pillows, but the flashlights of the night nurses sought them out every hour at bed check. Many only pretended sleep, their anxieties hidden from view by silence; in others fears flared at night, causing them to scream out. Kristen, dazed and dizzy, stood up and leaned against the side rail for support.

"Are you ready now?" The red-nailed nurse put her arm out to steady Kristen. "Juanita said to give you these," said another white form nearby. Kristen listened to the new voice; glancing up she saw two forest-green booties in her hand. Kristen's hand quivered, thinking of the wild-eyed woman in the bathroom patiently knitting. She clasped them to her and put them on. Enemies and friends are difficult to distinguish. "Let me show you the way," the first nurse gestured. Kristen, cold and pale, followed. She inched along the hallway as if blindfolded. Once she stopped, winded, and drew a deep breath. Shaking her head, she noted that the halls smelled differently; at night they smelled of caustic ammonia, during the day, rancid breath. She shuddered. The night attendant had done the job well, but Kristen knew the room would puke again the next morning.

Kristen's breathing quickened again, grew more shallow by the time the two women reached the room where Jamie waited. She was finding it hard to breathe and staggered a little. Jamie held out his arms. With small, uncertain steps she inched toward him. The nurse called, "Kristen, wait, take these," handing her the beige boots Jamie had brought. "I couldn't give them to you before. Put them on when you are downstairs, and don't come back, Kris," she said softly, genuinely. Kristen tried to focus upon her. Her alligator-face looks different in this light, she observed, rather young and vulnerable. Not trusting herself to speak, Kristen nodded her head in agreement to the nurse's words. Mrs. Kranz unlocked the elevator and pressed the call button. Kristen listened to her brother thank the nurse. Finally the steel door opened. Jamie and Kristen stepped inside. It was a shock to be free, Kristen reflected, if one called this freedom. She leaned on her brother's arm. As they moved out of the building Kristen kept her eyes straight ahead, fearful that a glance in another direction would produce the desire to run, to where was uncertain. Her feet felt cold; she looked down. Frost dotted the knit socks. With stiff fingers, Kristen pulled the boots on top of them. She expected to fall. At any moment she was sure dark blood would ooze from her, break loose. But nothing happened. They reached Jamie's car. Thick and twisted by silhouettes, the night passed through her. She stood shivering, but Jamie ushered her into the car, repeating, "It's all right, Kris, you'll be home soon."

It was after midnight when they crossed the Throgs Neck Bridge and headed toward the New England Thruway. The warmth of the car made Jamie feel better; being on the move eased the nervous stomach he'd had all day. As soon as he was sure that Kristen wasn't going to act up or protest, he slowed his speed, keeping an eye on her. She had wound herself into a tiny ball scrunched at the far end of the seat. They rode in silence. Kristen blinked, then lapsed again into the comfort of sleep.

Jamie swung onto the thruway at about the same moment Karl West adjusted his cap, narrowed his eyes to inspect the instrument panel of the plane, adjusted the radio earphones, and called into the speaker, "LaGuardia ground, this is King Air five-niner Turkey Trot, ready to go."

"King Air five-niner Turkey Trot, you are

cleared for takeoff on runway one-four. Contact departure control airborne and have a good trip."

The sleek, white and blue Beech King Air he had rented moved smoothly onto the runway from the taxiing strip, and he spoke in a low tone as he completed the takeoff checklist. Slowly he pulled back on the wheel to put the plane into flight altitude. Very soon the nose wheel came off the ground and the wheels cleared the runway, gear up, plane airborne. Pride surged in him as the plane climbed. Flying was a matter of feel, he thought, like knowing when to take the women you wanted. And better than most, Karl West understood the power of touch. He could anticipate what the gauges and dials would read and how the engine should sound when well lubricated, and as the plane reached its proper altitude, he listened until the right sensations clicked into place. Only then did he forego handling everything himself and switch to autopilot. Until this moment, he hadn't paid much attention to his two passengers. Now his gaze wandered to them. The pushed-in faces of the two men made them look like ex-boxers, but they were nattily dressed in dark business suits. The smaller of the two kept tugging at the corner of his moustache, while his bald-headed companion stared straight ahead. What were their names again? He searched his memory and tried to remember being introduced in the hangar and of whom the two reminded him. He scrutinized them again. Suddenly he knew: the warders in Kafka's *The Trial.* He thought back to the last scene of the book. Well, he mused, you may be sure when I go, gentlemen, it won't be as a dog. Hell, he thought, I must be getting paranoaic from visiting Kristen. I haven't read Kafka in years since ... what-was-her-name. He pulled his earlobe thoughtfully—the tall auburn one with sky-high legs and a succulent black mound. He laughed to himself and looked around.

Something inside the cabin did not feel quite right. Karl fingered the compartment in which he always carried a gun. The short man had begun grooming his moustache back and forth beneath his finger. Karl half-turned toward him in order to get a closer look, and spoke in the deep placid voice he reserved for in-flight communication. "The weather is overcast, gentlemen. Please keep your seat belts securely buckled until we reach cruising altitude. The approximate flight time between here and Keene is one hour. If you wish to smoke, you may." The men said nothing. When Karl finished talking, there was a strained harsh quiet. He shrugged. What the fuck is wrong with me, he thought. But the hemmed-in feeling in his chest gained momentum. He kept his guard up, watched as the potato-headed passenger pulled a magazine from his briefcase. Silence prevailed except for the occasional snap of a turning page. Karl turned his attention back to the plane. He inspected the radar. A cloud build-up and a moderate amount of turbulence. He navigated around it, flew through light, wet snow. Then suddenly the red warning light came on.

THE SPLINTERED EYE

Checking the left pressure gauge on the panel in front of him, he saw that it was low—too low. Carefully keeping his voice emotionless, he spoke to his passengers. "Extinguish cigarettes. Buckle in." Apart from the oil pressure gauge, things appeared okay. Then the indicator for the left engine started to drop. "Shit," he muttered to himself, annoyed. "I'm going to shut down the left engine," he said loudly and calmly. "The plane is perfectly capable of operating on one engine. I'm turning off the other's fuel supply and feathering it."

The taller man's head shook vigorously. The other's face greened and Karl handed him back a paper bag.

Almost as if Kristen in her sleep sensed Karl's danger, she cried out, *"Kyrie eleison, Christe eleison."* Jamie studied her restless form intently, distress gathering at the corners of his mouth. He did not know whether to stop the car or pick up speed. *"Benedictus in Domine,"* she intoned.

"Kristen, try to rest," Jamie flushed. "We'll be there soon."

"Hail Mary, full of grace," her voice continued.

"Good Christ," he muttered, "she's hallucinating. Get hold of yourself," he begged her, growing exasperated. What was he supposed to do now? The hospital was a good seventy miles back. Jamie's hands shook on the wheel. I should have left her there; fuck my father. He pulled in his chin, momentarily overcome with bitterness. Everything had to be done the old man's way. Meanwhile I play errand boy while the old guy probably sits smoking his pipe at home. Later, if anything went wrong, I—not Dad—would be the scapegoat. Jamie gunned the car's engine disgustedly, then noticed Kristen's body twitching. Jamie rubbed his eyes. Maybe she *was* crazy. What could he say or do? But if he did not bring her home, his father would be uncontrollable. In the isolation of his thoughts, anger fibrillated, rising, falling. He saw Kristen jerk about. Indecision rent him. He placed Wicklin's number on the dashboard, thinking he might have to turn back to Brookhaven anyway; self-disgust filled him. His stomach growled. "No wonder my father gives me no authority," he muttered to himself. Even now he was stuttering over what to do with this wretched scene and the rope which tethered him to it. Annoyed, he accelerated again, only to see Kristen grasp the door handle and call, "Let us kneel and make an act of contrition."

    His foot hit the brake, "Goddammit, Kris, stop this crap!" The car lurched. Kristen's head struck the windshield. A small sound broke from her mouth.

    Quickly Jamie pulled off onto the shoulder of the highway and, terror-stricken, stared at his moaning sister. A bloody bruise grew on her left temple. "My head, my head." Jamie's heart pounded. Kristen rocked back and forth, "Karl—

the glass—you're hurting me." Even more frightened, he saw that she was hallucinating again. What if she was dying?

"Kris, please—" he put his arms around her. The cars roared past as if they were inside his chest. He wept openly as shame filled him.

Karl West tightly grasped the rudder of his plane, struggling to regulate his failing engine. "The damned thing won't feather." He cursed it to himself and turned off the engine's fuel supply and accessories. The gauge showed no oil pressure. Karl began to sweat profusely. Whether the wild spinning would cause the propeller to break off— that was the important question. Reducing airspeed, he waited. The fucked-up thing wouldn't stop. Carefully he threw the radio switch and called traffic control. "Ground, this is King Air five-niner Turkey Trot. Unable to maintain altitude. One out, can't feather it."

"Roger, squawk ident," ground replied.

He pushed the button, "Squawking, what is the nearest suitable airport?"

"Are you declaring an emergency?"

"Not at this time. Clear me for a lower altitude."

"Cleared for four thousand feet," ground replied.

He began descending immediately, relieved that there was no traffic in the area. Just then, ground control called in.

"Aircraft at twelve hundred."

THE SPLINTERED EYE

Ten minutes later the voice again reported, "Aircraft at forty-seven hundred feet." His two passengers had begun to react to the trouble. As the noise and vibrations increased, the man with the moustache screamed, "What's happening?"

Karl explained quietly, calmly, "Left engine failing. Sit tight. Everything's going to stabilize."

Suddenly the plane began to lose altitude. "We're going to crash, you bastard," the bald head growled.

"Shut up," Karl nodded warningly.

The left engine whined like a wounded animal. Karl battled the plane. The moustached man crossed himself.

Snow iced the maze of silver light through which the crippled plane made its way. Visibility was decreasing. Shit, Karl thought, what next? Then, with a last dying shudder, the engine hushed.

Karl sighed deeply, his eyes widened with the pleasure of conquest, he felt his cock harden. Momentarily he felt an exultation which startled him with its intensity. He had felt it before during combat. He savored the excitement. Taking a deep breath, he steadied his thoughts. The only possible danger now was fire. Karl's eyes squinted upward. It's just you and me, he thought, daring fate.

"Slow," he murmured to himself, "easy does it." On the instrument panel in front of him, the radio bleeped its signal. Karl pushed the ident button, listening for further instructions.

"King Air five-niner, you are twenty miles south of Tarrytown. Do you wish to land there?"

"Negative," Karl replied. He would make Keene where the passengers had booked. He needed the five grand they had promised. The answer was to put more power on the good engine. Slowly, Karl moved the rudder forward.

Less than an hour later he located the rotating beacon at Keene, where the tower reported strong crosswinds and patches of frozen snow mixed with ice—a slippery runway, the last contest.

Karl sucked in his breath. He was ready for the landing. But before he could begin, the bald head interrupted. From his briefcase the man took a revolver, cocked it, and shouted, "We'd better make it, West. We have business with you."

Karl stiffened, but his voice remained steady as he answered, "We'll make it. Take it easy."

Then, betraying his annoyance only by the tic in his eye and the sweat which covered his forehead, Karl returned to the immediate problem. He would have to use every foot of the fucking runway to bring the plane in, and braking would be tough.

"Place your heads in your laps," he ordered, "now!" He was very much in command. Fearfully, the men did as they were told. Putting on the approach light, Karl prepared to land. A bleeper blipped. Karl pressed firmly for the landing gear. His heart hammered. The gear opened and a moment later locked. Thank God, he thought, wiping the sweat from his forehead and wishing some stewardess was near, something worked.

THE SPLINTERED EYE

The approach of the airport whizzed under the aircraft. Karl threw off his safety belt, primed to throw every pound of his weight against the brake. The plane vibrated to and fro. Finally it halted. Slowly Karl taxied to the waiting runway and cut power.

"Go on," Karl said, straightening up and running a sleeve across his wet forehead. "Go on. You were saying you wanted to speak to me . . ."

The man with the moustache drew his revolver and answered, "We're going to leave this plane. Him first, you in the middle. No problems."

Karl almost laughed as he considered the plot. He could make a grab for the revolver. He decided against it. The two men were obviously serious, even though they seemed like comic-strip characters. They had the advantage of preparation. He would have to bide his time, wait his opportunity for better odds.

Slowly Karl adjusted his flight cap and looked squarely into the eyes of the man who held the gun. Then he saw the reflection of the man's partner in the windshield, his own revolver cocked. Karl nodded his acquiescence.

The three men got out. "Okay, lover boy," the bald man scowled, "let's see how you do with men instead of the women you shove around."

An old Chevy coupe waited in front of Butler Aviation. Karl's pulse raced. James Bond always utilized these situations to his advantage. Emulating him, Karl pivoted, ramming his fist into the shorter guy's jaw. He grabbed the man's elbow and flipped him over his shoulder; the ground spasmed. From somewhere behind him, the man's partner materialized. His lighted cigarette came close to Karl's eye. "One more fucking trick, West," he growled, "and you won't make your next date."

A hammer fell. Karl West felt the top of his head go hollow. From a distance he heard a weight drop down . . .

He awoke in the back seat of an automobile, and saw a powerfully built sixtyish man seated beside him. Fixing the man's steel-like expression in his mind he heard, "This is a rather unconventional way to meet Mr. West. However, I thought it best that you make your request of me in person." Without changing his expression, the man lowered his voice. "I am Eben Blakely."

Karl West smiled wryly. The man's quietness alarmed him. Dimly he understood there were to be no excited outbursts, no fevered accusation. The face of Kristen's father, only a thumb's breadth from his own, remained inscrutable, but there was a look in his eyes that Karl recognized, had seen before in the streets from which he came—the look of a cat given the freedom of a ghetto tenement. Instantly, he had a startlingly clear insight into Eben Blakely. Karl shook his head. His own cunning would gain no edge here.

Realizing the vulnerability of his position, he said slowly, "I think, sir," he paused as if this were a chess game and his pawn had been checked, "you have the advantage."

THE SPLINTERED EYE

"Well then," Eben said crisply, "we shall talk when we reach our destination."

A silence fell. Nearly an hour elapsed. The car swung onto a vaguely familiar dirt road before they stopped. The moustached man opened the door and motioned to Karl, who climbed out. He looked around in amazement. This was the cabin to which he'd brought Kristen one month ago. Obviously Blakely knew everything. Damn it, he muttered to himself, knowing one-upmanship when he saw it. He looked up. Dark clouds covered the chalk moon.

As the night snow and rain formed ochrebrown patterns on the glass, Jamie tilted his head this way and that, surveying both the road and his sister who rocked frantically, chanting Karl's name. Then, just when he breathed a sigh of relief as she stopped, Kristen made a rasping sound he recognized. Kristen had always been asthmatic. She was having an attack.

Jamie felt his stomach muscles tense. He wanted to vomit and leaned back against the seat, his hand resting on the shelf of his pelvis. Suddenly, his whole back was equally cold and wet. All at once, a sinister thought struck him. If he did nothing, made no move to aid Kristen, he would be free. The thought wandered down his collar and through his innards. The pressure of the moment was intolerable. Momentarily, he did nothing, waiting, waiting. The rasping continued. There was a sudden constriction. Kristen's head rotated back, her lips open and held apart as if with surgical clamps. He visualized Gayle. How he wished he could be with her now. Hide in Gayle's arms . . . the sound of rattling breath interrupted his thoughts. Quickly he returned to the present. He got out of the car and ran around to the trunk. Kristen always carried Theophylline. Blackness made the search difficult. Strewing the contents of the suitcase around, he located the pillbox in the makeup case. Clumsily his fingers closed around the pills inside like a blind man's around a pencil. He scooped up snow in his cupped palm and ran toward the other side of the car, pulling the door open. "Kristen, swallow these." She resisted. He grasped her arm, pulling her from the car. Unable to get her balance, she fell to the pavement. Jamie knelt over her, pinched her nostrils, then reached for more snow and pried her mouth open. He placed the pills far back in her throat and poured the melted snow in afterwards, taking care to massage the larynx.

"Inhale, exhale, inhale, exhale," he shouted.

Like a wax doll, Kristen stiffened then obeyed. Her eyes slid sideways and she slipped from consciousness, but only for a moment. When she awakened her breath began to come in short gulps, then heavy sighs, finally becoming normal. The attack was over. Jamie picked her up from the pavement. Gently he placed her in the car.

"Kristen, I'm going to stop at the next diner," he said in a subdued tone. Sporadic sobs shook the girl. Jamie drove on, his frustration mounting. He bit his lip until it bled. Sporadically Kristen coughed, spitting phlegm out the window. Jamie tried to lighten the situation.

"As one bloody mess to another," he said, trying to joke, "how about a makeover." He tossed over Kristen's cosmetic case. Slowly she pulled down the visor until the mirror appeared. Her long auburn hair was matted and a purple bruise covered most of her face. Jamie tried not to stare. "Comb your hair. Put on some lipstick, too. You'll feel better," he said gently.

Without enthusiasm, Kristen smoothed her hair with her fingers. Then darting a look at Jamie, she reached inside the makeup case to grasp the silver bullet which she usually wore about her neck. Staring at herself in the mirror, she put it on.

Jamie sighed. Her vanity made him feel better. She couldn't be too badly off if she cared how she looked. Inwardly his stomach unclenched and he turned his attention to the road.

Fifteen minutes later he caught sight of The Spindletop Diner. "I usually stop there," he said more to himself than Kristen. His thoughts flicked back to Gayle, but he brought them back to the present. The moon bared a few razor-sharp teeth as he pulled the car into the diner's parking lot. "I wonder if that's a damned sign," he murmured. Kristen, not listening nodded. Weary, a dismaying flatness filling him, Jamie got out slowly, his head down, and came around to open Kristen's door.

She looked tiny and vulnerable. "Kristen, I'm sorry," he said, giving her fingers a soft squeeze.

There was no answer, but she moved closer to him and they walked up the steps to the diner hand-in-hand.

7

Inside the diner, phosphorescent signs proclaimed Budweiser king of beers, John Denver records purred, and somewhat groggy apple pie still made the best-seller list. A few joking truckers were bunched together at the counter, their wisecracks punctuated occasionally by a loud guffaw or a resounding backslap. The flat, yellow slab of light from the ceiling fixture produced a murky atmosphere that Kristen thought rather in character with the place. They took a booth far to the rear, away from the jukebox. Kristen watched the beehive hair-do of the fortyish waitress who had been behind the counter increase to mountain-like proportions as she grew legs and appeared at their table.

"Hi, Jamie," she said with a wink.

"Grace, um, ah—" Jamie stuttered, "this is my sister Kristen. I don't think you've met."

Kristen tried to affect a smile.

THE SPLINTERED EYE

The waitress nodded. "Hi, what'll you have?" she asked in a flat, small voice.

"Two glazed doughnuts and coffee for both of us."

Jamie darted a sideways glance at Kristen who was about to say nothing. The effort wasn't worth it, she thought. Instead she asked, "Jay, could you let me have some change?" He handed her a quarter. "Excuse me," she murmured walking away. A telephone call box hung on the wall next to the ladies' room. Kristen put a quarter in. "Reverse the charges, please," she said to the monotone-voiced operator who came on the line. Listening to the buzz, she fiddled nervously with a twist of hair. "Is it the wrong number?" No one answered. She hung up and tried the procedure again. This time the operator cut the sound off just as a female voice came on. Kristen stood trembling, receiver in hand, trying to make up her mind whether to ring again. Fear pounded and glossy-ridged thoughts twisted within her. Shaking her head, she remembered she had no more change and made her way into the bathroom. A white-hot feeling came toward her with a stabbing pain. Then she noticed the bullet around her neck glistening. She pulled it off and pried the bullet open. Inhaling the white powder up her nose, she looked up to see the bee-hived waitress staring. Kristen gripped the side of the wash basin. Bending over, she scooped up some water and swallowed it. The waitress disappeared into one of the stalls. Light-headed now, pain ebbing, Kristen made her way back to the table. As Jamie watched her she bit into the pasty-sweet doughnut, and it mixed with the bitter taste in her mouth.

Jamie's voice broke in, shrill and angry. "What the hell is going on, Kris?" He hunched forward, leaning on the table, face flushed. Kristen laid her fork down carefully and lifted her eyes to stare a few inches to his left.

"The narc, huh," she said, indicating the starched uniform up front.

"Don't use that Haight Street crap with me, Kristen. It doesn't suit you." His face had come alive with anger.

Kristen closed her eyes; his voice blurred. She felt disoriented, and trembled with panic. I am trapped here, she thought, doomed to sit attentively and listen. Her body twitched; tiny pinpricks struck one after another until it became hard not to move around. The coke, she guessed, and fought the impulse to sleep.

"What are you on?" Jamie glared.

She shook her head. He sounded furious, like Karl. Karl—what had happened between them? Was there someone else? He had sworn not, but she had heard—

"Kristen," Jamie interrupted. His voice, loud, struck her. "What drugs are you taking?" He grabbed her arm.

"Please, Jamie," she pushed him away. "I don't know what you mean."

"The hell you don't," he said sharply. "Do you think I'm an idiot?"

THE SPLINTERED EYE

Kristen squirmed on her side of the booth. She pressed her fingers against her temples.

"Tell the truth for once," Jamie pleaded, his face now pinched, drawn.

"I don't want to talk," she murmured softly, helplessly. "I don't want to. Why can't you all leave me alone?"

And then something loosened within Jamie, some element of control which had always been part of him. "Alone! Christ, I'd like to leave you all alone," he said in disgust, "but you need caretakers. Whenever the going gets tough, the nominee is me. Do you think I want to play perpetual babysitter for you, or be an errand boy for Dad? I want to get away— Have you ever asked about my problems? I have a girl, Kris—Gayle. She's *black*."

Kristen couldn't stand it any longer. "Jamie," she stammered, "I can't help being this way."

He stared at her, furious. "The hell you can't. What are you trying to tell me? You're crazy and need to be coddled forever? I'm sick myself." His arms swept out, knocking some dishes off the table.

"You hate me," Kristen said tearfully.

"Grow up Kris. That's bull. I'm up to here with it." He clasped his own neck. "You're all choking me; I feel nauseated. I want to throw it all up to concentrate on Gayle, on me, on our life," he continued.

Kristen tried to concentrate, but her head pounded. Everything in it mixed together: her brother's face blended into Karl's, then her father's; their speeches rushed together, words broke into syllables, then letters. She was carried upon the jangling noise back in time toward the smearing yellow light on the ceiling and beyond it.

They have been together a little more than a year. Almost as soon as she moves in, the pattern changes. In the first few weeks, even when he was away half an hour, he telephoned incessantly. Now, except for infrequent interludes—trips to Martha's Vineyard, New Orleans, or Texas, when she sits quietly in the rear of the plane working on her thesis or fucks him passionately in the various motels in which they stay after he has dropped off his clients—he hardly seems aware of her presence. Kristen spends hour after hour alone at the apartment window, staring at the street below. She flattens herself against the casement, her bright excited eyes fixed on the silhouettes which pass. She tries to catch sight of him before he knows she is there and is irritated at being scrutinized. At those times he lunges up the stairs and shouts in a cruel unrecognizable voice: "Don't press me. I can't take it." Once he makes it up the stairs without her knowing, grabs her from behind, sliding his forearm beneath her chin, choking her. "Who told you to watch me?" he screams. She feels paralyzed, unable to speak. Her mind squirms, veering out of control. That day Karl undresses her like a child and puts her to bed. When she awakes, her face and body are bruised. He wears a stricken look and kneels beside the bed, his head next to hers. "Kristen," he says agonizingly, "we'd better say goodbye."

But she can't, won't give up. Later that night she doesn't want to—afterwards, when he makes love to her, timidly at first, seeming almost afraid to touch her, yet unable to restrain himself, he repeats again and again, "I'm sorry." So she stays. There had never really been a question of leaving. She had come too far.

That next morning she covers her bruises so no one will notice them. For almost a week there are no more pointed, cutting words. They spend almost all their free time inhabiting each other's bodies, until Kristen feels that she has become all sensation, his flesh constantly against hers. She prays it will never end.

When winter's mahogany-burnished colors play upon the window, she stands in a garnet-colored knit dress, searching for Karl who has promised to take her to a concert. It is Sunday afternoon. He has been gone since nine—another "unavoidable appointment," a string of fake, lusterless pearls.

As she waits, something in her, something which has chipped, begins to sliver, shatter into irregular jagged pieces which cannot be simply fitted together again. She cannot stop shivering.

Karl comes up behind her. He has seen her at the window watching him and stolen in to catch her. He begins to shake her. One wrong word, one mistaken gesture can ignite his temper, or, worse, make him leave forever. "Well, Kristen . . ."

She doesn't answer. Instead, while an iron band tightens about her forehead, she gets her plaid coat from the closet, slips a glossy red Seconal into her mouth, and stands waiting at the door.

"I feel numb," Jamie interjected, "confused. Sometimes it's hard to remember things. Have you ever felt like that? Am I cracking up?"

"Of course not," Kristen murmurs, trying to extricate herself from the past, from Karl. But Jamie, absorbed in his own thoughts, doesn't notice Kristen's eyes wandering away again.

"Let me do it," Karl says.

Smiling hesitantly, Kristen hands Karl the coat, like a dog bringing the ball to his master. As Karl fastens one button after the other, his mood suddenly lifts. "Come on, hon," he says, "Ozawa's conducting."

They walk down the stairs, Karl's arm about her. A giddiness begins in the back of Kristen's head.

He hails a cab with a funny comic gesture that endears him to her. Her eyes fill with tears. When he pats the seat beside him, she slides over. Close to him at last. "Gorky's meeting us there," he says. "She has a late class."

Dvořák's "New World" symphony receives them in the lobby of Philharmonic Hall. As they

THE SPLINTERED EYE

hurry to their seats, it pours like a waterfall, shimmering and crystal-colored. The music—all brass and strings—flows toward her, enters without any effort. Momentarily, Kristen relaxes. Gorky, a few minutes late, smiles a greeting, slides in beside them, and without further comment they turn their attention to the music. Kristen steals a glance at Karl. The tension in his face eases, lines melt, and the blue of his eyes seems to soften. Grateful, she sighs and soon the oceanic rhythm captivates her also, cools and smoothes the throbbing of her head.

During the second movement, Karl leans toward Kristen and rests his head upon her shoulder. Then she feels utterly at peace. She wants to tell him but doesn't. In that single, delicate moment, with Karl's head on her shoulder, Kristen feels ecstasy. It pierces her like starlight.

And then, too soon, the music stops. The audience stands, hands beating wildly, the young Japanese conductor, Seiji Ozawa, bowing over and over. Kristen would like to remain there, but Karl's arm half-lifts her upward as he shouts, "Bravo." Afterward, the three happily and dreamily stroll toward the Russian Tearoom where Karl orders blinis with red caviar and champagne. As they eat, Karl reaches out to squeeze Kristen's hand or brush her forehead with his lips. Gorky, too, is caught up in high spirits. "Marvelous, marvelous, wasn't he?" she asks. "Almost as though the music burst from direct communion between the compose and ultimate conductor." Karl and Kristen

122

nod. Then Gorky asks, "Where have you two been keeping yourselves, except for the obvious—off on one of those holidays Kristen brags about?"

Karl's face darkens. Kristen stiffens, watching his mood change again. She tries not to be frightened. He doesn't like me to talk, she thinks, dismayed . . . I should have been more careful. Gorky, noticing Karl's quick, angry gesture, leans over and pats his cheek lightly. "Comrade, this spy will not reveal the deep, dark secret missions on which you go—except, of course, to the C.I.A." she says, whipping out a small notebook and pencil from her pocketbook.

"You two are practicing nuts," Karl grimaces, "walking advertisements on the dangers of over-education."

"Ah, comrade," Gorky jokes, " 'tis 'red' true, 'tis 'red' true."

The play on words, Kristen understands, but she looks searchingly at Karl as if for a signal as to how to react.

When he laughs, Kristen momentarily relaxes.

"Speaking of the dangers of over-education, how would both of you like to come to a lecture I'm giving at Haines Hall Friday?" Gorky entreats. "Warm bodies are desperately needed."

"Gork, your lectures are usually adventures in a sardine can," Kristen says warmly.

"Not, I fear, the week preceding Christmas vacation," Gorky petulantly pouts. "Anyway, this one's my favorite: 'Santa Lists for Grown-ups.' "

"For this the university pays you?" Karl interjects, shaking his head in mock disbelief.

"If not," Gorky retorts, "my unique revelations will not be forthcoming."

"Well, old girl," says Karl laughing, "I fear I shall have to refuse the honor of your invitation. I'm jockeying some half-assed executives to Canada this weekend for fun and games."

Kristen's heart pounds. He hasn't mentioned going away. She grimaces at the thought of the long, lonely weekend ahead.

"Kris," Karl says frowning, "I have to go."

"I know," she replies. "I just hate being alone," she says wistfully.

"Look," Gorky interrupts the tension developing, "one unembalmed victim is better than none. You come, Kristen. We'll have dinner afterwards. I'll pay. Call it just compensation."

"Kris would love to," Karl answers quickly.

For Kristen, the rest of the evening proceeds in slow motion. She has visions of her lover far away, of an accident, with no one contacting her. She sees Karl falling from the plane, his scalp lacerated, his ribs cracked, blood rushing from the wounds, dead, alone without her. She wonders if it could really happen in a different part of the globe where they cannot reach each other.

Somehow she manages to smile at the appropriate times, to interject "oh's," "of course," and "I see" in between. Finally the night ends. From the back of her head Kristen feels her lips move, overhears herself mouth goodbye. She feels near tears.

Inside her the trembling has begun again. She casts a glance at her love and is relieved. Fortunately, he doesn't seem to see.

Finally they are back in the apartment. In the next few hours, as Karl touches her body, enters her, she grows satisfied again. But the next morning she is sick to her stomach, her head aches, the room spins.

Too many pills is her first thought. I have to cut back. But this time the headache doesn't go away. Dates pass, revolve in her mind. Mechanically she beings to count. In a frightened daze, she stops, forgets, adds the total again. "Jesus," she murmurs, "what if I'm . . ." She doesn't finish the sentence, pushes it back into some unthought dimension of her mind. But days later it resurfaces. This time she cannot avoid it and makes an appointment with her doctor.

"Come back in a week, young lady," the gynecologist says later that day. "It's too early to tell if you're pregnant. Take these twice a day. Call if you get your period. Now don't look so unhappy. There are alternatives if you decide not to have it."

For the next two days Kristen waits. Nothing happens; her period does not come despite the medication. She thinks of telling Karl but doesn't. She fantasizes much of the time, daydreams of their blue-eyed son or daughter. For the first time she is glad he is away so much or preoccupied, and does not watch her closely. But when he leaves for the weekend Friday morning, an odd, prickling nervousness fills her.

THE SPLINTERED EYE

She spends the morning in bed, blinds drawn. At two she rises, opens the drapes, and dresses slowly, wondering if it is her imagination or if her denims have suddenly become tighter. She swallows two red capsules to ease the trembling, and too early she grabs a cab and arrives at Haines Hall for Gorky's lecture. Twice, before anyone comes, she slips into the ladies' room, whether from nervousness or the strange sensation within her pelvis she is unsure. Already the lecture hall is hot, airless. Finally students begin to enter and find seats. Kristen spots Gorky among them and relaxes. She watches the professor move onto the stage, toss the portable podium to the floor, and perch on the scarred wooden table edge.

"Make yourselves comfortable," Gorky says. "Coffee is in the rear. Groan loudly in unison if I ramble, but God, if He exists, better come at grade time to the aid of those who leave before my conclusion." Students laugh, then applaud. They begin to rearrange the chairs from designated rows to the informal clusters Gorky prefers. She is dressed in a forest-green smock with black leggings, at ease and smiling. She looks around and then begins.

"Since the existential era has begun, learned men viewing the uncircumscribed new world have proclaimed the modern atmosphere a wasteland. They have bemoaned the loss of certitude, that drying up of a somewhat dubious sea of faith, into a blob of unformed clay. Of course, the fact that in the past charted seas often proved to be different from their mapped definitions makes little impact.

THE SPLINTERED EYE

The ideal world, at least as a concept, was comforting and comfortable. Even if there is and was no Santa Claus, no universal truths, gods, or perceivable other worlds, just their notion and the kind ministrations of parent figures in hiding, presents of various colors and shapes helped to perpetuate fantasy and ward off fears of deprivation. Since Darwin, little childlike creatures have been stamping their feet in dismay as holiday figure after figure have been revealed as nonexistent. Those who have posted and had returned their requests for presents in the form of threats, letters, or prayers have been doubly disappointed. As the twentieth century advances, they have turned from free gifts and fulfillment to insecure advertisements and parental largesse or psychiatrists, drugs, or lovers. Unfortunately, these momentary appeasements of angst are also usually followed by chronic disillusionment. To grow up one must become his own source of illumination, his own present-giver."

From a blue canvas bag, Gorky takes a plastic globe lamp, the cord of which she plugs into the nearest outlet. Then she pulls the shades down, blocking outside light. The stationary globe begins to cast colored shapes all around the wall behind the speaker's platform.

"This small globe," Gorky explains, "provides the illusion of reality. Study it for a moment."

Then she pulls open the drapes, unplugs the light and passes it to the audience. A few minutes later Gorky says, "Please pass it to me." As soon as it reaches her, she takes the globe's translucent pieces apart and exposes the inner shade which has a multi-colored design stamped upon it. Then she spins the shade slowly. "So Plato was correct.

You have been fooled once again by preconceptions, misconceptioons, promises of rainbows, or colored lights. You wish to be perpetual children supplied with magic fireworks by parent figures in the sky. When success or power or love disappoint your expectations, since they are not adequate replacements for God, wombs, seas of faith, or Santa Claus, you complain of being cheated by history, the mass media, and promises made but not kept, when really the liar is yourself. It is time to form a new concept of what life is and can be, to define fulfillment in terms of commitment and involvement. This is the delusional state of perpetual innocence—the 'gimmees.' But if you relinquish this stage of being and move through experience toward vision, you will find new gifts. It is true in such a world there will be uncertainty and despair, but in this new universe grown people need not look for what they want under decorated trees or be in bed by ten or brush their teeth in a prescribed manner at a designated hour each day. The magical world of Santa's elves didn't exist anyway, except through your child's eye. Forget bedtime stories. A person journeys between two fixed points—birth and death—but within this interim without fantasies he may build an expansive creative space, whatever the setting. This Christmas, if you give up the non-existence myth you can begin to create a multi-dimensional reality. Of course, it is transient, but it is, and nothing else ever will be."

Kristen sits quietly. She struggles trying to make sense of the concepts about which Gorky speaks, but they are too abstract to be an antidote for her own pain. Gorky's philosophy seems distant, unclear, and somehow unrelated to her or anything. Kristen hears a sudden burst of applause. It, too, seems far away.

Gorky is speaking again. "By the way, when these various ideas have been digested, disjointed, or dispensed with, spend the rest of your vacation walking, looking, seeing, and feeling. Don't agonize too much. Remember what that pragmatic English playwright of Stratford said happens to those of us who do, despite Descartes' advice to the contrary."

Gorky leaves the stage to mingle with her audience. Thank God it's over, Kristen thinks, unable to sit any longer. She likes Gorky, admires her in fact, but she is anxious to get away from her words. They weigh her down with their complexity and girth. They remind her of those old philosophical discourses, or of Nero playing on his fiddle. Such things make sense only in the classroom, where student robots listen intently in order to pass future exams. Kristen shakes her head slowly. What difference does it all make? Only Karl makes a difference, being in Karl's arms. She shakes her head wearily.

Gorky looks pleased and content. Kristen watches her, wondering. Every night Gorky is alone. She has no one, probably won't ever have anyone. A meaningless lifetime interim of time. No matter what she says, Kristen sees the truth, the emptiness. She cringes. How could one not need love? Love is a center so that one's elements will not diffuse, come apart, as she would without Karl. People like Gorky, like Sister Margaret Rose, their lives were smoke. She was quite sure that, alone on dark nights, away from their convents or schools, the notions of which they speak with such authority lost meaning even to them. What good were they? She shook her head. Exposure to Karl, to the sensation of him, the excitement made all this pale and bloodless.

"Kristen," Gorky says, tapping her gently on the shoulder, "we can make our getaway in just a few minutes. Be patient."

"Whatever you say," Kristen says politely. "Don't hurry. I've nowhere to go." Gorky gazes at Kristen, about to speak, but just then another professor propels her away.

Immediately Kristen regrets her perfunctory politeness. She needs more pills to get through the evening but she is afraid to take more, wondering how many she has already had. Thoughts flutter through her mind like scraps of paper with undecipherable messages which jar and exhaust her. She sits down again. A student from one of her classes walks by, asks for a cigarette, lights it, sits near her. "I love her, don't you?" the Levi-clad man says, indicating Gorky.

Kristen nods. She hopes he will go away.

THE SPLINTERED EYE

"I'm not a philosophy major, so a lot of stuff passes over my head. But it's the first time talk about the cosmos interested me. You too?" he asks earnestly. For the first time Kristen sees him. He has strong Greek features, the kind an artist might want to sculpt. Kristen's hands twitch; she wishes him away. Finally he goes.

Unexpectedly Gorky stands behind her. "Okay, we're out." Kristen nods. Unsteadily she gets up. "The night air will make you feel better," Gorky says pensively. "I've fixed dinner at my place. The quiet will do us both good."

Soon they are at Gorky's apartment. Kristen notices a red linen-clad bridge table set up for dinner. "Festive, eh?" Gorky hands her a sherry. "And now, *voila le diner*," she says, disappearing into the kitchen. Kristen stands there awkwardly fingering the glass. In a few minutes Gorky reappears to light the logs in the fireplace. Then she waves to Kristen and is off again. The heat from the fire makes Kristen's skin feel clammy, ghost-like, but she stares into the flames, entranced. Suddenly an attack of nausea hits. First she squats down on the floor trying to wait out the feeling. Gorky, catching sight of her from the kitchen, rushes in. "Kristen, what's wrong?"

"I don't know," Kristen says, her voice low, hesitant. "Please just leave me alone."

There is silence. Gorky looks away. "We need music," she says, turning on the stereo.

The rich heavy sound seeps into Kristen, pleasures her. "Who is it?" she asks.

"Deodata I," Gorky answers.

"He feels good," Kristen murmurs.

At dinner Gorky does most of the talking while she ladles the rich Beef Bourgignon into brown earthenware bowls. "One of my favorite students made these," she nods and passes heavy French bread to dip. "This will help." She watches Kristen and pours burgundy into thick, apricot-colored satin glasses.

"I knew someone like Karl once," Gorky goes on. "Another spring, a different campus. She was a vibrant, intense girl, perhaps too vibrant, too intense. She couldn't stay anywhere very long. I tried to hold her; she tried to stay. Neither of us achieved our wish. One night after a fight—" she paused, "—it seemed like a lot of others—she drove over a cliff. No note, just got out. Maybe it was us, or the excitement leaped out of bounds. I wasn't there, will never know. But her eyes, they were the same strange blue as Karl's," Gorky sighed.

Kristen stared at her. She had been right; Gorky's ideas had nothing to do with life, not even her own.

"Kristen, intense fragments are not all—"

"You don't understand. I need something, someone to hold onto," Kristen moaned audibly.

Gorky regarded her levelly with clear gray eyes. "Kristen, don't—" Gorky pleaded.

Kristen's lips trembled. "Do you know how I have spent my whole life?" she asks. "Being talked to, at, about, or away from. Until Karl, I thought life equalled talk plus a preposition."

THE SPLINTERED EYE

"And with Karl you have discovered life, albeit a somewhat demented one," Gorky says sadly.

The two women gaze at each other for a moment and then look away.

"My pain is real, not imaginary," Jamie was saying decisively. "I can't think of anything else." In Kristen's mind, Jamie's words kept disappearing, dissolving, and then reuniting as she tried to focus.

"I don't know, I don't," she stammered, beginning to sob.

"Kristen, you haven't heard a thing I've been saying," Jamie shook his head. "I just don't exist for you."

"I'm sorry," she murmured, tears in her eyes. "I feel sick to my stomach."

"So do I," he retorted, "sick of putting myself last while you get involved with jerks like Karl or do dope; sick of having no life while you or Dad pretend to be ill or dying or crazy. Do you know how long I've been waiting for dear old Dad to turn his business affairs over to me, to let me handle your property and mine the way I want?"

"My affairs, Jamie, why should you handle my affairs?" Kristen protested.

"You're crazy," he said bitterly. "You can't even handle petty cash. You both need me to straighten things out. You'll be locked up in an insane asylum and the old guy isn't going to live forever."

Kristen was startled. "Do you want him to die?"

"I want to be free. I'm sick of following orders."

"But why didn't you stay in the Navy; you could have been an officer."

"Make sense, Kristen. How could I? I had to come home to you and Dad."

Kristen shook her head. Jamie was wrong. She had never told him to come home. Had her father? She couldn't be sure. Her head ached. It was so hard to remember. She wanted to console Jamie, to tell him everything would be all right. He would be all right. But there was only silence between them whether they talked or not. Kristen sighed and looked away. Finally Jamie spoke.

"Let's go," he said, and picked the check up with shaking hands—so much like her own.

There were few other cars on the highway. Everything seemed to be dormant, the houses they passed, store windows, trees, all covered with stillness. She wanted to sleep a silent sleep where no dreams blared; but each time she slid into unconsciousness echoes rapped upon her skull and shapes accosted her. She was too tired to fight; they dragged her toward them, her eyes wide open. "You're exhausted," Jamie said, glancing over. She turned toward him. In a soothing tone he spoke again: "Close your eyes, Kristen. Rest."

PART TWO

8

Eben Blakely stood somber-faced at the liquor bar in the New Hampshire cottage he had rented. He glanced at his watch. It was one A.M. Jamie and Kristen should be on their way home by now, he thought. Worry knit his thick brows together, but he struggled to make his voice agreeable.

"Would you care for something to drink, Mr. West?" Eben glanced toward his daughter's lover who, slumped in a faded chintz armchair, mumbled an inaudible reply.

"Pardon?" Blakely asked. "You must forgive my hearing problem. One of the ravages of time, I fear."

"Ginger ale," Karl said sullenly. "Liquor and flying are a combustible mixture."

"No doubt you are prudent, Mr. West," the dour-faced Scot answered solemnly. He poured the soda and then a stiff whiskey for himself. "I ought to abstain for health reasons, but the pleasure of good scotch from Aviemore or strong ale from the old brewhouse at Innerleigh makes longevity less desirable and savoring life more to my taste." Eben sipped his drink while he studied the other man. Nervously, Karl drummed his fingers on the table beside him. Eben handed him the soda and sat down. He proceeded with caution. Explosives were a poor method for clearing land, and anyway Eben had by sixty-eight learned how to curb the quick tongue of his youth. He had long ago learned of the relationship between West and his only daughter. Though he hadn't liked the initial reports about West, he had hoped the affair would end Kristen's obsession with the Church. He hadn't anticipated that Kristen's new commitment would entail total enslavement to Karl West. He was damned if he was going to permit this new nonsense. Nope, even if a purge was necessary, Eben was going to make sure it took place one way or the other. Eben's lower lip tightened. He was used to making decisions alone and then acting upon them.

Holding himself in check, he stirred the scotch, whose ice crystals dwindled, and sought to use the impatience of the man he observed. Eben began slowly, "Mr. West, you must admit—" and he touched the letter which protruded slightly from his breast pocket, "—that this plus Kristen's unknown whereabouts are reasons for a parent's concern."

Karl nodded slowly.

"And these," Eben went on decisively, "have prompted me to suggest my solution to our mutual problems."

"A perfect solution, no doubt, Blakely," Karl said cryptically.

Eben flushed. "I think, West," he watched Karl intensely, "I have a proposition which will interest you, one which will fulfill certain of your desires, release you from a difficult situation, ensure a certain amount of profit, and permit my daughter the opportunity to create a satisfactory life for herself—" He paused. There was an edge in his voice. With an effort of will he steadied it. "—without the martyr complex she would surely develop if your removal from this situation were anything but voluntary. My strategy may not be perfect but—"

"Is a reasonable facsimile of," Karl interjected sarcastically.

Eben's voice came strong, the burr more pronounced. "A compromise of mutual benefit to us both."

Karl looked up in astonishment. Certain breaks came without planning or effect. Somehow he felt this was going to be one of them. It was sheer good fortune. On first seeing Blakely, Karl had not known what was to come. Now, if he played it right, he might win after all. Luck was going to be with him. He could tell. He felt like smiling, but kept his face serious. Meeting Kristen had been fortuitous after all.

Karl spoke in a cool tone. Conveying what he

thought would seem distant interest, he said, "Good business deals are hard to come by. Explain what you have in mind, Blakely."

Eben produced his pipe, leaned back, and lit it. He regarded West levelly and did not miss the way Karl tightly gripped the chair arm. "It is strictly business, West. An old friend of mine has a large interest in a petrochemical company in Cali, Colombia, on the northern coast of South America."

"I see," Karl said flatly.

Eben nodded and continued. "One of the problems has been transporting raw materials down there."

"Go on," Karl said, more attentive now.

"There's little bulk, so trucking isn't cost-efficient, and everything else we've tried is too unstable: doesn't reach the factory on time to meet schedules or gets there damaged. What we're proposing is an air ferry. We'll hire your outfit full-time on a monthly basis."

Surprised, Karl looked up.

Eben went on. "Your main base will be Santa Mara. The spot is perfect; it even has a landing strip."

Karl leaned forward. "I get the general picture. How often will I get back to the States?"

Eben's eyes met his directly. "Not often. Most of our dealings are in South America or the Caribbean."

"You mean I'm not to see Kristen again," Karl said sarcastically.

Eben nodded. "If you choose to accept the benefits of this proposition you will not tell Kristen where you are based, nor subsequently acquaint her with your travel schedule, and you will terminate your relationship with her by whatever means necessary to ensure the separation will be permanent." His voice had sharpened.

"I may take your money and not fulfill the other conditions," Karl cut in angrily.

Eben considered before answering. "I think not, Mr. West. Although most of the proposition will be funded by friends, it is under the direction of an ex-New Yorker who makes his home in that country and his organization is not one to think of in connection with false transactions. Moreover, the letter you have sent me applying for a loan is more than enough insurance."

Karl sensed a trap being set. He could tell the old guy to shove it and everything might still work out, but that was a long shot. The strong probability was that without a transfusion Air Scape would go under, taking with it the investments of his uncle and friends. Momentarily, the thought struck him that there might be something illegal in all this maneuvering, but he shook it off. An opportunity now lay within his grasp. He would have to do whatever needed to be done to take advantage of it. This was no time to worry about morality—that equalled minutiae when weighed against the possible benefits of Blakely's proposal. He had swallowed dirt before and for less reason. Marriage to Kristen was out, and her father wasn't about to let the status quo remain. The old man's attitude toward him hardly equalled that of the good Samaritan. But he couldn't run the risk of Blakely's going to the police nor afford an investigation. He had no future that way. The bit cutting his mouth, Karl West quickly did what he perceived necessary, but couldn't resist saying, "You play Godfather rather well, Mr. Blakely."

"No, Mr. West," Eben cut him off somberly. "My family is everything to me. You have a daughter; you can understand." Karl's eyes widened. He had taken pains to keep the past hidden. Some men were not made for family life and he was one.

"I don't discuss my private life with strangers," Karl said icily.

Eben said deliberately and carefully, "We weren't speaking of your family problems, West, but of mine. When you are my age, the future closes in and one's end is meaningless if one's children are not prospering. They link me to that time of which I cannot be a part except through them. Especially Kristen."

Wearily, Eben took another sip of his drink. His eyes were doleful, and his veined hands trembled. For the first time Karl became aware that Blakely was old and perhaps ill. Karl's mocking tone changed. "Perhaps you ought to let Kristen find her own way."

"That isn't easy to do, West," Eben nodded bleakly. "I'm aware that people learn by different methods, but reality is too harsh for some to meet head-on. And Kristen," he sought the right words, "hasn't the spirit yet to fall and get up again."

"That's bullshit," Karl said bluntly. "If she's weak it's because you've given her no reason to learn to stand; you've made leaning very comfortable for her."

"Of course that's partially true," Blakely stroked his chin thoughtfully, "but she's fragile; I want to cushion the falls. At least for now." He looked away.

Karl threw up his hands. "Have you picked someone out to complelte her future? Hers and yours?"

Eben smiled faintly. "For a man who doesn't like to answer questions, you certainly pose a few." He nodded. "Yes, I have a man in mind, one who could handle my affairs and hers. My son just isn't ready. The man I am thinking of would give Kristen the kind of life which will be good for her."

"You're a hundred years behind the times, Mr. Blakely. I may have, as you have intimated, not been the best father, but I give other people, even my child, space," Karl said bitterly.

"Space," Eben Blakely replied slowly. "That doesn't seem to me much of a legacy."

Karl moved forward in his chair, his face darkened. Then he paused, thought better of it, and shrugged.

Eben drained his glass. "I take total responsibility for my action. Long ago I learned that that is all each of us can do anyway. I am an old man,

Mr. West. My ways are set, and to me they make sense."

Karl did not reply. The whole thing was no skin off his nose. He changed the subject.

"When do you want me to leave?" Karl asked, the resentment in his voice surfacing again.

"Today," Eben said shortly.

"That doesn't give us much time to wrap up my affairs," Karl grimaced.

"Everything will be accomplished in accordance with your wishes," Eben added dourly. "You will lose nothing by complying quickly. All your debts will be immediately paid and receipts sent to you. When you get to Cali, our associate will make all further details known and deliver the necessary funds. We will probably not meet again, but I shall be apprised of your progress. You will be paid on a monthly basis. At the end of every four months, if everything is in order, a bonus of twenty thousand dollars will be added."

Karl smiled. The old guy might be a tyrant, but he was also generous. "Done," he said briskly.

Within minutes a contract was produced, signed, and witnessed by Karl's two escorts, who had been waiting in the bedroom. "Wally and Chet can give you some facts about Cali. We've taken the liberty of arranging suitable lodgings for you. Expenses paid, of course," Eben paused, adding mostly to himself, "and now I must be on my way." He leaned over toward Karl. "You may rest assured you will be treated fairly. There is, of course, considerable self-interest in my generosity, but I am a

THE SPLINTERED EYE

man of my word. Moreover, there will be no retaliatory acts because of the episode resulting in Kristen's recent hospitalization." Eben sighed. "I have doubts about your reasons for committing Kristen—" he shook his head, "—but there's no doubt she was taking too many pills. I've checked that out myself. Whether or not that stuff would have killed her, I don't know, but it's certainly possible." His voice became softer. "You did get her to the hospital, and for that I'm grateful." He stared down at his empty glass, walked over, and poured himself a short drink. He rolled the liquor at a certain angle in his hand, admired the color, and swallowed the rest.

"Am I free to leave now?" Karl called out.

"Of course, Mr. West. Wally and Chet will take you to your plane. I would consider it a great favor if your apartment would be vacated by sundown. You were promised a thousand dollars for the trip tonight. Here it is—with a five-thousand-dollar bonus." He took a manila envelope from his jacket and placed it on the table in front of Karl.

The tension increased. Karl picked the money up; his face tightened. He seemed about to say something, then changed his mind. "Good night, Mr. Blakely."

"Good luck to you, Mr. West," Eben passed his hand through his gray, wiry hair; his craggy face was expressionless. "I am grateful for your quick response."

Then, waving the room to silence, he walked hurriedly to the front door and out to a small pickup truck. As he walked, thoughts coursed through him. There was something unhuman about Karl West which he'd seen before. What had it been? He visualized the man and saw again the penetrating eyes, almost ice blue. They glittered like a glacier. He paused. The transaction with West had been resolved in the best possible way. He could not be sure that Kristen would not be in touch with him again, but if West did not keep his part of the bargain, there were avenues of recourse. Of this Eben had made sure. On the other hand, if West kept his word, he would probably become a successful entrepreneur, probably but not certainly. Eben shook his head. He would have liked to ensure West's downfall, but first things first. He had gotten him away from Kristen. A calamity had been averted. Perhaps Kristen would go under anyway, but he could do nothing about that eventuality. Choice—that's all there is, time and choice. He had exercised his will tonight to give Kristen both those options. And whatever the outcome, it was worth the price.

Slowly, Eben opened the truck door. He wanted to arrive home before Kristen and Jamie. He'd never run from his responsibilities nor was he about to at this late date. As he got in, he felt a slight heart flutter. "Damned nuisance," he murmured and stopped for a moment to take the nitroglycerin pills he always carried. A few stars quivered. Eben looked up, enjoying the comfort of darkness interlaced with splashed tiny lights. Opening his mouth, he smiled, catching a few snowflakes on his tongue. "Still playing child games, old man," he said aloud. Only the night sounds answered. Rabbits and field mice crept about under the blanket of darkness. He patted the door tenderly, as if it were the shoulder of an old friend, and climbed in. Turning the key, he listened intently to the motor starting up. Then deliberately and cautiously he backed the truck out. The drive extended long and pleasant before him. Along the dirt road, the headlights picked up the outlines of dogwood and forsythia, soon to bud; the live oak and laurel still slept. Nothing escaped the old man as he rode along. Breaking through the rain clouds, the silver moon lighted the way. Eben luxuriated in the earth sounds vibrating about him. They renewed him. As he moved through patches of light then darkness, his spirit revived. The future's promise ticking, he thought, like this night. "I've done what I can," he murmured, and made himself comfortable. Now, he was content to let events happen as they would without further interference.

Less than three hours later Karl West had hangared his small aircraft at LaGuardia and made his way back to his Greenwich Village apartment.

As the door swung open, only moonlight shone through the small window, but he immediately perceived the silhouette of a woman asleep on his couch. "Oh Christ," he muttered, imagining the figure to be Kristen. Drawing closer, however, he saw Candice Shelton and called out to her, "Didn't

I ask you not to come here without my permission?" His voice conveyed exasperation.

"Damn right," she answered, startled awake, "but things like that don't bother me much once I make up my mind."

"You're too much," Karl shook his head.

"Not for you," she swiftly retorted. Karl laughed heartily.

At sixty, after a grim divorce, Karl's father had quickly married his long-time girlfriend. Candice was born five months later, and Karl's mother committed suicide. The two men successfully ignored each other for twenty years until Max had convinced him to see the old man one last time. On that visit, he met his half-sister. He had gone to Vermont for her wedding. The attraction between them had been obvious even then. Her husband, Larry, had some money but no other obvious attributes. Right from the beginning, rumors flew about Candice's antics and Larry's ineffective efforts to control her, but Karl, who was the subject of plenty of hearsay himself, discounted most of what he heard. Then a letter from his father mentioned Candy's arrival in New York a few weeks later. He'd made up his mind not to see her, but somehow did. And, despite everything, they had ended up in bed. Even during his affair with Kristen they'd continued to see each other. People who saw them together took them for father and daughter. Perhaps it was the similar color of their eyes or the way neither could sit still.

Quickly now Karl began to switch on lamps and gather his things together. "What the hell is going on?" Candy asked, stretching sleepily.

"I have to get out of here," Karl's eyes blinked wearily and he clenched his fists. With Kristen he had been unable to confess any problems or inadequacies. But Candy was family. She'd better understand.

"Really, right now?" she responded, in that half-satiric way which reminded him so much of himself.

"Company business. My ass is on the line. I'm taking a job in South America where I can make some real money and be free of this cheap shit."

"South America sounds intoxicating." She put an ashtray atop her head, jumped up on the sofa, and stuck her thumbs into the pockets of the tight denims she wore.

Karl grinned. "I haven't asked you to join me yet."

"Now that we're partners, I don't have to be asked; I'm part of the decision-making process." She laughed and struck a lewd pose. "Larry bought out one of Uncle Max's cronies and gave the write-off to me."

Surprised, Karl flushed. "No wonder your husband couldn't handle you. That would require a CIA agent." Karl paused, searching her eyes for a response. He shook his head. Fooling around with Candy was going to be more hazardous than his past affairs. She wouldn't be easy to lose. They were too much alike and she obviously had the adhesive strength of Crazy Glue. Still, her presence would be a happening. He smiled a slight teasing smile.

"And what about your husband?" he asked quizzically.

She nodded sagely. "In as few words as possible, leaving out all nauseating details, I've left him. It was never any good for either of us anyway," Candy's face clouded. "The only thing I've brought with me is a few clothes and a twenty percent partnership in your company. He knows damn well any court would give me a hell of a lot more. Her voice held a note of triumph. "This way the break will be clean and Larry can curl up with his father's money and the alimony he saved." She reached out and stroked Karl's back with long tapered fingers and gave a luxurious yawn. "Well, partner," she said, running her hands down the sides of his body toward his hips. Momentarily his cock hardened. "When do we leave?" Her eyes followed his every movement.

"Immediately," he grinned, lifting her up in his arms and carrying her toward the bedroom, "more or less."

"Hell, I never did approve of strict deadlines," she said quickly. Catching his heel on the carpet, Karl stumbled. "Maybe *you* want to be carried," Candy said mischievously. "I'm heavier than I look."

He tossed her up in the air and caught her

again. "You sure as hell are. Any other surprises brewing?"

"Plenty." She bit him on the shoulder.

"Have you had your rabies shot?" he asked, dropping her onto the bed.

"Find out," she suggested and began to throw off her clothes. Reaching across the bedcovers, she flipped the shiny silver dial of the stereo on. "Let's introduce a little more rhythm to the proceedings," she announced.

He started to undress. Moment by moment he could feel his organ grow still harder. His heart pounded as he reached out to touch the inside of her legs where the skin appeared so soft. It must be nearly four, he thought, as he nestled in her succulent fur and prepared to mount her. Her pulsing mouth swirled in front of him as he knelt.

"Fuck the time," he cried. Her arms opened to receive him.

Karl licked his lips; his throat felt dry. He leaned to the side, resting on one elbow. Two hours had passed.

"Let's pack," he said, and then noticed Candice's suitcase propped against a chair in the corner of the bedroom. "I see you came to stay," he chuckled, and slid from the blanket wrapped about them.

"Yes, to both semi-questions," she said, and lay back smiling.

Naked, Karl strode about. Abandoning his usual neatness, he snatched two valises from the closet, then began grabbing clothes from the drawers, throwing them in. Candice shot up and began to help him.

"Anything that should be left behind?" she asked.

"What we forget," Karl answered curtly.

Quiet, then, she began to dress. From across the room, Karl watched appreciatively. She's different, he thought. She returned the look, not missing a beat. Suddenly he called out, "I like the way you move."

"You too," she replied and blew him a kiss.

"By the way, your ex-girlfriend called before." She watched him closely.

Karl stared at her, his mind elsewhere.

"Kristen, remember?" she asked. He shrugged but didn't reply. "I didn't accept the charges."

"No matter," Karl nodded. "Are you tired?"

"A little bit, but I don't need much sleep," she shrugged, "a family trait."

"Hungry?"

"Are you suggesting an encore?" Candice asked. He laughed heartily, liking the way she spoke, the breathy voice and her quick responses.

He shook his head.

"Then I'll go scramble some eggs and make coffee while you finish up."

She moved languidly, half domesticated cat, half jungle tiger. Then from the kitchen came efficient sounds of cabinets opening then closing.

When Karl ambled in the food was ready. "Christ, I'm hungry," he exclaimed.

"Another family trait," she replied and began to dish out huge quantities of scrambled eggs and pass toast. The food was hot and simple. Karl thought of Kristen's breakfast banquets—*l'oeuf Benedict* complete with kitchen devastation, plus Di-Gel prognosis.

"You suit me," he said slowly.

"Thank you, sir," she murmured softly.

"We'll be meeting some business associates at Kennedy. They'll give us our tickets and the itinerary. You'll have to make do with whatever accommodations they've arranged."

"If you can, I can," she scratched back.

"Humility is not one of your character traits, I see." He grinned.

"Nor yours, either," she smiled back, "so let's can all that pretentious crap."

She got up, stretching her shapely legs, and stood in back of him, watching as he pointed out the route.

"Maybe I'll learn to fly," Candy said.

"Why not? You're not afraid, are you?"

"Don't be a fool. I'll try anything once—maybe even countless times."

His mind raced ahead to their destination. What would they be like together? They'd have one hell of a ball. His eyebrows shot up. That was the main thing. There was an easy recklessness about her which was bewitching. He watched her clear some of the things off the table and heat more coffee.

"Your husband should have hog-tied you."

She threw back her head, guffawing, "The hell he could."

"You're probably right," Karl frowned slightly.

"You can depend on that, partner," Candy added. They sat at the table, laughing and drinking coffee. Suddenly the telephone rang. Karl searched her face knowingly. The phone kept ringing. Finally he rose and said, "They're not giving up. I'll take it in the bedroom."

Candice shot him an annoyed look. He sighed. In some ways all broads were alike, he thought and strode toward the rear of the apartment. Picking up the phone, he spoke softly into the receiver. Candy pressed her ear to the cool, damp kitchen wall. "I don't know, honey; it may be several months. No longer than necessary, but I can't be sure. . . . Yes, yes of course I still do." Then a pause. "Kris, I have no choice. It has to be this way. As soon as things settle down, I'll be in touch." His voice changed to a whisper. From the kitchen came the noise of clanging plates. Karl put his hand over the receiver, and called, "Hey, keep it down." But the noise kept up. Not long afterward, he came out dressed and obviously ready to go.

"I thought you were rid of her," Candy said angrily.

"And I thought you could mind your own business." His eyes darkened.

"Look," her smile had faded, "I've played similar games. Don't think you're going to hand me that 'misunderstood' shit, and a few months from now a *ménage à trois* with a cuckoo bird," she snapped impatiently. "If and when we select added attractions, we'll do it simultaneously."

Karl laughed again. He shook his head, "I've never met anyone quite like you."

"And you won't, so cut the crap," Candy's mouth tightened. "No one fools around on me without my permission, and any attempts to do so could result in a load of buckshot where a necessary organ has previously been attached."

Jokingly, Karl put a hand over his crotch. "Hey, let's not go too far," he said with mock hysterics.

"No screwing around." Her voice held a distinct coolness.

"That I don't think I can promise," he said skeptically, "and neither can you."

Candy reached out to rake a fingernail along his arm. "Just remember, my trademark is on you." They stared at each other. She laughed, baring sharp, cat-like teeth.

"You pull shit like that, baby, and you'll be minus one arm," Karl countered.

"Don't try it," she said softly. "Is that how you got your kicks with what's-her-name?" Candice leaned over and faced Karl directly.

"That's none of your business," he answered sharply, and fixed his glare outside the window behind her. Apricot streaks of light appeared in the pre-dawn sky. He thought of the impending journey and the excitement always latent within him began to pound. This trip would be different, he thought, and began to visualize the ranch which awaited him and his Uncle Max's face when they bought it. In Karl's mind he could see horses grazing and thousands of miles of waving grass stretched out in the background. "Lock the suitcases," he commanded, looking at his watch, "and let's get out."

"I'm ready anytime you are," Candice responded coldly. Karl nodded knowingly.

"Only one last thing; I'll check whether the flight will leave on time."

The line buzzed; Karl became impatient. "Forget it. Let's dump this place and move on to better things." He snapped off all the lights.

"Hey, how are we supposed to find our way out of here, blind man's bluff?" Candice called.

Karl did not answer.

"Oh well," she continued, "I've cat eyes anyway."

"And that's not the only similarity," Karl countered, visualizing the bright red scratch mark on his forearm.

"Insults will get you nowhere," Candice called, having already found her way to the front door.

For a moment she stood suitcase in hand, waiting for Karl to join her. When he didn't she called out, "Well, hurry up, slowpoke."

Quickly he stepped up behind her. "Who's calling the shots here?"

She shrugged, "Who's got the louder voice?"

He grinned at her, the drollery between them returning. At the door, Candy crouched like a runner before the opening gun, her motor obviously racing. He shook off any foreboding. Thank God, though, he shook his head, marriage isn't even a distant possibility. Grabbing the two valises, he followed her down the steps. At the first landing they almost collided.

"You all right?" he asked, grabbing her elbow.

"I don't break," she said decisively.

He nodded. "Then let's get a move on. I want to be off the road and in the air before the half-assed begin their day, okay?"

"Okay," she answered tartly, jumping over the last few steps.

Weighed down by the heavy suitcases, he lumbered after her.

"Any problem?" she chuckled, hailing a cab.

"None," he answered as they each reached for the cab's door.

9

"Let's take a vacation," Kristen suggests in her lightest, most appealing tone. "We both need a change, perhaps somewhere warm."

Karl looks impatiently at her.

She feels her heart beating loudly, erratically. In such a place, Kristen thinks, secrets could be revealed—she could tell him easily about the child. Perhaps on a secluded beach they can communicate, talk about how they feel. Their future. Her thoughts pulse. She tries to read his expression. Impatience or pleasure? She cannot be certain. He is mercurial—one moment his eyes widen, laughing, the next, narrow to slits through which she cannot see to determine shade or meaning. Her lips tighten and forcibly she uplifts the corners of her mouth, trying to smile.

"Good idea, Kris." He toys with a pencil, his

thoughts skipping ahead. "Burt Cald rented a little cabin in New Hampshire for the month." Determinedly, he faces her.

Pressure snaps within her head. She can't stand Cald. There is something about him. The way he slips unnoticed in and out of rooms. Like a snake hugging a garden wall. She knows he is a threat. Karl's quick-fire friendships, like his moods, come and go. Cald is the newest in a long line of combustible relationships. At this moment he and Karl are igniting each other, but as soon as Karl talks Burt into investing in Air Scape and Cald becomes disillusioned, Karl will quickly drop him like all the others.

"Karl, please," she says in a whisper, "please, let's not take Burt; let's go alone."

"Sure." He pauses. "Why not."

Relieved, she suddenly feels better, but he quickly injects, "I'm going to spend most of my time skiing anyway."

Kristen opens her mouth to protest, to talk about going South, but decides not to.

"You pack," he points toward the bedroom. Kristen's thin face flushes. "I'll phone Burt. We'll leave in an hour or so," he says.

Kristen is startled. "Karl, I didn't mean today; I thought sometime next week." She rubs her eyes wistfully.

"Kris," he says decisively, "you wanted to go; we're going. Now."

Arguments are useless. She sighs. Nothing can be done. Whatever plans they make must be immediate, and she will have to accept that fact. She needs his pounding excitement coursing into her; she will have to do whatever she must do to get it.

Like an overly-wound toy, Kristen scurries about Karl's rooms, pushing things into bags and dumping the contents of drawers onto the bed. When Karl comes in, she sits amidst the chaos she has created, trying to decide how to re-order or eliminate things. The suitcase is too bulky to close.

Karl looks at the mess. "We only need one suitcase, honey. This isn't a resort in the Jewish Alps. Anyway, I intend to spend half the time skiing, the rest fucking."

She laughs at his teasing but then notices his bright impatient eyes and winces. Something will go wrong again. She sees the signs. Her hands tremble and grow more uncoordinated. Why does she do such stupid things?

He is shaking his head. "Kris, let me pack this stuff," he says, grimacing.

I'm failing, she thinks, before my chance comes. She goes over to a corner, an admonished child.

"It's all right," he says, tossing most of the things she has pushed into the suitcase out, "you can clean up later."

Kristen closes her eyes. I must do better, she thinks, frightened. This time her fears are groundless. His movements are calm . . . everything but his eyes.

"Why don't you check the ski report."

THE SPLINTERED EYE

"I don't know the number," she replies. "MU 2-3556."

Trying not to make mistakes, she dials slowly and repeats the monotonously spoken words: "Hazardous driving conditions, winds up to forty miles an hour, and heavy snow." Karl pays little attention; his course is set.

Within an hour a taxi takes them to Dodd Car Rental Agency. Heavy rain mixed with snow begins to fall as they move from the city onto the Hutchinson River Parkway. An hour later ice drifts blow across the road, blinding them every few minutes. Hypnotized, Kristen stares at the damp lumps of white tissue on the windshield.

Karl drives carelessly, much too quickly on the ice-strewn parkway. As they get further north and the roads become mountainous, he accelerates speed. The car sways and slides back and forth on the road, veering out of control. Kristen begins to perspire; she shuts her eyes, but they blink open again. Suddenly, she sees a red steel hulk lunge at them from across the highway. The other car shudders and spins around, landing near their right fender. Terrified, Kristen screams, and in that split second before impact Karl half-turns and covers her with himself. For Kristen it is a moment of utter contentment. Then the sound of collision impacts inside her head. Karl brakes to a stop; gravel splays about. He jumps out of the car, angry and incredulous. Kristen reaches for the door handle, ripping at it. Her fingers bleed. Suddenly the door springs open as Karl screams, "Stay in the car!"

But Kristen rushes out into a gray-white

streaked twilight and runs toward the hill beside them. Panting, she climbs up. Crouching on the hilltop, she watches the crowd gather, sees first Karl's silhouette then the other driver's bob up and down. The flashing red searchlights of a police car burst on the scene. People shout, their voices crash through ice-prickled air. I won't go back, she thinks. I'll stay here. No one can follow.

For a few minutes she rests, but then the sound of her name flashes through the dusk. Stepping forward, she stands exposed by the police car's headlights.

"Get down here, you crazy nut. Do you want to freeze to death?" Karl shouts into a microphone.

Slowly she begins to edge down the hill. She falls back as the wind strikes her. Several times she stumbles, only to pull herself up, recover her balance, and continue back to the car. The right door and fender are smashed in. She moves away, shaking.

Karl grabs her arm, pushing her along. "Open my door; get in. You're making a scene."

Once inside, her head pounds as she sees Karl's anger. "I'm sorry," she whispers.

"Forget it," he retorts. "Just stop chattering." His knuckles tighten on the wheel. "If I weren't a defensive driver, we'd have both been killed."

"Karl, maybe we should go back. The car's a mess; I feel awful. You—"

Karl cut her off savagely. "I'll drop you off if you want; I'm going skiing."

Afraid, she stares at him, watching his reck-

THE SPLINTERED EYE

less mood catch fire. She knows danger arouses Karl, whets his appetite, and her resistance will spur him on. "I won't leave you."

"I know," he says flatly, his face an impersonal mask. With a rough gesture he floors the gas pedal, the car sputters, and then, infused with a burst of energy, lurches forward. The muscles of Kristen's stomach clench. She bites her lip. "Don't push me away," she moans. Why this is so important hardly matters. That it is, she does not question.

Afterward, Kristen forces herself to remain silent, as if this too is a test. They pass other vehicles abandoned on the side of the road. The thickening snow is beginning to cover them. Soon they will be huge white mounds. And this their cemetery. Their car hurtles onward. She visualizes Karl as a kind of adventurer claiming new territory. Nothing can stop him. She wonders if this isn't real courage, pure and unadulterated, not to always be plagued by indecisiveness and alternatives but to move like Karl, swiftly and surely toward his goal. At that moment she loathes herself. She wishes she could throw herself into Karl's body—Karl, who surely knows without doubt where to go and how to get there. Yet she cannot even do that; there is a void between them. A void spawned, she is sure, by her; a void Kristen cannot step around. Yet she cannot seem to change and does not know how, except by clutching at him. Now he acts oblivious to her. Sometimes she thinks he envisions another woman. She considers this idea for a moment, then discards it. Even if it were true, she would not believe it. Her thoughts float to the small, white shimmering forms falling outside the window. Snowflakes twist and turn as she moves her head back and forth, her eye melding their shapes together.

"Look, Karl, they're like sequins on a ball gown."

"Kristen," he muttered, "do you know how many accidents will occur tonight, out here tonight?" He searches her honey-colored eyes. "Of course not," he shakes his head, a kind of sad wonder creeping into his voice. She smiles back. He pats the space between them. "Come closer."

Sighing, she leans against him, his body, a dome of pleasure within the vibrating car which slides about on the icy road.

The cabin is only ten miles away, but it takes nearly an hour to get there. Ahead she sees Mt. Snow—snow-dashed evergreens and wide, smooth trails. She nods. Coming here with Karl was the right thing to do. She twists a strand of her hair. Things would be better here.

At the cottage Kristen and Karl run hand-in-hand to the door. Her heart beats fiercely. Surely this is a good omen, she thinks, feeling him close beside her. Laughing, he lifts her up and carries her inside. For a moment Kristen envisions herself a bride.

Light but no heat has been turned on inside the cabin. Shivering, Kristen looks around. Wicker furniture covered in faded chintz and starched, red-checked curtains indicate former owners who had probably been content with very little. Kristen could see them clearly—a stiff but pleasant New England couple who wore faded clothes, had birthed several children, and grown old but not feeble.

"I'll cut some wood," Karl says. Even his voice seems to take on the New England twang of her fantasy. She watches him grab the axe from above the mantel and go outside. Then from the kitchen window she sees him again, jacketless, his hair wind-tossed, his face ruddy. He chops the logs with deft, graceful strokes as though he had been born to such labor. Kristen takes a deep breath. Her spell of bad luck must be over. She thinks of the future. Silently answering her need, Karl comes inside and builds a fire.

"Are you warm enough?" he asks. Gently he puts his head in her lap and they remain silent, close together there. Finally, the bright splashes of light ebb.

"We'll let it die down now," he says, indicating the bedroom, into which she follows happily. He reaches out to touch her and their bodies come together, lovers who know the rhythm of each other and do not have to hurry. With a sensuous drowsiness, she floats toward the feeling. Hair, flesh, bones, and blood are his. She holds nothing back. Karl bends over her, body against body, face toward face, and she tries to hold fast to him as he throbs inside her. But as they come apart, the warmth ebbs. She tries to think of the child in her womb, his child, but cannot. Only Karl sleeping beside her is real.

At dawn Karl, dressed in red ski gear, brings mugs of steaming tea. "Let's get in a full day, sleepyhead."

She laughs vaguely, discombobulated by the cold and early hour.

"Come on, slowpoke, come on," he urges, his voice leading her on. Shivering, Kristen gets up and pulls on her black sweater and ski pants.

They are together only intermittently during the day. Karl skis far too well for her and likes only the expert trails with their canyons and icier ranges. She wants to brave the more difficult runs, but every time he comes to claim her, she reneges. The glaring white mountaintop frightens her. Laughing, he races ahead leaving her far behind until all she can see of him are two blood spots of color. Near sunset, inching up the mountain she spies Karl, his jacket open, paralleling on a high peak among snow-ladened trees. Without noticing her, he speeds past, taking each turn with the ferocious abandon of some wild thing at ease in his own element. He leaps over ice moguls and then executes a flip as though the sheer joy of the challenge propels him on.

Thank God, she thinks, the lifts will close soon. Slowly she picks her way down.

Just as she is about to let her skis run, a fierce wind ricochets across the hill. Ice needles pierce her face. Her body becomes numb. In the distance the lodge grows blurry. Fast-moving skiers speed by. Fearful, Kristen scrutinizes the trails trying to find the easy path, but snow flies up in her face. "Damn you," she sobs. Somehow she has to get back to Karl. He will be furious that she is late and she wouldn't blame him. If only she could stop picking at herself. "I'm sick of this endless bickering," she cries aloud. "Fuck it all." No one is there to hear her. She points her skis straight down the slops and narrows her eyelids to shut out obstacles.

In what seems moments, Karl stands before her, arms outstretched. "The mad bomber," he says, and she topples skis and all into his open arms. He pats her ass. "What a funny duck you are. Fearless one moment, scared shitless the next. You need some hot grog." He gives her a bear hug. "You're the color of chalk." She presses her half-frozen face into his shoulder.

That night he lies beside her. The sheet has fallen away. He sleeps completely nude as always. Shivering a little, she burrows into his side and almost involuntarily his arms shut about her. To belong is what matters, she thinks. Her heart pounds erratically. She has a sudden new vision of them; while she reveals her secret, he buries his head in her breast, joyful about the baby, their baby. He needs her and the baby, of this she is quite sure. Near her Karl moves ever so slightly, wrapped in his dream. His cock stiffens as she watches. How beautiful it is, how responsive to her. She remembers how earlier that night Karl's caresses, his excitement, steered them from orgasm to orgasm as he hardened again and again. If only they could stay entwined, unlike those ordinary people passing them on the street, the others with awkward bumbling relationships which sent them scurrying to sexologists or shrinks.

Her eyes envelop Karl; she longs to be possessed by him again and smiles, wondering how to bring him back to her.

At breakfast he hurries her along, anxious to ski again. Not quite ready to divulge her secret, she makes up her mind to wait for evening.

They stop for dinner at a quiet restaurant close to the slopes. His attentiveness makes her feel quite beautiful, happy at last.

"I want to be close to you again," he whispers, lightly kneading her shoulder.

When they arrive back at the cabin, it is near midnight. She is tempted to delay the words she has been rehearsing but stiffens her resolve.

"Karl," she says softly. (How quiet everything becomes, each word pauses, suspended on the edge of a cliff, only to fall smooth and white into a ravine somewhere unseeable below.) "I'm pregnant, darling."

"What the hell do you mean—" his eyes widen as his fingers dig into her shoulder.

Minute particles of whiteness outside the window scream silently wherever they land.

"—pregnant? Are you crazy?" he shakes her back and forth, a flush of blood suffuses his face. She tries to pull away, but he locks her shoulder blades into a position where she must stare directly into his eyes. "What are you trying to do to me?" he shouts.

"You don't have to be afraid to belong," her voice chokes on tears.

"Are you crazy?" he yells, his nostrils flare like those of a stalked animal. "I don't want to belong to anyone. I want to be free."

"Karl," she pleads. She is beyond stopping. "Please, think about it—about our child."

He seizes her by the hair. A clump rips away in his hand. "Get an abortion right away. Do you understand that?"

"I won't." Her upper teeeth cut her clenched lips.

"I don't want any more strangleholds on me," he groans. He jerks her head around. Cries arise in her throat, but she does not draw back. Trembling, she speaks. "I want our baby."

"Well, I don't, damn you, you fucking bitch. This is a psychological horror. I trusted you. I've asked you a dozen times if you were using something and you lied to me. Why, why?" He is moaning now.

"I did, Karl," she protests, "it just didn't work."

His voice broke. "Don't give me that shit. This is no mistake. It's a fucking trick, and I'm not falling for it. No one is going to lock me in again— ever!" He shudders, his fists clenched.

Panic grips her. She stands there, stunned,

idiotic, watching Karl grab a wooden chair and come at her.

"Get rid of it or I'll get rid of you," he screams, throwing the chair. She ducks, but slats break off, shattering against her body and face. She feels the stabbing deep inside. Karl, not looking at her, is already at the door. "I'm going to a hotel. Call me when you come to your senses." Kristen, tasting blood, sobs incoherently.

But Karl has already rushed out into the night. He doesn't look back and she knows she has lost.

10

Morning bleeds red-white checkered curtains, fades them almost indiscernibly until one color runs into the other. Caught in a swatch of light, Kristen steps back, tries to blend as easily as that thin cloth into the surrounding air, or merge with the other objects scattered around the room. She stiffens her body until it is motionless, still. What kind of scalpel, she wonders, could dissect thoughts, cut them out like clots of dark red blood and confine them to some distant pathology lab in some obscure bottle? "God damn it," she mutters. "Hopeless, it's hopeless." What an absurd joke on those of us whose thoughts or experiences drive them forward or mad.

Finally she stretches her body. How do crazies remain in one position for days on end, she wonders? Probably a lie, like everything else. A strategy to confuse the sane. When their attendants leave, such patients undoubtedly yawn, move about, and then resume their stolid stance when spectators reappear. On display always. Especially when we love—perhaps more than ever then.

Kristen forces herself to concentrate on the thing inside her. She no longer refers to it as her baby and so hopes to confine moral conjectures as to its reality to nothingness. But even this fails. Her body fails her mind. She feels like vomiting, not only in the morning, but constantly. Vomiting until there is nothing left. But even when her stomach is empty, frothy yellow bile sticks in her throat. Bad luck, she thinks, always without end.

None of the hotels she calls have a Karl West registered, so sprawled across their rumpled bed she waits, nauseous, pretending to herself that he will appear. By the next afternoon she admits it will not happen. She walks to the ski slopes, moving jerkily, feeling out of place, awkward. The mountain looms ahead, curiously gray, strangely comforting. She reaches the lodge in time for the daily bus back to New York. Once aboard, fragments of conversations from weekend skiers rumble about her. Their voices strike her like chimes gone mad, pealing without reason. How young they look, she thinks, especially the girls. They gab continuously. "Do you like Rossignols?" "Have you tried wearing Bonne Belle on the slopes?" "Who are you going out with Saturday?" Kristen listens and nods pretending to be part of the conversations, but in the end she is sure they know she's alone. Whisper about her. She tries to fall asleep. But their sounds and movements intrude, whining and elbowing for her attention. Unknowingly, they taunt her.

Finally they arrive at the Port Authority bus terminal. She tries to visualize Karl inside the apartment when she arrives. But when she opens the front door she is met by silence. Turning on the overhead light, she notices the letter on the floor, stoops to pick it up, and sees disappointedly that the sender is Dorothy, her old nurse. She still works for her father and brother. Kristen rips open the envelope. She reads: *Something dark is coming for you.* Kristen stares at the message, mystified.

"Damn," she utters. She crumples up the letter and tosses it on the floor. "No more today," Kristen cries.

She runs outside, down the stairs to Gorky's apartment. In front of it she stops short, a shadow hovering in the hallway, a spectre leaning on the doorbell. Answering, Gorky sees Kristen's anxious face.

"I have to get an abortion." Kristen keeps her eyes riveted on the frayed loops of the worn gray carpet.

"Oh, Kristen," Gorky protests. "No."

"As soon as possible," Kristen sobs. "Help me."

"Is money a problem?" Gorky asks, sitting next to her on the couch.

Kristen shakes her head, "No."

"It's the only way," Gorky sighs.

"Yes," Kristen says flatly, turning away.

"Kristen, I know that sounds like a crock, but sometimes life is."

"I love him," her voice trails off.

Gorky shudders, "We love oranges and we squeeze the life out of them."

Kristen shakes her head. "You don't understand. Without Karl I'm nothing, no one," she says brokenly.

"And with him?" Gorky asks, not unkindly.

"I don't know. Love sometimes involves pain."

"What a fucked-up word it is then," Gorky answers savagely. "If love isn't based on a desire to grow freely and a wish for one's partner to do the same, it's doomed anyway."

"Knowledge gathered from your ivory-tower perch," Kristen bitterly interjects. Gorky winces.

"Ah, Kristen, must one experience to see?"

"Gork, no lectures. If you want to help, convince Karl to marry me. Abortion is a mortal sin."

"Come off it, Kris. You can't invoke the gospel when it's convenient," Gorky answers quietly.

"But it's true," Kristen agonizes.

"Then it's true for Karl too, Kristen," Gorky protests.

"Don't you understand that Karl really needs me too?"

"In what way, Kristen?" Gorky shakes her head.

"I'll do anything to keep him," Kristen's upper lip trembles.

"Perhaps anything won't be enough; perhaps it will be too much." Gorky's eyes meet Kristen's.

Kristen feels herself shaking again. Gorky's words sweep through her, fill her. She gags upon them.

"Kristen, do you feel sick?"

The girl nods.

"Stay here tonight," Gorky says gently. "I want you to. You'll have to bed down on the couch, but it's comfortable. A friend of mine can supply us with a reputable doctor. I'll make the arrangements tonight and get any necessary instructions."

"Will you go with me?" Kristen implores, pressing Gorky's hand to her cheek.

Gorky shudders. "Yes, of course," she nods her head. "Let me get some linens and set up the couch. It's late and tomorrow will be difficult."

Kristen doesn't answer. Soon they are finished making up the couch. The silence is awkward and Gorky retires. Kristen lies down. She pulls the rose-colored quilt around her. Tears glue her eyes open. They ache. She does not care. In the darkness ghost-like shapes fill the room. She wonders when they will attack. The thought makes her head pulse. Feverish, she waits without rest until morning comes.

The clinic is in Long Island City. Kristen huddles in the cab next to Gorky. The memory of Karl gouges, lunges through other thoughts to wound her again and again. What if all this is a

THE SPLINTERED EYE

dream? What if she isn't really here or anywhere? No, she isn't that mad yet. On the side of her cheek a huge red-black swelling proves this. She feels stricken, helpless. Without warning, the taxi stops.

"I must have dozed off," Kristen says hesitantly.

A grayish brick building is directly in front of her. On the left a small, black-lettered sign bears the letters *T.L.C.* "Tender Loving Care, no doubt," Gorky grimaces. Kristen stares at her without understanding. "Never mind," Gorky murmurs, "bad joke." Slowly they make their way up the entrance stairs glazed with ice. "Careful," Gorky calls. "Don't slip."

For a moment Kristen stands motionless, longing to do just that or have someone, something push her forward. But of course, no one comes. She reaches the front door and stops, waiting for Gorky to open it. But Gorky, one step above, moves aside. Unsteadily Kristen opens the door. A brown-haired, angular woman with bifocals pushed up on her forehead sits at the front desk. "No doubt a spinster," Gorky jokes, "who has never been laid nor has the desire to do so." In spite of herself, Kristen smiles. Tears sting her eyes. She watches the woman nibble off a huge chunk of Danish then snatch it into her mouth with her tongue like a furtive rat.

"Please sit down," the woman commands, emphasizing the last two words. Quickly Kristen obeys, but Gorky remains standing. "I'm almost done with these," the woman rattles a few sheets of paper. "The paperwork here is horrendous. Everything in triplicate. Just give me a few secs and I'll be with you."

The woman speaks with a nasal twang which seems to resound in the plastic surroundings. "I'm sorry to have brought you here," Kristen whispers, leaning toward Gorky. "This mess is unforgivable."

"It's all right, Kristen," Gorky nods.

"I'll need to get some information from you." The woman at the desk points to Kristen and then turns to Gorky. "Are you her mother?"

Kristen stammers, embarrassed, "No. She's just a friend."

"Then you'll have to fill out this form yourself. Be sure to press the ballpoint really hard, so all three copies are marked," she instructs tartly.

"Even these questions seem too complex," Kristen sighs. She keeps crossing out words or putting them in the wrong blocks. "Could I have another form?" The woman looks oddly at her. Perspiration soaks Kristen's blouse and her heart beats rapidly. Finally she returns the paper to the receptionist. She looks up at some spot on the wall. "After completion of this form, wait in the outer waiting room until one of our volunteers takes you inside. After which the doctor will examine you and a nurse will escort you to the second floor."

Kristen looks searchingly at the woman, "I beg your pardon?"

THE SPLINTERED EYE

The woman turns to Gorky. "She does understand, doesn't she? We don't like to undertake patients who are unstable."

"You must have trouble filling your quota, then," Gorky replies curtly.

The receptionist tilts her head sideways. "Kristen, perhaps you'd better follow me. I'll take you back. You can come if you wish," she gestures to Gorky.

The syrupy yellow and orange outer waiting room has a plastic motel glare. A sharp pungent odor, more cloying than sweat, seeps in from somewhere. Nausea wells up in Kristen's throat.

Looking around she sees perhaps ten or so women, some with small untidy children. Some stare straight ahead, others slump down and their eyes cannot be seen. On the left one woman speaks Spanish to another who nods every few syllables. Suddenly, the second woman begins to sob incoherently.

"Kristen, here." The receptionist hands Kristen a slip of paper with the number seventeen. Kristen turns the sheet over quizzically.

"Your number," the woman explains.

"Of course," Kristen says.

"It will only be a few minutes," the woman pats the air.

More meaningless gestures, Kristen supposes. She wonders how the women seated near her feel. Which ones have regrets, which ones relief. Amazing, modern technology. She visualizes quarter-sized creatures oozing out into basins nearby, while still more quarter-sized creatures crouch in readiness. It is all she can do not to scream. Trying to forget, she searches out the tiles on the ceiling, then counts the objects nearby. On the bright gold formica table to her right are several children's books. *Sleeping Beauty* falls into her hand. I have been betrayed, she thinks, by these same fairy tales. She tilts her head forward, flipping the pages, seeing the falsehoods pronounced in print. Within her somewhere these lies still lived, of this she was quite sure. And no instrument, no matter how sharp, could reach that far inside and pluck them out.

The number seventeen flashes on the wallboard. Gorky nudges her.

"Kristen, it's time."

"I don't know." Kristen grips the chair arms.

"Hurry up, please. It's time," the social worker yawns. Slowly, Kristen walks toward her and watches the social worker make penciled check marks on the sheet in front of her. "Over there," she gestures toward a door.

Once inside, piped music comes from somewhere. Next to her, a frizzy-haired blond woman snaps her fingers, out of beat. Kristen tries to stare straight ahead, but the woman leans toward her. "Second time this year. I have multiple sclerosis. That's why I'm here."

The girl with the squared-off bangs on the other side of them joins the conversation. "Hell, this is the first and last for me. I'm going to have my tubes snipped, then relax."

THE SPLINTERED EYE

Kristen fumbles for an answer, but cannot think of an appropriate one. A freckle-faced brunette in a wrinkled surgical gown runs out from the area of examination rooms.

"How long do you think they can keep me waiting?" she asks, scratching her arm until crimson gashes appear.

Kristen wishes she were unconscious. She longs for the large, numbing shot of sodium pentathol. Finally a rotund nurse calls out, "Seventeen." Kristen nods, following her into the examining room. Without flinching, she watches her own blood being drawn.

"We want to make sure it's red," the nurse jokes. Kristen turns away, beginning to cry again.

"First one?" the nurse asks.

Kristen nods.

"Don't worry, it will be over soon—not as bad as a tooth extraction." Kristen stares at her. She presses her free hand to her face.

"I'm sorry." The nurse pats the girl's shoulder sympathetically.

Upon the table, Kristen's legs ache in the stirrups, but she cannot move. Finally the dark-haired doctor comes in. "How are you doing?" he asks jovially, squinting under the bright lights.

Kristen looks away. There is nothing to talk about. There is no backing out.

"You're taking a masters in social work, aren't you?" The cold speculum slides inside her vagina.

"How? . . ." Then she realizes, of course, she had written it on the information card.

"Why don't you apply for a job here?"

For the first time she stares at him: a tall man in his thirties with acne-pitted skin and piercing brown eyes. Kristen shakes her head.

"Well, you're about eight weeks pregnant, all right. We'll have you fixed up in a few hours' time," the doctor says firmly.

Suddenly, three or four others surround the table. In the corner is a large barrel. She wonders how often they empty it and where.

"Come on, hon," another white figure says, strapping a black wire around Kristen's arm. "We've got a long day ahead."

The white porcelain ceiling shines in her eyes. Looking down, Kristen sees weblike hands in flesh-colored gloves poised above her.

"We're ready," the doctor says crisply.

They place her feet in white wraps. She hears herself counting, and then her voice becomes vague. In a moment the room is gone. In another she awakens on a small cot, lips dry, throat aching. A Kotex is lodged between her legs. A nurse reaches down, pulls it away and scrutinizes the blood. Kristen half-raises herself to protest, only to see the pad soaked in blood.

"Don't fret," the nurse explains, "it's normal." She tosses the Kotex into a nearby pail and sticks another between Kristen's legs. Kristen's too weary to protest. And even if she weren't, what

THE SPLINTERED EYE

good would it do? She wills the room to vanish and, for the time being, it does.

Gorky was wrong, Gorky was right. Kristen does not try to decide which. Within a few days of the operation, Karl West calls and Kristen begs him to come back. Her womb aches, but Kristen knows she must not wait to reclaim him. She clasps him to her and neither speaks. There is blood all over the sheets after they make love. She hardly sees it and falls into a deep sleep. Waking suddenly, she rises and finds Karl standing at the window, gazing outside longingly.
"What are you looking for?" she asks fearfully. Shaking his head, he takes her back to bed and they make love once again.

Each morning she awakens, terrified he will not be there. Sometimes the red or white or yellow pills she has taken shut off thoughts or make them stand still. But perpetual unconsciousness does not come easily. They always seem on the brink of a quarrel, stormy, strained. She tries to narrow her mind to a slit to shut out light. In her coat pocket is the number of the young doctor from the clinic. Sympathetic or flirtatious, he prescribes Demerol shots and is willing to make housecalls.

Karl is out often, day and night. His breath smells of liquor. He smells of other women. Lipstick stains his shirt collars and the crotch of the underwear Kristen scrutinizes. Carefully, she examines the garments again and again and hides them in her drawer. Later his bright staring eyes seem to dare her to accuse him but she refuses, holds on, won't acknowledge defeat or relinquish him. On the nights he still comes to bed, she holds him as tightly as she can. But he comes to bed less and less.

He is gone days at a time.

One evening she lies alone, restless in the darkness only to find herself bleeding unexpectedly, heavily. Shading her eyes, she nevertheless feels the ugly blood tears dripping and reaches down vaguely to touch the moisture. Her hands come away sticky. Off and on she sleeps, but then awakens to recognize Karl still hasn't come home. A kind of chilled disbelief begins. Has he gone on another trip? She cannot remember. Pills lie on the bedside table. Kristen swallows several without water; thoughts pass from her, become glossy, unidentifiable pictures. Her thoughts turn, spinning into new places. Here it is neither day or night. She is drawn down a steep, dark hillside. Her body floats on. Even the veins of the trees become clear—dark green encrusted beads. Their greens merge, divide, and spill over the mossy surroundings. Suddenly a massive wind comes. Almost unconscious, Kristen reaches for more red pills. The wind sweeps leaves and branches from the trees until there is no more forest—only gray stone fields where tumbleweed grows. Kristen's hair and dress fly violently around her, pinning her down so that she cannot move. Then as she turns, a door appears. Underneath the door, light seeps. Kristen wrestles to free her arms; they are weighted to her sides. She wakes sobbing and runs to the bathroom to gulp more pills down. Familiar, yet unknown, silhouettes appear one after the other in the mirror—hair roughed, disheveled as if by wind. Back in bed, darkness returns.

Then suddenly something grabs, straddles her. "You bitch," it screams, "get up . . ."

Another voice calls, "Is she dead?" A long slippery image glides past then falls away beneath a gray boulder. An angry form holds up some fingers, slaps her face over and over.

"Wake up! I won't let you do this to me!"

It is Karl. He looks broken, twisted into ribboned silhouettes of skin and bone which entwine and choke her. Inside the dream, she begins to slip down the hill, knocked backward, spinning upside-down, until something breaks the fall. And then she is lifted onto a flat surface and tied down so that she cannot move. More voices call. She doesn't answer.

A siren whines, whirls through space. She is inside an ambulance. Nearby there is whispering. She wants to run back to the dream, but they will not let her. Suddenly white-coated doctors come into a long white room. She protests "the baby." *Run*, something screams, *they're taking it back*.

She struggles to rise, but large, dark figures hold her down, stretch her skin taut, and then blackness covers her and everything.

Time passes, how long is uncertain, but it is day. Kristen squints. There is too much light. She twists around to see a uniformed woman call out

"Walk." Kristen nods, but she cannot move, she grows heavier, numb. And then more darkness. When she returns there is blood everywhere—smeared, streaks of red. Everyone seems to recognize her. They call, *K-r-i-s-t-e-n*. Her body stiffens and she beings to scream. She searches for Karl.

His black, mouthless face screams, "Kill yourself next time when you're alone. You're not going to do this to me!"

A thick form slams her into unconsciousness.

Now she walks slowly along a corridor.

"How have you been?" a clown-like man dressed in starched white asks politely.

They walk past other whimpering, rumpled women on benches and toward another room. She sees him pull back gray blankets. Then she lies down gratefully upon a metal cot. The room isn't recognizable, but she somehow belongs there.

Fragments swirl, then change places and identities. She is in an office. Another man sits across a desk. He repeats his name. Harold Wicklin. The window blinds are closed. She is appreciative of the shade, but still her hands vibrate, fists clench then unclench. It crosses her mind that she has been in this room before, but there is no way to be sure, so she waits. Suddenly her eyes burn and she scratches at them until he protests.

"You must try to relax, Kristen. Here, look at me. Hang your head over like this. Breathe in. Let yourself go." Wicklin's voice is hypnotic.

Suddenly exhausted, Kristen's body goes

limp. Perhaps she has been given something; she isn't sure of this either.

"Please let me sleep," she says. "Give me something to sleep." The room blurs.

"Why are you crying?" Wicklin asks. Kristen does not answer. Answers are lies. She keeps her mouth firmly closed.

11

Suspended between darkness and dawn, a few moment fibrillate, neither night nor day. Slowly, Kristen lifted her head to watch the sky turn from opaque blackness to steel.

"I wish he would come," she murmured.

"What?" Jamie muttered. Suddenly, the car skidded over an icy patch. "Fuck it!" Jamie cursed and hit the brake. For a second or two they slid about. Then, with a sudden jolt, the car and past stopped revolving. She was not in the hospital now, nor at Karl's apartment; she was not twelve, expecting a miracle, or twenty-three waiting in a hotel lobby, heart frantically beating, sure that magic would come.

"Karl can find me anywhere," she said. He'd told her that once. Shouted it across a theater lobby. *Once.* The word tasted spoiled, rancid on her tongue. She spit it out in disgust.

THE SPLINTERED EYE

"For God's sake, Kristen, get hold of yourself," Jamie commanded, watching her. She began to tremble. A sense of terror spread through her. Even Karl wouldn't find her here—didn't even know she'd left the asylum, or if he did, would think she'd disappeared. Kristen caught sight of Jamie, his face grim. She knew he was disgusted with her. Phlegm rose in her throat. She felt the same way he did.

"Jamie," she said in a small pleading voice, "I need to use the comfort station."

"You mean toilet," he interjected. "Let's let a little reality in here." He seemed about to say something more, then abruptly shrugged and said, "The next one we pass."

A few minutes later he pulled the car into a gas station. Quickly jumping out, Kristen rang the outside bell to rouse the owner. "The bathroom key, please," she half-whispered to the gray-haired man who'd obviously been asleep.

"We don't lock things out here, girlie," he said stiffly. "No need to."

He stared at her dishevelment disapprovingly, shaking his head. Embarrassed, she looked away.

"Use the one straight back across from the phone," the old man called.

Jamie pulled the hose from the pump and began to fill the tank. Grabbing a well-worn lumber jacket from a hook atop the cash register, the proprietor strode out toward him. "I'll do that, sonny."

THE SPLINTERED EYE

Fumbling in the semi-darkness, Kristen made her way to the phone. Let him be there, she thought. With a kind of desperation, she grabbed the receiver. Perspiration soaked her. She heard the connection made, the ringing.

"Please," she murmured, "please don't do this."

And then his hello, jagged but distinct, rang out. A giddy feeling coursed through her.

"Please, please come," she pleaded.

"Kristen, I'm leaving."

"Leaving," she echoed. In her stomach nausea forced its way up. "But you can't. Where are you going?" she pleaded.

"I can't tell you," he answered.

Tears flooded her eyes. "I've got to see you, I can't lose you, not now, not yet . . . you can't."

"I have to," he said sharply.

His words were shapeless, blurred, like the fog which enveloped her mind. Suddenly Karl's face floated before her, part boyish, part worldly, gliding by at their first autumn meeting. Then she saw his hand caress her at their first picnic. In her thoughts he skied past, silver pole raised, iridescent in the twilight. She whimpered, "Don't go."

His goodbye, thick and musty, rushed into her with a brutal swiftness and left her standing numbly, receiver in hand.

She shook her head. How was she to get from this place to another? Her body trembled. Even putting one foot in front of the other seemed a forgotten skill. For a few moments she wept, empty, mollusk-like. Perhaps had she spoken more clearly, found an eloquent argument. What use were such thoughts? Slowly, as she walked from the phone, objects passed near her, dark things collided with her. She felt like a sleepwalker.

"Can I help you?" the old man mumbled from the office.

She shook her head.

She stumbled toward Jamie's car. She reached for the chrome handle. Within it the features of her face multiplied, became a distorted, gleaming spectre glaring back. She could not confront her own gaze and froze. Jamie reached over to open the door from inside.

"Get in, Kris," he said wearily. She obeyed.

Bits of light struck the unfocused eye like a blow. They were driving north into dawn. Call it curious or imagination, but as Kristen stared at the sky, the prismatic effects of the wet snow seemed to form a rainbow above the surrounding countryside. Despite her agony the sight intrigued her. She watched them pass gray old barns and chestnut newer ones, the fresh wood still retaining color, unbleached by this first frenzied winter. An old yellow corn chopper, half-rusted, leaned against a silo. Nearby the forsythia, taking its cue from the tarnished tool, cast a peculiar haze of gold against the whiteness. A mottled deer ran across the road and Jamie stopped to allow it to cross. The deer's fur glistened, snow-jeweled. Kristen sighed, almost soundlessly. The tree branches, except for the evergreens, were bare of leaves, wearing instead crystallized ice.

They were nearly home. Kristen recognized the surroundings: the river, translucent and restrained with only a line or two of gray-blue flowing water, the rest almost motionless. She remembered her father each year at this time perched atop the stone crags, anxious to get out to sea once more, watching the ice floes intently, as if he had wanted to sail upon them to some open bay and onward.

Jamie turned up the narrow lane and shut off the ignition. Slightly off balance, Kristen stumbled as she got out.

"Careful," Jamie called. She felt herself begin to shake again. Cold, fresh snow swirled toward her; snowflakes nested on her clothes and caught in her mouth. She wiped them away. Watching the day break, she had the feeling that her life lay about her, half-encased in the gray fog, half in the bluish-white light of near morning. Jamie sighed, "We're home."

Home. The huge white house stood undaunted. Her heart churned.

"Better go inside. You'll freeze," he said, pushing her forward toward the door. "I've got to garage the car and finish some chores, and then I'll be along."

She nodded but stepped back, resisting his advice. She stared at her breath misting in the

THE SPLINTERED EYE

sharp winter air. Tears fell on her face, but in the pale fragmented light they mixed with rain-like snow.

The granite steps had been carefully shoveled and strewn with salt. All the summer's wicker furniture had disappeared from the wide planked porch, but from the past Kristen heard the sounds of rocking chairs creaking. Her hand reached out to rub the familiar stone pillar atop the last step. The gesture had always signaled whether she or Jamie was the winner of childhood races. Somehow a quick feeling of triumph returned, had not been wholly lost. At this she smiled, surprised, and turned the door knob.

As always, the front door remained unlocked. Her heart slowed near rest. A fire had been lit in the hall hearth. The copper woodbox glowed, obviously polished by Dorothy, who had been with them since Kristen's mother's first illness. The logs overflowed onto the floor. Kristen pulled off her wet boots and stood in front of the fireplace trying to get warm. Firelight flickered, faded, grew bright again as the wood burned. For a moment, as she stared into the fire, her thoughts vanished. Almost hypnotized, she watched the blue-orange blaze cast umber images across the windowpanes. Even the glazed surfaces of the furniture shimmered in response. She paused to let the warmth seep in and then walked toward the parlor.

Nothing had changed. Her father still sat straight-backed in his favorite brown-and-olive-flowered armchair reading. Silently she watched.

THE SPLINTERED EYE

Had the leaves faded ever so slightly? No, she was almost sure the chair's material had looked old even when she was a small child. For a moment she felt calmer, relieved that the outside realities had not penetrated here. At that instant her father lowered his book absent-mindedly and looked up. Seeing her, he smiled.

"Sit down, Kristie," he said, gently pointing to the rocking chair which so long ago she claimed for her very own.

"Dad, your glasses," she said affectionately, repeating an old admonishment. He shook his head absent-mindedly.

"Read this, Kristie." He handed her the book, carefully marked in the margin.

She wondered if it was another of the history books he liked so much or some myth which had stirred his fancy. His reading matter was catholic, so unlike her own. Her mind drifted like a balloon high above the page and then floated down toward it.

> The earliest people of all, the Cyclops, were built with a special organ with which to register the finer vibrations of the physical world, the realm of the others. This organ was known as "The Third Eye" and had its seat near the pineal gland. They used this eye to see all non-solid matter, which was all that existed at the time. As the earth solidified, human beings developed and man had two physical eyes with which to view the solid world, and his special organ recessed, its etheric sight spreading all over the nervous system having its seat in the

solar plexus. It is said each of man's five senses spread all over his body in the same way.

As physical sight developed, the etheric eye recessed, but although dormant at present in most people, it is only awaiting development and training to be reawakened. This training is part of deliberate mysterical movement which was well understood and thoroughly provided for in the ancient temples. No pharoahs were eligible without such training. The face of his finished apprenticeship was announced by a knob upon the forehead of his statue representing the awakened Third Eye or by a serpent's head rearing from his own to show that he had raised the Kundalini serpent.

The Chinese Mandarin wore a peacock feather in his headdress to represent the same development.

When the Third Eye, the eye of the soul, is opened, individuals begin to see all the manifold creatures and activities of the other levels of existence and they approach much nearer to the causes and realities of life.

Her father watched her intently. "So the spirit is not dead yet, Kristen, just hibernating, eh?"

She handed him back the book, shaking her head, not trusting herself to answer.

"To reawaken what has been so long asleep requires more than idle wishes. A new beginning perhaps?" Eben paused, his eyes thoughtful.

"It's really too late for that—" Kristen said softly.

"Are you dead then?" Eben said amusedly.

She laughed out loud; the sound rang out, astounding her.

"Kristen, pain is a survivable affliction; distance gives you a measuring rod—perspective."

Such words only distressed Kristen more. She would have preferred future numbness or the promise that what she fervently wanted would be hers if she had the courage to wait. But the future her father foresaw—filled with tranquility provided by philosophical musings—repulsed her. Endless monotone days followed by endless colorless nights. She had thought that destiny had brought Karl to her and fate would ensure the permanence of their relationship. To acknowledge that it would not only made her feel more vulnerable, more alone.

Kristen felt her father touch her arm. "Stay here a while, rest. All of us want to believe in magic and forever, and when the trickery is exposed there is always a brick-wall crash. When you are young, such wounds heal much more quickly. Young bones are not so fragile."

Kristen felt dizzy. She clutched her stomach.

"Fear is your real obstacle," Eben observed. "Remember the old lady and her apples?"

"Daddy, I was only four or five then."

"Late enough for your character to have molded sufficiently. Remember how every Sunday Jamie, you and I would ride our bicycles through the surrounding roads with me in the lead?"

Kristen smiled, knowing how he relished the

memory. "You would never let us go first," she mused.

"I wanted to protect you both. I still do," Eben said decisively. "The old lady, the apple orchard." Eben closed his eyes.

"You always went that way," Kristen protested. "I never could understand why."

There was a pause.

"They were wild apples, Kristie," Eben said patiently.

"She screamed at us anyway," Kristen trembled.

"One can't twist truth or steal freedom, Kristen." Eben objected sharply. "One can only give them away. Fearful, timid people, ones who don't resist or allow others to rule them, can never flee far enough. That from which they have run usually catches up with them anyway."

"Dad, I feel empty, useless . . ." Kristen leaned toward him.

He patted her hand. "The two have different cures, but one hinges upon the other. For the first, turn outward. One day you will find your own pain diminished." Eben paused. "For the second, strip your life down to basics for a while and then seek new nourishment." He shook his head. "Men like Karl West provide quick energy but no substance. You must find real nourishment or grow anemic even as your body swells with fat. Kristen, have you thought about what you want," he paused, "to do?"

She tried to think. "I'm not sure."

THE SPLINTERED EYE

"Once you wanted to work with children."

"It isn't enough. I want Karl. I want to be happy."

"Kris, neither of those goals is graspable. You cannot get happy nor can you hold someone who wants to be free. Love, in such a case, becomes a prison and you the armed guard."

"Have you turned philosopher, Daddy?" she said softly, with sudden seriousness.

"Approaching death has that effect."

There was a silence between them as a coldness gripped Kristen. "Death." She winced. She studied her father apprehensively. There were pale brown spots strewn on his face, soft blue pulsing veins on his temples which she could not remember having seen before. Her eyes filled with tears. "Your death is eons away."

Eben's voice had lost none of its force. "When one is as lucky as I have been, life has a natural cycle whose closure is as much a part as its beginning. Neither dying nor living is a cause for fear, Kristen. Only those who spend valuable hours trying to escape the inevitable instead of utilizing the interval between have reason to cringe." He looked searchingly at her. "Kristen, have you walked along the sea lately?"

She shook her head.

"The sea is at the apex of all being. When you walk its shores each day as I have you reinstate your place in the scheme of things," he met her eyes.

Kristen nodded. Her father's prescriptions

were always so simple. If only they worked. But of course, they didn't—not for her. Had they for him? Of course, he was rich, the shipping lines prospering, supporting all the other companies he had so carefully nurtured. She shot him another sideways glance, measuring his mood.

He seemed content now, serene even, but in another time she had heard him curse loudly, protest fate's unfairness. Suddenly she again saw her mother lying in a dark velvet coffin, her father crying nearby.

She leaned over to kiss her father on his cheek. Her own problems with Karl seemed so immense they obliterated all others. She wanted no more pain, not now. Turtle-like, she crept back into herself. "I think I'll go rest now."

"Rest is good, but the sea is better, Kristen," Eben said steadily.

She nodded, unable to trust speech.

"I'll be going out soon to check the riggings with Jamie. When we come back, we'll lunch." She leaned over to kiss him again, but he had already found his place in the book and turned his attention back to the reading, or pretended to.

She wanted to lie down; she made her way back to the bedroom.

In her room, nothing had changed. The walls were still rosy-hued from the pastel-print paper her mother had chosen. She walked toward the big brass bed with its plump down quilt edged in lace from her mother's wedding gown. "To dream upon," her mother had said. How good it still felt, she thought, plopping on top. Her books lined one wall. Glancing toward them, she was disturbed by their remoteness. They seemed to belong to someone else, yet not long ago each had an assigned place on the shelf, just as the cluster of dolls which were now heaped together in the corner. Kristen walked over to the bookshelf and ran her fingers across the volumes slowly, as if the print were Braille. A nuisance, Dorothy used to call them. One toppled into her open hand: *The Psychology of Learning and Instruction.* "Dececce," she murmured, remembering the author. She glanced at the fly leaf but could read no more than a few sentences. The meaning seemed to blur. Quickly she placed the book back on the shelf.

Hurrying into the tiny bathroom, she smiled again. Bunches of slender white lilies in painted earthenware pots were grouped around the room. Evidence of Dorothy's green thumb. On the back of the commode, lilac foil and giant pink satin bows waited. Already a few petals had turned brown. Kristen looked in the mirror. The patch of white in her hair frightened her. She began to weep noisily, helplessly, like a child. And then, just as she had when those small disappointments of years past occurred, she disrobed, turned on the shower and squatted on the bottom of the tub. The warm water streamed over her. It soothed her. Images rose to consciousness, then diminished. The stream of water scattered them.

As she showered, voices filtered through the wall. They came from the next room: her father's room. At first the sounds were indistinct, but snatches of conversation soon became clear. They were talking about her.

"Has she said anything about West yet?" Jamie asked in a weary tone.

"What more is there to tell?" Eben's voice was grim. "We knew most of the story anyway. What good would an interrogation do?"

"Did you make your deal with him?" Jamie asked sharply.

"Of course," Eben said decisively.

"And does she suspect who's *really* employing West?" Jamie asked in a hollow mocking tone.

"Hell no," Eben snapped back, "and let's see that she doesn't. That might make a martyr of him."

"Or her," Jamie said softly.

Their voices became barely audible and Kristen pressed her ear to the wall, her head aching.

"Have you noticed just how disturbed she really is," Jamie mused.

"Crazy, you mean." The voice of the older man took on a cutting edge.

"Dad, look." Jamie paused and took a deep breath. "She's out of control, cries out for no reason, talks to herself, even tried to jump out of the car. What would *you* call it?"

"She's not crazy," Eben said sternly.

"What is she then?" Jamie asked softly.

She heard her father's sigh. "I won't have it. Jamie, I'm sixty-two years old. Maybe I have four or five years left. Don't you think I want some peace?" Eben said bitterly.

"I'm more than willing to handle everything myself," Jamie injected.

Her father sighed again. "One of these days, when you prove yourself, you will. Until then, we need a senior navigator."

"Well, you'd better scrutinize this, Captain," Jamie said sarcastically, "before you plot a course."

"What?" Eben asked slowly.

"The hospital evaluation. Here, read it."

"My glasses." Eben stopped.

"You don't need them," Jamie responded harshly.

There was a pause. "You read it, James," Eben said, his voice surprisingly strong.

She heard loud rustling of papers, then Jamie's voice again.

"Referring physician, Dr. Harold Wicklin. Physician in charge, George Hayward, charge nurse, Nancy Alba—"

"Get to the point," Eben said bleakly.

"Whatever you say, Father," Jamie snapped back. "Reason for admission: During the day or early evening prior to admission, the patient made a suicide attempt and was involuntarily committed to Brookhaven State Asylum. Brief summary: The patient is a twenty-four-year-old single Caucasian woman, a doctoral candidate in social work at New York University. Her past psychiatric history includes at least four known suicide attempts, as reported by Burton Cald (credentials unverified), identified by Ms. Blakely's companion as the psychologist of record. Two of these attempts required hospitalization, and the reports have been forwarded here. During the past year the patient has had multiple emotional crises involving physical abusiveness with her present companion with whom she lives. Her life pattern demonstrates numerous instances of immature decision, inappropriate dependency upon her father, brother, and other figures, ambivalence about life goals, and pseudo-independence reflected in oppositional behavior and rash decision-making. Her conflicts have been consistently experienced as external and she has, thereby, learned to manipulate her environment to achieve some release, but not resolution, of these conflicts. She has demonstrated only ambivalent motivation to change." Jamie drew a deep breath.

Eben broke in. "Jamie, what's the result of all this hocus-pocus?"

"Dad, this problem can't be waved away by your command. You might as well hear it out. The doctor's diagnosis is Hysterical Personality 301.50 with passive-aggressive and obsessional trends," Jamie said fiercely.

"And the prescription?" Eben's tone was withering.

"If you mean treatment," Jamie shot back, "intensive therapy and/or long-term hospitalization."

Eben answered savagely, "What is suggested, then, is solving her reality problems by sticking her in one of those places where she can further escape life or decision-making and legally be a drug addict." There was a silence, then Eben said heavily, "I'd rather see her dead."

Kristen's eyes glistened with tears.

"If you take that attitude, you just might." Jamie's voice was husky.

"Which means, my boy?" Eben said sternly.

"Don't call me that," Jamie said quietly. "I'm thirty-two years old, and as long as the information is piling up, here's more."

"Yes?" A trace of impatience.

Jamie snapped, "Another one of those weird poems you always encourage. She gave it to one of the shrinks the day before we left. Words to the wise, no doubt.

>'They locked me in a thin white room
>of Conical stars and apple cores
>While moons rummaged in my head
>They thought I lay upon their bed
>Tantalized by hours
>They drove the purples
>   from my brain
>They drove the pain
>At intervals of time
>   they came
>But I erased their smooth white sheets
>The daily bath
>The pulse they pressed
>I laughed that they thought me sane
>Passing from the earth
>again

> But they return each night
> Whisper sight
> names recite
> pretend to see me
> on this
>   crystal bed
> But I am dead.'

"Now you understand," Jamie said.

"What is there to understand?" Eben sounded weary.

"Dad, you know damned well what I mean. Kristen's got one hell of a lot of problems."

"As do we all," Eben shot back.

"I'm thinking of her future security. You're getting on. It's fairly obvious she won't be able to take care of herself, no less participate in our business. You have to give me the opportunity of protecting us if trouble comes." Jamie's voice took on a barely controlled urgency.

"How?" Eben asked gruffly.

Jamie hesitated, then went on. "By having her sign a power of attorney in my favor right now. Then we'll be sure none of those kooks she gets involved with marry her, get control, and piss the whole thing away."

"You think that best?" Eben asked thoughtfully.

"I've proven my loyalty," Jamie said sharply.

"Loyalty is not always a stable quality," Eben observed quietly. "Over a period of time, circumstances cause people to shift allegiances, change or rationalize past oaths, sometimes because of new insights—" he calculated and weighed his words "—to say nothing of less honorable motives."

"Don't be insulting," Jamie protested heatedly.

Eben shook his head. "No, my boy, just realistic. One can't be eternally sure of any living thing. I have hopes just as you do, but certainty—" he paused. "If life has brought me any real insight, it is that permanent certainty is an illusion." He sighed. "Maturity is not an easy quality to come by, but when you have it, Jamie, I'll know, and then I'll gladly step aside. But for most of us wisdom comes late."

"When I'm eighty perhaps," Jamie interjected bitterly. "Do you know how long you've been sticking that same old carrot in front of my nose? If this keeps up, I'll ditch the whole thing. Do you think I'm going to work my ass off for all this to let it end up in the hands of Karl West or a senile old man?"

"I won't stand for disrespect," Eben stated quietly.

"Dad, don't start that."

"Start what, James?" Eben asked. "Are we talking of Kristen or you now?"

"Don't be ridiculous, Dad. I just spent hours getting her out of that place bringing her up here."

"I know you did, son." Eben's voice grew quieter. "And this could be a turning point for Kristen. She could rethink her way if we just give her some time."

"We Christians wait hopefully for Christ's

return, but there are no imminent signs," Jamie said sarcastically.

"Jamie, look." Eben paused. "I need to cogitate for a while, read the weather signals, and figure out the right direction. I want to allow Kristen a little settling-in time instead of forcing her to sail around trying to find a breeze when a shift in the wind will come naturally. Let's sit tight for the moment."

"And lose everything, including Kristen, because we've taken no precautions?" Jamie said bitterly.

Eben's voice was still tending to gentleness. "Jamie, you've always been too impatient. That alone may cause the loss of what you desire. Come on, son." His voice grew stronger. "It's time to check the boats. This is the time the waters unlock. First things first."

Kristen heard the sound of things being gathered up, doors closing, and then silence. Without further delay, she jumped from the shower, grabbed a towel, wrapped it around her, and hurried back to the safety of her bed.

12

"Kristen, are you sleeping?"

Nervously, Kristen jumped. No one was around. Listening through closed eyes, she felt her heart pound, then skip a beat. In an instant, another jerk of her body propelled her up, another down. She could not remain quiet, the motion continued against her will, forcing her mind to accompany the irregular rhythm.

"Are you sleeping, Kristen?"

A voice lurked somewhere in the room. Behind her, perhaps, or beneath the bed. She was being watched. Someone knew she was really awake, pretending sleep.

"Do you hear me?" the soft voice called. "Open your eyes, darling."

Kristen's eyelids felt heavy, sluggish. She let in a moon-colored crevice of light. On the wall in front of her, she perceived the outline of a thick figure. She wrapped her arms around her stomach to dull the rising panic.

"It's Dorothy, my dear." Kristen nodded gravely, but when she tried to answer, the sound grew elongated, the reverberations swelled, enlarging the confusion.

She forced herself to speak. "Dorothy?" Words like pinpricks tingled in her throat. She wanted to reach out to touch her old nannie, but could not seem to move. "You're here."

"Don't be afraid, daughter." The black woman paused with ethereal grace near the bed.

"Dots, your letter was too late." Kristen shook her head. "That night the ambulance came. I think it was the same night. It's so hard to remember." Her head swam.

"I knew the hour to be close at hand," Dorothy interjected quietly.

"How could you?" Kristen asked, and suddenly she felt a terrible urgency to understand, despite the pounding at her temples. Questions, fragile as ancient iridescent seashells, hung in the air. There were so many to ask, but the older woman waved them away.

"Questions are answerless," Dorothy said, her dark eyes fixed upon Kristen, "unless you believe. I have been fasting that you may pass over and inquire of the ancestral spirits." Kristen looked away, giddy. She could not catch her breath.

"Open yourself," Dorothy commanded. Something seemed to be happening to Kristen, a thing she could not stop. Unsure what it was, nevertheless she obeyed Dorothy.

Dorothy sat down on the side of the bed and placed her hands on the girl's shoulders, gently lifting Kristen towards her. "My bones are clean, the flesh scraped off, the bodily fluids thrown away, eyes torn from sockets. Now I have new flesh and the spirits have instructed me to find the soul of you who are sick or carried by demons away. Let my spirit guides lead you." Kristen trembled with expectation.

"Please," she pleaded.

"Come," Dorothy called.

"Yes." Kristen heard her own voice softly reply almost as if she were outside herself.

Dorothy placed a cream-colored candle and a small vial of water on the night table. Like a sorceress, she knelt on the wood floor, tapped three times, and from a blue canvas bag took out bones, dice, and shells—her instruments of divination. From somewhere a piercing sunlight fell across the bones, yet the blinds remained closed and the room dark. Kristen felt the light ray strike her eyes and raised her hand to shield them. Dorothy did not look up. She picked up the bones, blew on them, and cast them down. Then she blew upon them three more times and threw them to the floor.

Kristen gasped. Dorothy placed her fingers to her mouth. "Shush." She quietly chanted a mixture of Christian and pagan prayers. In a high-pitched tone Dorothy called out. Kristen raised her head and the gold bracelets on Dorothy's arm caught her eye. Rapid flashes of metal blinded her momentarily.

"No, don't turn away," Dorothy instructed. "This is the bone of the impala." Dorothy's husky voice paused. "It lives with its brethren until the time comes to go. Then the deer travels through dense brush, is cut by sharp branches and often lost and alone. But it must journey onward." Dorothy paused, then her voice grew stronger. "This is you. Much pain but also a new path will be your destiny. What you will learn is what the spirits teach you. This is the only way." Puzzled, Kristen continued to watch Dorothy intently.

The old woman threw the dice again. She stretched out her hands in a gesture of supplication. Kristen leaned her head out over the bed; she frowned in concentration. Dorothy's eyes appeared dilated, dazed, as if the focus of her vision lay somewhere else. There was a silence. "You and the flyer. Your bodies met. There was a shock of recognition. You drank from one another and were fed. This is time past." Kristen drew in her breath and stared in amazement. What was this woman about? It was as if she knew Kristen's own mind. Kristen's thoughts whirled. She could not remember telling these feelings about which Dorothy spoke to anyone, yet now they were being repeated aloud. Kristen grew more giddy.

"How do you—" Kristen whispered and her voice cracked. Something is happening to me, she thought; pieces of me are crumbling. I will disappear before I can escape. Baffled, frightened, she tried to signal Dorothy to get her attention, but she was mute and paralyzed, waiting helplessly for this new madness to subside.

Dorothy began to wrap Kristen in a white gauze. Like a shroud, Kristen thought, and she shivered. She hadn't the nerve for this—not now. She must tell the woman to stop. But the stricture of the sheet was more calming than freedom. Suddenly her body convulsed, a seizure spirited her mind away.

She felt as if some berserk being grabbed hold of the hollow core of her being. Nor was the thing human; in the distance she saw it—half-man and half-horse—throw her on its back, and it did not draw back though Kristen bit her lip and screamed in protest. Together they rode over obscene and terrifying scenery. There was no stopping. Dangers half-seen, half-forgotten in childhood passed and Kristen sat upright, buttocks raw, rooted in the saddle. More bitter memories returned, threatening to encompass her. Her eyes fastened upon terror after terror as she and the beast rode on. Everything within her wanted to burst, only the straitjacket of gauze held her sweating body rigid. Certain now of her own madness, she yelled and tried to grab hold of the wild horse's flanks; she felt a fierce desire to hold the stuff of which madness was made. But the horse executed a series of twists and turns and zigzags, and the last connected coherent thing within gave way. Her head hammered, about to split open, and poured out tumors of sound. She wanted to warn Dorothy, who seemed to be placing cold compresses on her forehead, to watch out. . . . Her lips formed the letters in a silent scream: *Help me.*

Then shadows came and rocked her within them, and the sharp peaked past grew quietly inert. Moments like cast-off dead lined the road, and from them a soft, oozing sound of dying came; and she again sensed the presence of Dorothy holding her, she was still swathed in gauze. Fragments of people swirled by, and she became one with them, but then passed on from their presence to other figures in another time.

Dorothy chanted, "The spirits call. They are summoning you to their land. Enter. Do not draw back. You must journey through madness and let die your other self. When death comes, the spiritual power which has been turned against you may be reborn. It will become one with you. Accept it."

Dorothy stood over the bed, sprinkled three drops of water from a silver-encrusted vial upon Kristen's forehead and began unwinding the layers of gauze. "I commend her to your care," she called and raised her arms. Then, without looking back, she hurried from the room. Another seizure shook Kristen, spreading through her entire body. She was sure she would black out. The ordeal had gone too far. Yet how could she be sure of what had occurred? The room was empty now. How could she know what was real? She brought her shaking hand in front of her face and spread her fingers. In the strange light they seemed to have a red glow. Her fear increased. No proof at all. What if her

THE SPLINTERED EYE

body itself was the final illusion? Her heart drummed. She traced the vein on one hand with the other and raised it to her mouth. As she did so, the odor from beneath it accosted her. Truly, she thought, something had died, was decomposing. She gagged. There was a reality to the odor that defied repudiation—could not be denied. She inhaled it again and grew more calm. Bullshit; of course she was here. Out loud she laughed and her head responded nodding, "Yes, yes!" Still, her excited brain sparked more jumbled thoughts. Slowly she tried to get up. Her body bobbed, had a certain weightlessness; every nerve and fiber quivered as if its entire chemistry had changed.

"I am returning," she said, and felt no shame at her exultation. "The past is ended."

She wondered what Dr. Wicklin or her father would say if she told them what had happened. Surely they would commit her to some asylum forever, would not understand the salvation of such madness. She clutched the bottle next to the bed and threw water to the ground three times. Then she lit the taper and waited, but nothing happened. "I don't care," she murmured and lowered her eyes. She laughed breathlessly, shivering and feverish at the same time, as if a heat spell had broken leaving cool, moist air come to quell the inner turbulence. Never again was she quite sure of realistic explanations, nor that explanations define all events. Slowly her blood slowed its pounding; she wiped her wet forehead against the soft pillow.

There was a pause as if the very air held its

breath. The room darkened. A blue-white light streamed through the bedroom door leading to the closet. She stared at the light. It shone like a laser beam with an explosive power. She rubbed her eyes. Suddenly the light outlined a woman's body, her dark hair caught by a scarf.

The woman looked somewhat like Dorothy—the honey-colored skin, the dark-rimmed eyes. Kristen gasped. The eyes—she shook her head, looking into the woman's eyes. Never had she seen such eyes: they were tri-colored. Each layer distinct—black, then blue, then brown. Who was this? Surely she had never seen this woman before. Am I losing control again? She trembled. Near the upper curve of the woman's breast a character glowed with crystal light so exceedingly white and brilliant that Kristen had to look away. Where was the woman's body? Stunned, Kristen tried to calm herself, but then the woman spoke: "The events which have happened here were prescribed. I have brought you to this day because I wished you to see in this way. You have not slept."

As the woman talked, Kristen began to sway in agreement mumbling, "Of course, it has always been this way, yes, yes," over and over again. Then from the perspective of timelessness, she saw her life in retrospective and prospect.

"Relinquish your dreams of the aviator. Beware of her who whispers in his ear. They are illusions. All that you have desired before this day is only a consequence of false light. With vision, the true roots of consciousness spring up, bear new foliage, receive sustenance from the whole self, and create a supple fruit."

Kristen gave herself up to the words. She felt the substance of them flow into her body, nourishing her. In days to come she would wonder if the voice had really come from somewhere inside her, a long lost aspect of herself swimming dizzily to the surface, drunk on its first expansive breath. But now the voice's transcendent reality was something worth staking her life upon and putting her trust into—a buoy to hold onto while integrating and reconnecting the events of her life. As they surfaced, each could be viewed individually but also their parallel and cross relations became visible. The seer, the seeing, and the seen; the feeler, the feeling, and the felt were all one.

She saw suffering and the occurrence of her own death: "You must remember that it is hard for us here to estimate time. Because of these times, you will not live to an old age, still you may will a creative life. It is within your reach," the woman decreed.

She saw the death of others: "On the last day of his life the sun is strong in the sky. It must be summer. Your father will lie down facing the sea. Your child is near him, as are you. In this moment he will fall into his sleep. So will it be."

These moments of death did not cause fear nor contradict the eternal dimensions of life. Without pain, Kristen saw and accepted them. What was proclaimed was birth, death, and the law of probability. All else allowed freedom. Kristen plunged forward into the luminous world to which she had been given access.

"A man will soon come to you. To him reveal your dreams, for he is worthy of revelations. He will see always what is best within you, and you therefore will aspire to fulfill higher goals." Kristen drew closer, and it was as if she gazed from darkness into the light of stars. She felt the upsurge and outgo of energy all around.

"Come now, Kristen, visit the sea. I will bring you no more messages in this way, for you are too delicate to gain your knowledge from the earth. You are not like me or your father with the big antlers. Rather, you are the doe. The spirit is within your eye. A man comes who will guard this spirit, for he is like your father—yet like you—and he knows those like me."

Kristen watched the blue-white light about the woman ebb. The room began to fill with blackness. But for the barest moment before the vision completely disappeared, both waking reality and dream reality were clear and intact, superimposed and yet unjoined. And in that fleeting instant beyond time, Kristen perceived them both simultaneously. Sheer awareness narrowed to a wire-thin ledge. She stood on the precipice of pure being without fear. Whether seconds or hours transpired she never knew, but she wanted to remain there. But then effortlessly she felt herself rise into consciousness.

With fumbling movements, Kristen grabbed up her clothes and pulled them on. In the bathroom mirror her face was infused with new color. As if a hand guided her, she took an eyebrow pencil from the medicine cabinet and drew a letter on her breast. It seemed to blur immediately. A remnant of ashes. Suddenly a strange sensation arose in the pit of her stomach. "I'm famished," she murmured, amazed.

In the parlor she stood waiting. Dorothy must have anticipated the hunger, because near Kristen's coat was a tray of thick-sliced brown bread spread with coarse-cut marmalade. Hurriedly pouring the tea from the kettle into a coarse brown cup, Kristen raised it to her lips. How strong and delicious it felt going down her throat. Hungrily she devoured every speck of the toast and scooped up the bittersweet burnt-orange droplets of jam on the plate with shaking fingers. Then she mumbled to herself, "Go now to the sea." And pulling on her windbreaker, she ran, still trembling, outside.

Carefully crossing the property line and stepping on the mulch created by decayed autumn leaves and branches felled by winter, Kristen made her way toward the ocean. Last night's snow had melted into the earth, and her boots sank in. Somehow she would have liked to be barefoot—to feel the soil so long asleep beneath the frost. In the distance through the silhouetted silver tree barks, the ocean appeared. Kristen moved toward it.

During the night, the waters had come undone as if the last winter storm had caused the ice floes to break open and cast mixtures of ice and hoary driftwood to the shore. The waters appeared to cry out to her, a bombastic sound of flowing current which came alive. The tide breathed quickly, then slowly, a heartbeat rhythm. She watched the movement until, ceasing to be an onlooker, she began to feel the current moving back and forth within her and tasted the sea in every cell of her body. The sound was blue-green, an aural Cezanne. As she stared, the sound colored—became more turquoise—filled with a luminous clarity and depth. For a moment she closed her eyes to hear better, and when she reopened them the whole world was a living sea surging with life.

    Kristen walked slowly along the shore and saw the earth come alive again—a universe in which she had been for so long a ghost without substance. She realized now that such life had always existed. She had been blinded. Every level of life flowed from this source and back to it eventually. And she knew herself a multi-varied universe of time, space, motion, and desire. This was a new orientation to herself and the world. At that second, a feeling of cosmic tenderness filled her. Then the cold air spun through her senses. Morning swirled about her, and she moved more naturally, now sorting the fragments of the past, present, and future. They formed a spiritual mulch. Finally, the barriers between inner and outer reality faded. The real structure of creation and her part within it clarified.

    On a huge crag, Kristen sat down. She put

her hands to her face and massaged her red-lidded eyes. A pale honey-colored sun hung over the water. The warmth jostled her, coursed through her thoughtstream, an osmosis of heat and light. Moments of timelessness deft as butterflies emerged from their cocoons.

Dream completed, Kristen thought. Time to return. But she could not stand up without shaking. She felt fragile—as if lost pieces had been bonded and reunited but not allowed to dry. Nevertheless, she knew she would have to go back. Without time giving her the distance to accept what she had seen, felt, and heard this day. And Karl's image would still be with her—a craved addiction, a drug whose effects would remain gnawing in the pit of her belly.

How would she be able to begin? Suddenly sea spray splashed above the rock, drenching her. Trembling, she jumped up startled.

Her breath came in uneven spurts. From somewhere overhead pale-winged birds—sparrows, sandpipers, terns—spun down in shadowlike formations. Kaleidoscopic fragments of light grew stronger as she walked. Yellows, oranges danced on the frosted evergreens, glistened on the open fields.

"It must be almost noon," she thought, glancing up at the sun. "Dad will be returning." She wished she could remain here, safe. But she knew she could not make time stand still any longer. Something within her called, "Return." She leaned over and pulled up a sprig of onion grass which had found its way through the wet ground. How strong the taste was.

She climbed uphill now. The house grew larger, white and substantial. Later perhaps, she thought, I shall return to this exact spot to see it again. She cocked her head to either side, listening, surveying.

"Must get back," she mumbled and felt her mind quiver. She shook her head; even aching it could still make it work for instead of against her. She directed her thoughts forward, floating past fear. "Almost there." Kristen stopped. Her eyes brimmed with tears. She contemplated herself and felt a strange elation. She tasted the wind: it was strong and fresh as it brushed through her hair.

She took a deep breath and felt better. She was not crazy, not fated to madness. She heard the sea's presence and glanced back over her shoulder. The sea was a living blue-green. She sighed with relief. No, the whole incident had not been imagined, not at all. This was the proof for which she had always searched. No one could take such insight away. She felt momentarily reborn. She knew such intensity of feeling could not last but she would feel this way again. Perhaps not immediately, but one day. Of this she felt almost certain.

Suddenly, her heart beat very fast, loud enough to hear. But she shook her head. She would no longer be fooled by such trickery. She would go on. A pattern was emerging; a direction had been glimpsed. At last, in front of her, the back gate appeared. Her father always wired it shut against the winter storms. Painfully she climbed over the sharp-peaked wooden slats which scratched her legs and tore at her clothes. Finally she reached the back door of the house and went in.

Jamie and her father—their faces clear, beautifully open—sat at the mahogany dining room table. Its polished surface gleamed with their silver-gold silhouettes.

"There you are, Kristie. We were beginning to worry."

She smiled, the high-colored windburn making her look more robust. "I took your advice and walked a bit."

"The sea air, you look better already," her father sighed. "Join us."

13

Kristen felt her face grow warm. She looked around the table. Her father looked so hopeful, hopeful that she had instantaneously recovered and would immediately turn into his healthy girl once more—the one who had ridden behind him on the red tricycle twenty years in the past. She wondered if he noticed that she had become a woman who might have had her own child by this time. And Jamie, who sat there in the center chair staring at her with a grave frown, what was his true impression of her? A mixed-up spoiled post-adolescent brat who constantly needed to be watched over? She studied his face. Then again perhaps he was too lost in his own struggles to ponder hers.

"Kristen, sit here," Jamie said with an impatient gesture that made panic flash through her again. She wanted to run away from the panic but for the first time stood her ground and felt it quiet and disappear. Surprised, she heard that the voice which answered Jamie and her father was just her ordinary voice. Sitting down on the opposite side of the table, she met both their glances in turn.

"I feel much better," she said, and, watching them smile, knew she had given the right answer, the one they wanted to hear.

Lunch was already served, shepherd's pie heaped in a large, gleaming brown bowl that had been handed down from her great-grandmother. The mashed potatoes atop the pie were swirled about the rim of the bowl like organdy ruffles on a prom gown.

"How good it looks—like Mother's," Kristen reminisced. Everyone brightened. Kristen was surprised to find she still felt vaguely hungry. Had it been hours or minutes since she'd had the tea and toast prepared by Dorothy? The bowl was passed to her. She ladled out a large serving.

"Your eyes were always bigger than your appetite," Eben laughed. "Jamie, pass Kris the scones."

"Where's Dorothy?" Jamie asked, briskly helping himself to another roll. He passed the plate across the table.

"Don't you remember, I dropped her at the bus Thursday. Another of those endless sick relatives she supports. She won't be back 'til tomorrow. Lucky she left this stuff in the freezer or we'd all be on starvation rations 'til she returned," Eben winked.

Kristen felt the pressure return inside her

head. Alarmed, she leaned over the table to steady herself. "Dorothy was here early this morning," she protested.

"Don't be silly, Kris," Jamie grimaced. "Dad just told you she won't be back 'til tomorrow."

Eben looked at his daughter hesitantly. "You must have imagined—" He stopped.

"Dad, pass the butter." Jamie interrupted the anxious moment, noisily putting down the proferred plate and spreading a huge lump on his bread.

"Jamie, you don't need all that fat. Use honey instead," Eben ordered, his attention diverted.

"Yes, Daddy," Jamie grinned, feigning a small child's voice. Eben and Kristen laughed and the mood at the table returned to normal.

The rest of lunch went slowly but serenely. It must be Sunday, Kristen thought, looking at the antique lace tablecloth and the good silver. She picked up her fork, fiddled with the meat, and tried to capture the appetite she'd now seemed to have lost. She wondered if she should bring up the subject again but decided against it. They would think it evidence of her insanity, and anyway, how could she express what was unexplainable? Suddenly, her father stared at her with an intense look of affection and fear that agonized her. Jamie had the peculiar look also. Kristen sighed and knew she would say nothing. Perhaps a time will come, she thought, when other people's opinion of my sanity will be meaningless. She wondered when.

THE SPLINTERED EYE

"Is that so?" Jamie asked thoughtfully. What were they talking about, Kristen wondered, startled by Jamie's question.

"You all right, Kris? Do you have enough of everything?" her father asked solicitously. She nodded and took a bite of the dark-green flowery vegetable. Broccoli, her mind registered.

The telephone rang. Startled, Kristen's body twitched. Her thoughts raced ahead. She imagined for a moment that it was Karl and jumped up from her seat. Hurrying to the foyer, she stood there in a panic wanting to answer the phone, afraid to answer. Was he calling to say he loved her, wanted help, would marry her immediately? Kristen closed her eyes, letting the images drift through. Finally, she managed to pick up the receiver only to hear a strange voice say "Neddy." She tried to respond calmly but heard her voice break. She took a deep breath waiting for her emotions to stabilize and then slowly walked back to the dining room.

"Wrong number," she said unevenly, sitting down again. After an awkward pause the conversation between Eben and Jamie continued.

"I think we should tie in with Atlantic Fleets," Jamie said briskly. "Small companies are a thing of the past."

"Our whole country's past," Eben cut in sharply. "Our family's future. As long as I'm running the ships. I'm too old to have some ex-college man tell me where to fish, when and how, just because he studied the psychology of tides at some merchant marine academy."

THE SPLINTERED EYE

Jamie laughed uneasily. "I guess you're the boss," he said, "and I'm still the boss's son figuratively clad in short pants."

"I accept the innuendo," Eben said carefully. "But try to understand, to parents children never fully mature even when one of them gets to be thirty and the other's sixty. You'll find the realization as difficult to fathom as I do when your time comes."

"If it ever does," Jamie said half under his breath. Kristen's fingers moved restlessly on the old lace, tracing its up and down pattern. She had hardly touched her food. Suddenly her father noticed.

"Kristen, you've eaten hardly anything," he protested softly. It was a mild rebuke, but she wished he wouldn't. Guiltily, she reached over to pat his arm. The affectionate gesture seemed to bridge the communication gap between them.

"Ah, Kristie, I'm glad you're home," he said, his burr surfacing.

"Me too, Daddy," she said quietly.

Jamie and Eben appeared still hungry. Kristen squirmed a little in the chair. Jamie had already started his second or third helping. Kristen wished the food upon her own plate would disappear. For months now a peculiar lump in her throat had made swallowing difficult. Her stomach had shrunk so much that even very little food made her feel satiated. She wondered how to camouflage the mound on her plate. Should she slip into the kitchen and dispose of it? Edgy, Kristen dabbed at her eyes; she had thought this pressure would disappear after the vision, but the relief had been only temporary. Her nerves were still playing their tricks. Well, let them, she thought. I believe what I saw. She would practice until she could hold the glimpsed reality longer and longer. Her gaze fell on the other faces. They would have to accept as she would this slow healing, and the best solution was to stop pretenses of a miraculous cure now. She pushed her plate away.

"It's delicious, but I'm just not used to eating large meals anymore." Again an awkward silence.

"Don't force yourself, Kristen, go slowly," Eben said, his voice low-keyed and deliberately not forceful. She smiled in relief, relaxing a bit. Life would be easier to handle. There was nothing to be afraid of. After a while she felt more comfortable; the pressure receded.

Her father and Jamie went on talking. Every once in a while they tried to include her by soliciting an unnecessary opinion. But mostly they spoke to each other. She was grateful. She wanted to get up from the table and go back outside, but she tried to concentrate instead on what was being said. Suddenly she realized they were staring at her, obviously waiting for a reaction to something. She looked around.

"Kristen, answer the door." Her brother shook his head. The buzzer sounded. Mechanically, she arose and nodded, not really responding to the sound of the bell but rather to Jamie's directive.

Just as she reached the foyer, the front door opened.

"David," she said wonderingly.

And in that instant his large gentle hand reached out to touch her shoulder, and she saw him silhouetted against a glowing sky.

"Hello," he said smiling, and his eyes were as unexpectedly warm and earth-colored as the day.

"What are you doing here?"

"Your Dad asked me to bring up a first draft of his will."

"Is something wrong?" her voice quivered.

"Kristen," David said patiently, "it's prudent for a man your father's age to get his house in order."

From the other room came her father's impatient voice.

"Who is it, Kris?"

"David Hetherington," Kristen called back.

"Bring him in," her brother said. She had never noticed before how alike the voices of her father and brother were. It was hard to distinguish between them.

David smiled and she led the way to the dining room. "Join us for some lunch, David," her father said.

"Thank you, sir," the younger man answered courteously, holding out a chair for Kristen. He sat down beside her.

Small talk and McClouties Dumpling, her father's favorite pudding, completed the meal.

David spoke about the benefits of New England country living, the clean feeling of peace in the atmosphere. Kristen nodded, while Jamie and Eben remarked on the devastating effects of last night's storm on the other coastal areas of Maine.

After lunch Jamie excused himself to tend the docks. Eben and David retired to the study, leaving Kristen alone to clear up. She stood quietly at the sink and concentrated on the simple job of washing dishes. The hot soapy water soothed her trembling hands. Haphazardly, she picked up the coffee cups, slipping them underneath the suds and then out, covering the silverware with transparent bubbles which burst as cool water ran over them.

"Well, you'll never make a professional dishwasher," he said, walking up behind her. "Better finish your education."

"David," she gasped, "you scared me."

"Kristie, sorry. I'll make amends by helping. Those utensils need a master pot scrubber."

She looked over at them. "Definitely right in your astute judgment," she said, stepping aside. "They're the worst part."

"Not if you soak them first," he laughed. She watched him set up a precise system amid her clutter. With a flourish he placed the pots in hierarchical order.

"It will take you all day and night at this rate," she interjected.

"No, once the order is established, the rest goes quickly. Watch." Amused, she nodded. He seemed to understand her mood completely, accepted the easy silence and returned to his task. Once he reached over and touched her arm.

"Let's go for a walk afterwards," he said. She felt a tinge of alarm, but he was so comfortable to be with that she discounted it.

"Of course, I'd like that." Kristen smiled faintly.

A short time later he announced, "Ready," and with a bow, took off the dishcloth he had wrapped around his waist.

"We'd better let Dad know," she said.

"He already does," David answered.

They left the house together and walked down the ocean path. The sun-flecked wind, like mellow Alsatian wine, cooled and warmed them at the same time. Side by side they made their way to the beach. She felt momentarily tranquil strolling beside him.

She recounted her experience of that morning. "Do you think I was hallucinating," she asked, "or totally mad?"

He scrutinized her closely. In the now-bright sunlight his hazel eyes were golden. "Haven't you read Maslow's ideas on peaking?"

"School seems so long ago I don't even remember what he said."

He flashed a quick smile. "The problem of our age."

She looked at him, perplexed. "Why do you say that?"

"Just a pet theory. Anyway, for Maslow, peaking is a kind of transcendent experience. He considered it a valid psychological event worthy of scientific study. And you?"

"I don't know," Kristen said, obviously still puzzled.

"What?" he asked gently.

"—is real—I am open to possibility," she went on.

"As long as such insight isn't merely a turning on but is meaningful," David finished her sentence.

"Meaningful." Kristen echoed his word. They were relaxed and comfortable with each other.

"Making a contribution."

Her face lit up. "I agree."

David continued, "There are many paths, I think, to consciousness, but I don't know any way to bypass the hard work of integrating a glimpse of so-called 'divine purpose' into one's life except by living it. First one has to synthesize available inputs and then use the energy to implement the synthesis; that tends to be a life-long effort, not just a 'quickie,' to use the vernacular." He smiled ruefully at her serious look. "I do talk a lot."

Suddenly they both felt the spindrift and turned in the direction of the ocean. "God, that feels good," David said through half-closed eyes. Then he opened them to gaze back at Kristen. "Life and love. There's a huge difference between a great screw and earth-moving feeling for someone. I can't place all my faith in any moment, be it in the form of event or person. That's why I can't separate the immediate desires of my cock from the long-term ones of my head or heart."

She laughed out loud. The sound felt good.

He went on, "Which doesn't challenge the authenticity or value of your experience—it merely asserts other insights to be just as valuable. For me, the revelation is that kind of perception which leads to action and the knowledge that life means alleviating the pain of one's fellow man and not just being an adult nipple sucker. From here on you prove or falsify the claim that you have received a valid message, not just a visual message."

Kristen looked searchingly at David. For the first time, she didn't feel locked within her own consciousness. She didn't feel so isolated. Around them bits of spring vapor misted the air. Kristen took a deep gulp and watched David do the same.

"Would you like to see my old childhood escape hatch?" she asked.

"Of course," he laughed.

"It's really a somewhat lopsided log cabin built by Jamie and me eons ago."

"Oh, you're feeling your age."

"Doesn't everyone?" she asked, amused.

It was his turn to smile.

She changed the subject. "You remember those murky teenage years when one 'vants to be alone'?"

"That need goes on in varying quantities forever," he said, a slow grin crossing his face.

"Ah, so," she murmured, returning his smile. She led the way up the hill away from the deserted beach.

Frost-ladened dead branches were strewn everywhere; moist, decomposing leaves, murky brown, or grown transparent with shadowed veins, littered the ground.

"I hope it's still standing," she said earnestly.

"I do too," he answered.

Their steps, as they walked, had a kind of matched rhythm, a rhythm within a rhythm.

"Well, I'm out of it," she said. "Karl, I mean. At least part of me is." She folded her hands across her breast.

"That's very good news," he said. "I've been hoping you would escape. . . ." He paused. She stared at him, bewildered. He cares for me, she thought. Her heart beat frantically. No, perhaps, she thought suddenly, he is making fun of me. She wondered what he could possibly see in her, especially now. What could he want but an easy lay? But she didn't run from him, just turned her head away so that he could not see her thoughts.

"It's all right, Kristen." He shook his head and they resumed their walk. The path divided.

"This way," she murmured, and they trudged up a steep hill filled with bare trees, tall weeds, and small wild bushes. "Look down," Kristen urged. They stood for a long moment and let their eyes roam over the beach below. The sunlight had turned the sand to gold and minted the foam-capped waves.

"Wondrous," he mused.

"Over there's my escape hatch," Kristen said, pointing to the left.

"You're sure it's not a mirage?" David asked out of breath. She laughed and ran toward it.

"Come on."

Kristen opened the door. "We never lock it," she explained, and they stepped inside.

Mist-colored cobwebs laced the tiny cabin. "No one comes here anymore," she said sadly. "Everything has grown too small," she grimaced, glancing around. There was the pink easy chair from her nursery and the youth bed she had slept in until she was nine. Her mother's rocking chair, covered with dust, stood in the corner. Nearby, old mildewed books and magazines were stacked high. "You're too tall," she said. "You just don't fit in here."

"Neither do you," he said tenderly.

Then he walked over and kissed her. For a moment, she felt absolute peace, as though she had always known he would come, had been waiting. He stroked her very gently with his fingertips. She felt his excitement, his body hardening as he held her. Then suddenly her fear sprung at her, overcoming desire. She jumped away. "Please," she murmured. "I'm not ready, not now." In her eyes was a mute appeal.

David responded gently. "I didn't mean to rush you, Kristen. It's just that I've been waiting so long." His expression saddened.

She shuddered despite herself. "You mustn't wait for me."

"Why not?" he asked softly.

"I may not ever be ready." She shook her head tearfully. "I'm not sure." She moved out of the cabin. He followed.

"I'll take that chance," he answered slowly. "And what will you do now?"

"Probably go back to New York." Her mouth was dry.

"Good," David said. "Then we'll be able to see each other. Where will you be staying?" He leaned toward her. She edged away.

"Maybe a hotel at first." A nerve twitched in her eye. She rubbed at it. "I'm not sure." They sat down on the gray old crags which glittered in the sunlight, and she pointed out to him fossil marks in the rocks and secret tree bark landmarks she remembered from her childhood. "Then perhaps I'll get a place of my own."

His eyes met hers. "Kristen, I can have all that arranged for you. I know New York: the prices, the neighborhoods. Where the best buys are. If you'll let me you won't have to bother with any of the distasteful sides of apartment hunting. I'll see that everything is done and when you're ready you can move in," he said decisively.

For a moment it was all too tempting. He seemed so strong, so competent. And never had she felt her own fragileness so acutely. Her face felt hot and feverish as his offer replayed itself in her mind. If she would let him, he would take care of her: of everything as her father had, as Karl had, as Jamie wanted to. Her heart began to pound. She stared searchingly at him. Perhaps he meant what he said.

Perhaps they all had. But it didn't matter, not now, not anymore. For even if they did as they said and she allowed them, there was a place within her where the agonizing fear she had felt so often in the past would return. And when it did, it would have the pull of gravity, of death, just as Dorothy had shown her in the dream.

"David," she said softly, "you're so very kind."

"But—?" he asked sadly.

"I don't think I want anyone—not anymore—to do that much for me."

"You will call me, soon, won't you?" he said gently, prompting.

"Of course," she murmured.

But, of course, she didn't.

Only one week later, Jamie, Kristen and her father were having breakfast in the dining room when Kristen announced that she wanted to leave and go back to New York. Go right then.

"Kristen," her father entreated, "you just aren't well enough to leave here yet. You have to give yourself a chance to get your strength back."

She said slowly, carefully, "I have to leave."

"But why?" A nerve twitched over his left eye. "This is your home. Dorothy, your brother and I, we can help you here. If you leave—"

Kristen stared at the floor; she understood his anxiety for her, his fear. "Dad, staying here wouldn't protect me; sooner or later I'd have to go out again, and then what?"

"I think you ought to follow Dad's advice, Kristen." Jamie looked uncomfortable. Kristen stared searchingly at him. She had hoped Jamie would support her. Understand her need to get away. He cleared his throat. "I spent a lot of time discussing your case with the doctors at Brookhaven, especially Wicklin. They felt very strongly that you needed both support and supervision." He paused, his voice betraying agitation. "I don't think we should even consider letting you live on your own right now."

Kristen's eyes blazed. "I don't need anyone to tell me what to do," she said furiously.

"That's just the point," Jamie protested. "We think you do."

"You too, Dad?" Kristen asked, turning toward him, her face a mixture of pain and love.

Her father regarded her levelly. "I want you to stay," he said decisively. And so she acquiesced.

Another week passed, then two, then three. Through them she moved softly as if living in the past. And in that world she was a child, carrying the confusions of the present somewhere in the back of her mind. In a way it felt good. Good to walk the dunes in the rain, read old books curled up in her tiny cabin, eat her favorite foods cooked as only Dorothy could make them.

But one day, sitting at her father's desk, her eye caught sight of the calendar tacked on the wall. How many times she had seen it before she didn't know. But this time she checked the date, April 12. Almost trembling, she touched the number. Somehow she could not remember the past few months passing. It was as if fall, winter, and spring had coalesced into a single season without beginning and without end. I have to go, she thought to herself. If I don't, I may never leave.

She found Dorothy standing over the kitchen counter, lovingly polishing her mother's silver tea service.

"What's wrong, child?" Dorothy asked as Kristen approached her.

"I want to go back to the city."

"Aren't you happy here?" Dorothy asked anxiously.

"It's not that," Kristen explained slowly. "Of course I'm happy here. I'm forgetting, but—"

"Well then," Dorothy said patiently.

"That's not what I want to do, Dorothy, forget. I want to remember and go on."

Dorothy smiled. "And that is as it should be, Kristen. We can't cut out large chunks of our lives and throw them away like pieces of rotted wood. Our lives are meant to begin and end as whole vessels. And no one can decide except each of us deep in ourselves the direction we must take to complete our passage."

Kristen looked at her admiringly.

The next day, over the protests of both her brother and father, Kristen left.

14

The small, obscure residential hotel she chose suited her. It was neutral, blank, the way she wanted to be. On the wall near the bed she mounted a drug-store calendar. Each night before crawling back into the antiseptic-smelling hotel sheets, she tore off that day's date and prepared for the next. Wishing she could sleep through it. But sleep constantly eluded her. Images of Karl and the girl who had answered his phone filled the night hours. Exhausted, drained, she waited for each morning and then wished it would disappear.

Money was not an immediate problem. She still had the small inheritance from her mother intact. She didn't have to work, at least for a while, and she couldn't imagine sitting still enough to get through her classes, so she withdrew from NYU, notifying Roslyn Gorky.

THE SPLINTERED EYE

As she walked the city, spring, like a dream, floated up around her and spun on. Sunlit windows of Madison Avenue boutiques sparkled; red, yellow, and white tulips planted along Park Avenue's center strip budded and blossomed; the sparse green on the maple trees in Central Park multiplied. At first she barely saw these long, blurry days, not knowing or caring where she would find herself or when meals should be eaten or how she would get back. Serious, mute, she saw her surroundings as if from a great distance. Sometimes she felt bursts of anger at being surrounded; at other times she felt grateful that amidst the hurrying throngs on bustling sidewalks, or crossing congested streets, no one knew her thoughts and feelings. Unhappy yet glad people were there. One could be and yet wasn't alone. The city's worst and best virtue, she reflected.

She felt anesthetized. From what or whom she was uncertain. Was it out of loneliness for Karl, for her own lost dreams or in the knowledge that what she had tried to hold so tightly had slipped like sand through her fingers? Most of the time she didn't care about the cause.

Just when she felt most safe watching television, the banal soaps or the foolish banter on some situation comedy almost relaxing, she would close her eyes, shielding them from the glare for a moment, and see Karl's face or hear snatches of conversation they once had.

Still, the aching stopped sometimes. Unable to keep her body still, she watched spring explode into summer: a tangerine sunrise trailing scarves of lemon and gold rays, the pure warm colors filling her odd, cold thoughts. From her hotel room window, she saw streams of traffic along Park Avenue form patterns of dark, braided hair, and from the shabby-facaded brownstones nearby, fashionable and tattered people rushed down steps illuminated by rising or fading sunlight, their harried or happy expressions catching her attention as she stared down wondering where they headed and to whom.

By July, she was feeling moments of calm. Frequently she jogged in the early mornings in Central Park with Gorky, who had kept calling and seeing her despite Kristen's efforts to hide away.

"Why did you withdraw from school?" Gorky asked one day, panting.

"Why?" Kristen answered nervously. "I can't concentrate; my life is a complete mess."

"Whose isn't?" Gorky laughed.

Kristen shook her head. "Not like mine."

"Look, Kristen. Look around you. Did you ever see so much amoebalike consciousness?" As they jogged, Gorky pointed to a forlorn gray, ragged bag lady sifting through a rusty garbage can, two strung-out black teenagers tottering under an initial-scarred elm tree, an ageless drunk lifting a brown-bagged bottle to his lips as he stood on the cobblestones under the stone arch. "Is that self-actualization, I ask you?"

Kristen couldn't help laughing.

"Look, I've brought you something." Gorky

stopped short and passed her a crumpled brochure from the pocket of her white runner's shorts. "The psych department at NYU is developing an interdisciplinary exchange program with the University of Miami. Professor Kwasneski from philosophy and Holleran from psych will be visiting professors down there this year. They want to take two brilliant, humble graduate assistants with them. Probably in order to get more sun for themselves." Gorky grinned. "The pay is abysmal, but the experience and change of scene might do you good."

"Gorky," Kristen said quietly, "you're really a caring person."

"I always thought so." She laughed in embarrassment. "Not everyone does." Abruptly she turned away. "Come on. Let's sprint," she called.

"Sure!" Kristen raced after her.

That night, sitting on the bed, Kristen read the pamphlet. She looked at the strange anonymous room in which she now lived. No ties. Nothing held her in New York or might ever again. She winced. Here she was not even thirty, not married, not sane, not even a career. She snatched up the application form and stared at it, suddenly remembering her experience with Dorothy in Maine. Could such moments as that one and this change the odd, shapeless form of her life? She shook her head. Probably not, but what had she to lose? Nothing. She walked over to the small formica desk, sat down and began filling in answers to the questions. Then she put the form in a stamped envelope addressed to Gorky and laid it on the dresser. Undressing, she lay down. But she was too restless to sleep, pulled on some jeans and a blue Lacoste shirt, stuffed the envelope in her pocket and went out to run a few blocks. On the corner of 73rd and Lexington she dropped the letter in a mailbox and quickly moved on.

But the next morning she had second thoughts and rushed over to Gorky's apartment.

"I shouldn't have applied," Kristen protested. She sat cross-legged on the floor, watching Gorky pin up the story boards for her latest book.

"What's that supposed to mean?" Gorky frowned.

"I won't be able to make it down there on my own—alone." Tensely, her heart pounding, Kristen continued, "And even if I could, no one is going to hire me. I just got out of a mental institution—"

"I hope that bloody honesty of yours didn't cause you to apprise them of that news," Gorky shook her head.

"No," Kristen said hesitantly. "Of course not, but they'll know I dropped out of NYU."

"You didn't drop out," Gorky said, "I corrected that little faux pas on your record." She smiled mischievously. "It now reads 'one year leave of absence'."

"Gorky," Kristen said, "you could get in a helluva lot of trouble doing things like that!"

"I could get in a helluva lot of trouble breathing, Kristen," Gorky laughed, "but some things are instinctive and one of them is helping my students not to burn bridges they may later want to cross." Gorky stopped, her eyes reflective. "You're the kind of student a teacher waits a lifetime for. I couldn't stand back and see you ruin a very promising future with a futile gesture."

Kristen smiled wanly. "I don't know what to say."

"Don't say anything," Gorky said decisively, "just get on with your life. You have a chance now to retrench, to re-think your future."

"But why should they hire me? There must be plenty of more suitable candidates."

"Kristen, the machinations of academe are one step lower than the mafia's. The wife of the head of the psych department at Miami is a former sorority sister of mine. I've done them both a lot of favors, including a major editing job on his thesis. They owe me one and I'm calling it in."

PART THREE

15

Six weeks later, still agonizing, her heart beating fiercely, Kristen was searching for an apartment near the University of Miami. Being driven through an area called Coconut Grove, which appeared to have been erected for a Disney version of *Alice in Wonderland:* a funky jumble of pastel-colored buildings with pink and yellow minarets, spires, and steeples, gabled roofs interspersed with white stucco bungalows, rambling mansions set among palms, cypresses, and occasional orchids, a few metallic modernistic and Spanish-style apartment buildings, numerous natural-food restaurants, at any of which Alice might stop for her tea party with the Mad Hatter. A wonderful, wacky confusion of architectural and decorative styles where nothing made sense but everything delighted the eye. Kristen rather fancied the place, finding herself smiling, despite the continual, annoying gushing of the platinum-haired, glossy-eyed real estate woman seated beside her. Their white Cadillac stopped in front of a tall terra-cotta-colored apartment building with Spanish towers and Greek columns. On the tile was imprinted "The Eden House." To the right, a pathway and tennis court were shaded by orange and grapefruit trees leading to a cloisterlike cluster of bungalows, and to the left, a patio and pool were surrounded by hibiscus and bougainvilleas.

"You'll just love it; it's so artsy and quaint," the agent was saying in her Brooklynese accent, making Kristen doubt her own favorable first impression.

"But I'm not sure I can afford . . ."

The woman broke in. "Darling, you can, you can. That's the real beauty of this. The woman is really ready to deal. She's worth oodles, just got a divorce last month and took this place. Now, she's decided to go to Europe for a year and wants someone responsible to water her plants. They all have names, by the way."

Kristen smiled again.

A broad-shouldered man with curly black hair and a battered, kindly face opened the car door. "Hiya, Shirley," he said to the agent, who handed him the keys. "Got a new tenant for us?"

Shirley smiled. "She'd be missing the chance of a lifetime if she didn't take it, Tommy." As they passed through the doors, she called out, "Tommy Burley owns several car concessions among other things." Her face darkened for a moment, then she pasted back her saleslady bubbling look. "Anything you need after you move in, he's the one to ask."

Kristen was about to protest that she hadn't even seen the apartment yet, but thought it better not to waste the effort and smiled.

The lobby's idiosyncratic furnishings continued the wacky confusion of styles begun outside: tapestries of wool and sisal, Louis XV antiques, marble walls, tables of heavy glass and solid brass with mirrors everywhere. In one, Kristen came across the surprise of her own face; and she thought, looking for a moment at the reflection dressed in a black gabardine suit, the one she had worn to her mother's funeral, her hair tumbling down her back, her shoulders arched back, that she looked strong and confident. She stared in amazement.

As they passed the concierge's desk, Shirley stopped. "Mrs. Weisell, please," she said in her sing-song voice. "She's expecting us."

"Us?" the moustached pseudo-Frenchman behind the desk asked, raising his bushy eyebrows.

"Shirley Wolfe, South Keys Realty."

The man rang up. "Go right on up," he said gesturing to the elevator, "1604-C."

"How many apartments are there in this building?" Kristen asked, astonished.

"Maybe a hundred," Shirley answered seriously.

Kristen laughed out loud and then caught herself.

THE SPLINTERED EYE

The apartment door was opened by a petite, pumpkin-haired woman who said, "Hello, I'm Lydia Weisell," in a lilting voice.

The furnishings were early bordello: raspberry-tufted velvet chairs and couch, white lace draperies, touches of black and white, a marble cocktail table, an ivory French provincial wall unit, and a profusion of flowers and plants. They followed Lydia Weisell into a flowered bedroom of raspberry and pistachio silk. California chic, Kristen smiled to herself. But walking out on the twin balconies was heavenly. From the bedroom one looked over the sherbet-colored building tops toward the turquoise Biscayne Bay, and from the living room one felt almost suspended in an aquamarine sky. They passed through the sliding glass door onto the balcony.

Lydia brought out a Waterford crystal tray and frosty glasses filled with Pink Ladies. "You look like someone I could trust," she said in her soft choirgirl's voice, her veined hand trembling as she served. "It's really a lovely place." They sat on white wicker garden seats. "I've spent so much time making my plants grow," she said. "It isn't easy, you know, in a southern climate like this for azaleas, jade plants, and tulips. Palms always have a difficult time adjusting to the air conditioning and now they've been uprooted. I used to have a greenhouse for them at home. Of course, that's gone now. I'm newly divorced. My husband's already married his secretary; she's twenty-three. They're expecting their first baby." The woman's voice trembled. "I just have to get away for awhile."

Kristen covered her hand sympathetically. She looked into this stranger's warm brown eyes and liked her immediately. Despite the gobs of makeup and attempts to remain girllike after fifty, she was so basically decent and vulnerable one couldn't help responding. "I really want to take it," Kristen said, "but," she swallowed, "I'm alone myself and the price may be too high."

"Whatever you feel is fair," Lydia Weisell answered timidly. "I really want to leave them," she gestured toward the plants on the other side of the plate glass windows, as if not wanting them to overhear, "in good hands."

Shirley's raucous voice broke in. "I told you," she winked at Kristen. "I'm absolutely sure something satisfactory can be worked out."

Kristen moved in two days later.

Adjusting to her new schedule wasn't difficult. She rather liked the tanned, earnest students who sat in her classes and the other professors, especially John Kwasneski, an angular, charismatic man whom she met at the faculty tea to which graduate assistants were half-heartedly invited. The University of Miami, nicknamed Suntanned U., was better than she anticipated. A respectable faculty, fine facilities, especially the well-stocked library, and a lovely spread-out campus nestled underneath sun, palms, and coconuts. The tempo seemed leisurely and seductive, but the academic demands were such that, despite the warm breezes and blossoming trees, one could not completely succumb to the lulling rhythms and survive as a doctoral candidate. Of this she was glad, since the concentration necessary for reading and writing papers and preparing lectures for the two courses she taught kept her mind meticulously focused on necessities and away for hours at a time from vague ponderings about her past and future.

Weeks passed. Her life seemed to be consigned to square shapes, she thought, as the semester progressed. The classroom, the cafeteria, the lobby, her apartment, the television. Stolid and confined. Safe. She held tightly to the safety of confinement, for she felt unready to venture beyond.

Then late one evening, her doorbell rang—loud and without stop. She was in the shower washing her hair. She rushed out, wrapping the fluffy yellow towel turban-style around her head and pulling on her terrycloth robe. "Damn," she muttered as the turban slipped off and her dark wet hair tumbled down. Still the bell continued blaring. "Hold on, I'm coming," she called out, pulling on the doorknob with slippery hands. She peered out. Karl West, suntanned, muscular, and impatient as ever stood in front of her carrying a small overnight case.

"Honey, what took you so long?" he demanded in that boyish, endearing voice she could not forget. His eyes swept over her body. Kristen felt a nauseous faintness grip her. She steadied herself, leaning on the wall.

"Karl," she murmured.

"Aren't you going to ask me in?" he asked, reaching out to touch her.

Almost instinctively she moved toward him and then shrank back. "But why have you come now?" she asked wistfully. "So late."

"It's never too late for us, Kristen," he said huskily, striding into the apartment and eyeing it as closely as he had her. "I'm on a little business adventure."

"But why Miami?" she asked.

He smiled knowingly. "You might say it's the gateway to and from Latin America, some say for more than two-thirds of all the marijuana and cocaine entering the United States," he shrugged, "and for those of us engaged in other sea and air transport businesses like your father and myself."

"My father." Her voice sounded small and plaintive even to her as if the last months of growth had never taken place. As if she had put no distance between her and him so that he could easily return at any time and restake his claim to her. "My father," she repeated.

"I work for him," Karl said grimly.

"You couldn't," Kristen objected. There had to be a mistake. Kristen knew it was a lie, a word-lie. She wouldn't accept it, wouldn't let him confuse her again. But perhaps he didn't mean to lie, perhaps she hadn't quite heard what he had said. "He's never even mentioned knowing you," Kristen protested.

Karl made his mouth twist into an ironic smile. "No, I wouldn't think he would." He sprawled out on the sofa in front of them and patted the space next to him. "I run the transport end of one of his companies."

"Where?" Kristen asked.

"Cali, Colombia." There was steel beneath his words. Why had he come here? Kristen felt terribly sick to her stomach. He pulled out a check from his pocket. "Recognize the signature?" He passed the check to her.

Stunned, she stared at it and collapsed in the armchair. "It's my father's."

"That's what I said," he grinned. "Look, I need some money. Cash it for me." She nodded, putting the check on the table in front of her where she could watch it. Be sure. Karl's low, urgent, familiar voice penetrated her, breaking the concentration she had worked so long to achieve. Kristen shuddered. She began to shiver.

"How long?" she asked softly.

"How long what?" Karl said sharply. They faced each other briefly and then Kristen dropped her eyes.

"How long have you worked for my father?"

"Since we split," Karl said grimly.

An image of their last meeting flashed through her. What did he want after so many months? Why was he telling her these things?

"How did you find me?" Kristen asked, her voice barely a whisper.

Karl leaned forward, close to her. "I told you I always could." His bright blue eyes glittered, riveted on Kristen. Her heart began to race. Perhaps he did love her. As she had loved him: her thoughts, being, encircled by him. In some part of herself, she still remembered being totally absorbed by this man. Measuring out the meaning of her life in him. Tears stung her eyes. Kristen shaded them and stared searchingly at Karl.

"I want you so much," he said. "I had to see you." He had disappointed her; wounded her. Could she forgive him, return to him as he was asking? "Please come to me," he said gently. "Now."

Her throat ached unreasonably. She was trembling with anxiety. With anticipation. She had thought it was over, but nothing was ever over. "Yes," she murmured.

He moved toward her, lifted her in his arms and strode into the bedroom.

Afterwards, he slept restlessly, one hand slung over her, his fingers twitching. Kristen watched him closely, yet as if from a distance. He seemed a stranger, a stranger pressing a terrible, sudden intimacy upon her. She shook her head, wondering when it had happened, when she had begun to disengage herself from him. But there was no minute she could catch hold of. Just the certainty inside her head that it was a reality. She had been so dependent upon him physically, emotion-

THE SPLINTERED EYE

ally. And now what did she feel? Empty. Numb. No, there was more than that. Something remained. The memory of desire, the memory of feeling. A little while ago she had wanted him just as much as he had wanted her. She moved out from under his arm. She wished he would leave, leave her alone. Let her think.

"Why are you staring at me?" Karl opened his eyes, quickly raising up on an elbow. She shook her head, not trusting herself to speak. "I think what you need is more loving," he said huskily. She looked at him levelly with clear amber eyes.

There was a silence between them. It was gone in a few moments but it was deeper and more profound than any Kristen had ever felt before. When it ended she clasped him to her guiltily and saw his face relax in a grin. "I'm fine, Karl," she murmured, stroking his shoulder absent-mindedly.

This time he made love to her as if a frenzy had overtaken him. Bringing himself to the brink of a climax again and again. And Kristen came with him, her heart divorced from her mind. Their bodies remembering, tasting, touching, finding the union they never had. Spent, exhausted, she watched him fall into sleep and cautiously moved away.

Her mind swam up through the dense air. Her heart beat slowly, ponderously but steadily. She no longer wished him to go away. He could stay there all night. It didn't matter. She was no longer afraid. He stirred in his sleep. She patted him gently.

THE SPLINTERED EYE

"Happy?" he murmured.

She patted him again, reassuring him, out of habit. She wondered if it was cowardly of her, but thought it no more cowardly than keeping her real thoughts silent. As she had always kept them silent. After all, he was quite free. Free to come here and free to leave. Suddenly, she was overcome with a sense of dread. She herself had never been free. Had never even wanted to be. Before. But Karl. In this penitent moment she realized he had never wanted anything else. His vague, angry face with its gaze always set somewhere beyond her.

How he must have hated her as she clutched at him. She lay beside him, contrite, remembering the need she once had, the terrible power of it. She felt no desire for him now, had outlived that desire, in a way had triumphed over it.

What were his needs then? This man lying beside her. This man who had no claim to her. She could see his agitation. He was grinding his teeth as he slept, and a vague worry for him filled her. She fell asleep, dreaming.

The next morning he was gone. As suddenly as he'd appeared. Only silence awaited her when she rushed out to the living room. The check had disappeared from the cocktail table where she'd placed it. Shaking her head, she wondered if she'd imagined the whole thing until she walked back to the bedroom. His smell was everywhere: the tousled sheets, the cigar crushed in the ashtray beside the bed.

She wanted to forget it all but couldn't. For

hours, she scoured the rooms until her skin, reddened and burned with disinfectant, assured her he was gone. Then feeling guilt and anger rise up in her again, she pulled on her jeans and a shirt and went out to feel the fresh, clean air upon her face as she ran. She jogged along blocks scented by jasmine, shaded by swaying palms and lush banyans, with no sense of direction, no plan, just the need to move quickly and furiously away. She jogged until her shirt was soaked with perspiration and her body ached. And then, breathing hard, she walked very slowly back to Eden House.

One night Tom Burley stood on the circular drive watching her.

"Hey, Kristen," he said smiling. "No date."

She looked up. "I don't date," she said slowly.

"You don't." He smiled and seemed about to comment further but then changed his mind. "Do you like that modern art stuff then." A soft Irish brogue crept into his words.

"Yes," she nodded slowly as if thinking about it for the first time. "I do."

"Good. One of them artists just moved in Saturday. I helped move her stuff and she gave me a painting—not that I understand it. But I told her I'd send some people up. Kristen, you being a teacher and all I thought you might—anyway, you need something over that purple couch."

Kristen smiled, "It's raspberry."

"Whatever," he laughed. "Anyway, name's

THE SPLINTERED EYE

Ms. Radne. Apartment 1802. Wait till you see those huge jobs. I hear she gets plenty for them."

"Thanks for the tip, Tom. I'll go see her soon." Kristen went back to her apartment but the silence reproached her. She wanted to escape it. Quickly, she walked back outside again and pressed the elevator button. "Floor, please?" the sandy-haired boy asked.

"Eighteenth," Kristen said slowly.

Danielle Radne's heart-shaped face and huge hazel eyes seemed almost childlike as she answered the door barefoot, paintbrush in hand. Her long blond hair swung freely about her waist. "Hi. I'm Danny," she said, her throaty voice firm, direct, yet somehow seductive.

"I live in the building," Kristen said hesitantly. "Tom Burley said you might have some paintings for sale."

"Some?" Danielle laughed heartily. "I've got scores." She put out her hand to shake Kristen's. "Welcome to my inner sanctum or sanctuary, whichever term momentarily fits my wide mood swings."

The apartment suited Danielle, Kristen thought, looking around. Spare, modern furniture in soft beiges, a bit of brushed chrome and glass, track lighting and, grouped in clusters upon easels, stands and the sisal rugs, huge canvases. Even from a distance, their intensity of color and form drew the eye. Kristen walked toward one group. In the first canvas to which she turned there was the illusion of a vast blue space receding behind the prominent, floating shapes of color; in the next the dominant color key was yellow, so pure that the forms within it seemed to dissolve in the intensity. In the painting Kristen liked best, shades of violet and blue-violet whirled before the eye, advancing into vibrant yellow and orange.

"I tried to catch the movements of dancers there," Danielle said softly.

"They are quite wonderful," Kristen said, her face lighting up. "A synchrony of color—I used to paint," she said self-consciously. "Of course, I never found a vision like this."

"Perhaps you didn't search long enough," Danielle said seriously. "Sometimes, just as one is about to give up," she smiled, "the whole scheme comes together and then the only problem is getting it from the mind to canvas without spilling a drop."

"I'd like to buy that one," Kristen said shyly, pointing to the violet painting.

"It's one thousand dollars," Danielle murmured. "I don't know if that's too much."

Kristen's face looked downcast. She was beginning to be conscious of her dwindling inheritance and the pittance she earned.

"Perhaps you could pay it out," Danielle said, "something every month or so."

"Yes, I definitely could do that," Kristen said, smiling.

"Come on. Let's lug it to your apartment," Danielle said, "then I can help you hang it."

They shouldered the canvas and took it to

the service elevator. Entering Kristen's apartment, they leaned the painting against a wall.

"Do you have tools?"

Kristen looked mystified.

"I'll run back up and get a hammer and hooks," Danielle said. Quickly she returned. "This isn't you," she said, glancing around at the furniture.

"No, I've sublet the place," Kristen smiled. "I'll make us some tea if you'd like." Danielle nodded.

"You ought to start painting again," Danielle said as they sat sipping it. "I have a feeling you're better than you think."

"Perhaps, perhaps not," Kristen mused.

"You could use my stuff to get started."

"I don't have much time," Kristen said. "I'm teaching two classes at Miami and studying for my doctorate."

"In what field?"

"Abnormal psych and art."

"A strange combination."

"It's a new interdisciplinary program, in my case, with a view to art therapy." Although she had never voiced the idea before, she realized as soon as she said it that this was the direction in which she wanted to head.

"We could paint at night," Danielle said. "I do anyway."

"Are you sure you wouldn't mind?" Kristen said.

"If I did, I wouldn't have asked," Danielle

laughed. "I got away from that polite sort of shit long ago. One of the benefits of analysis."

"Is it?" Kristen mused.

"Sometimes," Danielle smiled at her impishly.

Never had a friendship come so easily; she was drawn to Danielle. Perhaps it was being alone so much or the black periods that snuck up on her just when she was least expecting them, or memories of Karl that flamed up like meteors and streaked through her. Or, perhaps, it was Danielle herself. Buoyant, sympathetic Danielle, who never pried or asked, but listened intently to Kristen as they painted side by side.

At times they talked incessantly, or sat silently smoking, trying to relax, reaching for private insights about the world outside or inside them. When Kristen was feeling especially low, it was Danny who took her shopping in the Grove, pointing out Mirande's with its handmade straw hats decorated by satin ribbons and cabbage roses. Danny hustled her inside to try on first a yellow, then a bright pink one, insisting on buying one for a present while they giggled, then hurried on to another shop, this one filled with giant ceramics in the shapes of paint cans, chunky plaster brushes clumped together and splashed with high-gloss primary colors. "And you worry about vision," Danielle laughed. "How'd you like to have that one?" Another day they stopped at Alfalfa's, a tiny courtyard natural-food restaurant latticed with palms and greenery and ate veggie burgers and salads with strange pea-green and mustardy-yellow sprouts. Kristen's happier spirit responded to the warmth and understanding Danielle so willingly gave and Kristen felt an ease of trust that amazed her. All the subjects she had so longed to talk of with Karl, Danny welcomed from their musty hiding place as if they were exotic black orchids blossoming for the first time.

Once, after midnight, having painted the evening away, Danny insisted on going to The Monk's Cellar. In the dark panelled room lined with books, they sat on wooden benches beside butcher-block tables heaped with wheels of cheese and wicker baskets filled with apples. "Bring us a bottle of good burgundy," Danny said to the watery-blue-eyed waiter with a drooping moustache.

"Which one, Madam?" the man asked.

"You choose," Danny responded, returning to the anecdote Kristen was sharing.

A few minutes later the waiter returned, ceremoniously opening the bottle. "We shall let it breathe, Madam," he said. Returning, he asked, "And now, will you taste it?"

"No." Danny gave him a ribald wink. "You do it."

"If you wish, Madam," he said, raising astonished bushy eyebrows, but pouring himself a full glass. They had laughed all the way home.

Not long afterward, on a wind-glazed Saturday morning, Kristen, with huge dark circles under her eyes, sat perched on the balcony ledge watching soft gray clouds cluster around the hazy sun like the seats of a ferris wheel before the carnival music begins. She had to study a boring text on behavior and techniques and write a term paper for Tests and Measurements for which she had been gathering notes but, like the clouds, she, too, was malingering. The telephone rang. She gave the caller plenty of time to hang up, but the ringing clanged on.

"Persistent son of a bitch," she murmured, annoyed as she walked inside and answered with a sharp-tongued, "Yes."

"I knew you'd be brooding," Danny said. "Come horseback riding with me. Too much thought deadens the spirit."

"It's been eons since I've ridden," Kristen said.

"You can ride with an instructor until you feel comfortable."

Reluctantly, Kristen agreed.

Misty Hollow, the ranch where Danny rode, was some twenty miles south of Coral Gables. They drove in Danny's bright red M.G. with the top down, first through suburban blocks, then through a desertlike area of greige sand and marshland, and finally toward a bright green oasis of cactus and palms and ferns and giant sprawling ranches on which brindled cows and dappled horses roamed. "Well," Danny laughed, "this is what Florida calls the country—a bit sparse, but interesting."

"I rather like it," Kristen said. "There's a

kind of rugged beauty. I feel like a million miles from Gingerbread City back there, suspended in the wilds. Any minute we'll hear coyote cries or a posse will ride out of some corral after a no-good cattle rustler."

"Well, you've certainly got a feverishly-working imagination," Danny kidded. "Sam Winfield, the owner, raises some fine anguses, a few guernseys, plus palominos, sorrels, and buckskins." Danny put an arm around Kristen. Kristen felt instinctively warm and relaxed, but when Danny didn't take her arm away after a few minutes, Kristen moved closer to the door. Danny looked wistfully at her. Then, turning back to the road, she said, "The place was once a stagecoach stop. So, if you're prone to daydreams of the old west, you can shoot the breeze with Sam and his ranch hands."

Danny drove through the rough-hewn wooden gates sounding the car horn. Ahead stood an authentic ramada of pine timbers topped by a roof of ghost sequoia. Among the eucalyptus and wild orange trees was an old adobe bunkhouse from which emerged a powerfully built, handsome man of about sixty, wearing worn jeans, a white western shirt, and a stetson. "Hey Danny," he yelled as the car screeched to a stop raising dust clouds. "Get out and use your feet, if you haven't lost their use with all that city livin'."

Danny bounded out of the car and the man enveloped her in a bearhug.

"Where've ya been lately?" he demanded.

"Practicing my craft," Danny said. "You're submerged in your love, so you can't begrudge me mine."

"Hell no," he laughed, taking off his hat. "Who's this," he asked, coming around to open the door for Kristen.

"A good friend," Danny smiled.

Neighing horses could be heard in the distance. A magnificent amber palomino with a tawny mane and long graceful legs was running free around the ring.

"That's one beautiful horse," Kristen said.

"Sure is," Sam said. "Name's Firebrand. Waiting for the right hand to gentle him. You ride much?"

Kristen shook her head. "Not since I was in my teens and pretending to be on Black Beauty."

"Well, Firebrand's too much for you right now then. But riding's like making love," he said, moving his hand in an undulating motion. "It comes natural and once it's yours, you never lose the feeling, no matter how long you lay off or how old and cantankerous you get." He winked at her kindly. "So, don't give up. You and Firebrand may be soulmates." There was a gentle light in his eyes.

Kristen smiled. She liked him instantly.

"We'll find you a tame steed today and then you can move on up when you feel ready. Rusty," he shouted to a lanky, brown-haired girl who galloped over on a high-stepping chestnut roan. "Saddle up Wild Spirit and Suede. Li'l lady here," he pointed to Kristen, who felt conspicuously awkward, "is going to need some lessons."

"More than a few," Kristen smiled.

Rusty brought out a frisky cream and chocolate Appaloosa and a gentle sorrel gray mare. Danny mounted the Appaloosa first and Kristen realized anew how long-legged and agile her friend was, as she expertly maneuvered her horse around in a circle waiting.

"This one's yourn," Rusty said, leading the mare to the hitching post. The horse was docile, but Kristen felt clumsy and nervous. "Don't worry," Rusty said. "Everyone's a little squeamish at the beginning. Just get the feel of it."

Within a few weeks, Kristen was galloping, and within a month she could canter, auburn silken hair flying behind her, feeling freer than she had in years. She and Danny went out to the ranch every weekend and sometimes during the week, if Kristen could take a break from the seemingly endless lecture presentations, the stacks of ungraded papers, and the reading lists prepared by graduate professors whom she was sure never thought of their students as having more than one class—theirs.

Getting out those one or two times each week became more than an escape. Sitting atop the black and white pinto she had been upgraded to, her eyes, like sentinels, took in the crystals of sun glittering, alighting in her hair like black diamonds. She breathed it all in: the warmth and the freshly-cut grass. "I'm alive," she murmured, her back straight, her hands curled over the reins.

"Hey," Sam said to her one Saturday, "good seat, good hands. You're going to be a fine horsewoman. Wouldn't you say so, Danny?"

"I would." Danny gazed at Kristen with such tender intensity that Kristen blushed and turned away, reflecting. What about Danny? There seemed to be no men in her life. Yet, she was obviously warm, sensuous. She stole a glance at Sam Winfield and then at Danny again. Was there some kind of relationship between them? Sam had to be at least thirty years older than Danny. Well, stranger things happened.

Going out on the trail was the next step, and when that day came, Kristen led out the pinto proudly, reins well in hand, following Danny and Sam past the bunkhouse and across the pasture. The alfalfa and broom smelled sweet. Before her a new world stretched: sweet fields of grassy dew, the balm of sun, the taste of the orange-honeyed wind. Tall grass bent down as they passed. They trotted slowly across a meadow where wildflowers burned fiery orange and magenta by a tart lemon sun swayed back and forth. Sam's horse broke into a canter. Danny's followed and Kristen turned her pinto in their direction. She never knew exactly what happened next—a rock or grass-covered ditch, a garter snake—but her horse reared, the world spun as Kristen flew through the air; again she saw Dorothy lifting the ancient bones and tossing them to the floor and then the sun's whirling golden light spikes crashed down upon her. Unconscious for a few minutes, she awoke to find herself cradled in Danny's strong arms. "We'll have to get her back to the bunkhouse," Sam said. "You stay here; I'll bring the station wagon around." He galloped off on the gray stallion.

"Kris, Kris," Danny cried tenderly, stroking Kristen's forehead. "I never should have brought you out here."

Kristen tried to sit up. She felt dizzy and bruised.

When Sam returned, Danny insisted on driving Kristen off to the emergency room at South Miami General while Sam took the horses back to the stable.

"Looks like just bad contusions," the lean, dark-haired resident said with a heavy Spanish accent after the preliminary examination. "We'll do a complete set of X-rays anyway, since this is a head wound and there's always danger of a concussion. If nothing shows up, you can take her home. Let her rest a few days, but call if there's any projectile vomiting or dilation of the pupils."

By the time Kristen finished the X-rays, the side of her face had turned red-purple; one eye was completely closed. Danny took one look at her and fainted dead away. They had to take a taxi home, but once there, Danny insisted on Kristen staying in her apartment. "You shouldn't be alone."

"This is the faint leading the blind," Kristen laughed, but she didn't feel much like being alone either and followed Danny upstairs.

THE SPLINTERED EYE

Tenderly, Danny undressed her, gave her a satin nightshirt to wear and tucked her into a giant antique brass bed with snowy linens and a profusion of lace and silk pillows.

"I feel like a princess," Kristen murmured, as she slipped into a quiet, peaceful sleep.

"How long have I been here?" she asked, awakening after some indefinable interval and seeing darkness.

"Two days," Danny said softly, spooning some beef broth into her mouth.

"Jesus . . . school," Kristen said. "I was supposed to have taught today, wasn't I?"

Danny nodded. "I called the chairman and explained about the accident. He said he'd take the classes himself and not to worry."

"That makes me feel worse."

"Problem?" Danny asked.

"Guilt. I've bitched a lot about the work he loads on."

Kristen smiled weakly. "I oughta go home and study," she said, rubbing her aching forehead.

"Not so fast," Danny said softly. "You still need tender loving care. And it's yours for the asking."

Kristen looked at her with astonishment.

"Kristen." Danny leaned toward her. "Have you ever been loved by a woman?"

Embarrassed, Kristen did not reply.

"I thought not. Not that I don't like men,

THE SPLINTERED EYE

Sam especially, but I'm a lesbian, Kristen. I really only feel close to women."

Danny leaned forward and clasped Kristen's hand. Quickly Kristen drew it back.

"I think I'd better go now," Kristen said.

"Don't be silly. I'm not going to attack you just because I'm gay." Danny smiled reassuringly. "You still need a lot of rest. I'll be out in the living room if you need anything."

Kristen drew in her breath slowly. Trying to steady herself, she tried to rise but lay back exhausted.

During the next few days Kristen grew stronger, but peace eluded her. She could not stop thinking of Danny's tender, ministering hands; silhouettes of Karl, Burt Cald, Jamie, her father accosted her. One face after another rose, shadowy then clearer, until the pictures in her tense mind snapped, clicked incessantly. Where do you fit, she thought, if anywhere?

By the weekend, Kristen could sit up for longer periods. Her head still ached when she tried to read, but she could get out of bed without becoming dizzy. Friday night she slept fitfully, awakening in the darkness to see light seeping beneath the closed door. Slowly, she made her way across the room and turned the knob.

Danny, dressed only in a lilac Qiana bikini, stood at her easel intently painting. How beautiful she is, Kristen thought. At that instant, Danny turned and they gazed at each other. Danny put down her palette and opened her arms. Kristen moved into them. The excitement rose between them, unspoken, unnamed, better than words. They walked arm in arm toward Danny's bedroom, sinking into the cool lavender-scented sheets. Kristen's heart pounded as Danny rained kisses upon her face. Leisurely unbuttoning Kristen's satin nightshirt and slipping from her own bra and panties, Danny lay naked against her, slowly caressing Kristen's breasts. And then Kristen lay back as that warm tongue, those same lips clasped, caressed, licked her until Kristen's own passion answered.

As dawn broke, Kristen watched Danny sleep. And she again remembered Karl and the events that had brought her there. Thoughts, images whirled as she half-dozed, and then they faded until she was only in that room where she found herself at the moment and in no other.

After that night, whenever they were together Danny was enchanting and piquant. Kristen watched her expressive face flushed with pleasure, her inquisitive eyes always looking for new beauty, her artistic hands creating canvas after canvas. Danny glowed, filled to the brim with the satisfaction of her work and life.

But during this time Kristen trembled with indecision. She could not determine what her real feelings were about Danny or herself. Danny was a sensitive, caring lover and kept telling her, "I don't want to enslave you . . . you and I must be free to have other friends, other relationships." But caught between needing warmth and the inability to pretend that such need was love, Kristen continued to hear echoes from within. Voices, sometimes murmuring, sometimes shouting, and she dared not speak about them to anyone . . . least of all Danny.

Danny, however, took Kristen's silence to be serenity. "Don't you feel the difference now," she asked, "between what women can share, and what men and women can hide from each other?" And Kristen had to admit this was partially true, for Danny spent hours listening, touching, and caressing her as no man ever had. Yet what they shared was somehow unfinished, left her with unspoken needs she could not or did not want to express, until Danny began to notice Kristen's brooding.

"For an idealist, you care too much about what others think," Danny said one night. "Our life could be open; we don't have to hide. What you say you want is possible for us. But you're ashamed of loving a woman."

"Perhaps," Kristen admitted, "that's part of it. But not all."

"Perhaps, what you want I can't give," Danny said.

"Someone else said that to me once," Kristen said.

"Who?"

"Look, I'm tired and irritable," Kristen said. "I think I'd better go home."

Danny gazed at her sadly and then turned back to her canvas. "Whatever you say."

Getting into the elevator, Kristen's mind was

crammed with so many possibilities, hypotheses, that she couldn't settle down. "I've got to get some air," she murmured and pressed the lobby button.

The evening was uncharacteristically cool. Kristen wore only a loosely knit shirt and jeans. Unconsciously, she began to walk faster, breaking into a run. Her mind raced. She was thinking of everything, of nothing; images darted in and out as she moved. Where was she going? She did not know. Behind her was Danny, the endless books, waiting. The night wind whirred and whispered about her shoulders. Nearby, Biscayne Bay softly lapped on the shore and the huge crystal moon lighted the way. Kristen breathed deeply, feeling the rhythmic movement of her legs and arms. There was a nice smooth flow to the night, to the drowsy world about her. She sighed, relaxing, continued on for a while and then turned back in the direction of the apartment, easing her pace.

In the lobby she stopped at the concierge's desk for her mail, expecting the usual assortment of bills and advertisements. Of course, they were there but among them a special delivery letter on beige parchment from David Hetherington's law firm. A series of addresses had been crossed out and a new one penciled in, in what she immediately recognized as her brother Jamie's handwriting. It was her Florida address. A shiver went up her spine. Kristen tore open the envelope. Dislodged, a newspaper clipping fluttered to the floor. She stooped to retrieve it. The large black print headline caught her eye:

THE SPLINTERED EYE

NAVY FLYING ACE FERRIES DRUG CARGO

Miami, December 5

Inspectors found 162 pounds of marijuana in fake United States Postal Service bags aboard a private air ferrying service owned and piloted by former Navy Ace Karl West. Customs officials seized the aircraft and took West into custody on charges of smuggling illegal cargo into the United States.

A customs spokesman, Christopher Sorling, called it the largest haul in recent months. "We got an anonymous tip," he revealed. West denied either knowing about or being involved in drug trafficking. "This is a set up," he said Friday night as he was led away after returning to the aircraft to unload his cargo. The plane, a Beech King Air, arrived from Cali, Colombia, on Thursday.

Lodged inside the envelope was a note:

> Kristen—
> Please contact me when you receive this. Karl is being held at the Dade County Jail. He can't make bond and insists you can verify his story.
>
> Sincerely,
> David

16

Going up in the elevator, she debated what to do, but once inside the apartment she walked somberly to the telephone and called David Hetherington's office in New York. Her heart hammered as the chilly voice of the law firm's receptionist answered. Luckily he was in. Hours seemed to pass but then, gratefully, she heard his deep, resonant voice upon the phone.

"Kristen, are you all right?" he asked with obvious concern.

"Yes, I am," she said hesitantly. "At least I was."

"Kristen, I didn't want to contact you this way, and of course your father has expressly forbidden me to—"

"My father," she interrupted. "What has he to do with it?"

"I'm sorry, Kris." David sounded genuinely concerned. "Karl is claiming your father is his employer. That whatever cargo Air Scape was carrying was at the company's request and if it was illegal, it's their business, not his." She clutched the phone more tightly, watching her knuckles whiten. "Kristen, are you there?"

"Yes," she murmured softly. "I'm here. But what have I to do with all this?"

She waited silently. Seconds passed. "He says you can corroborate his story."

"Testify against my father?"

Obviously he sensed her pain. "No, I don't think that will happen. But I don't want to kid you. If Karl is telling the truth, your father's company may have some responsibility." There was a pause. "Either directly or indirectly," he added gently. "But if you know something that can clear Karl, you might not be able to live with the knowledge that because you refused to speak, he went to jail."

Kristen sighed wearily. She felt dazed. "David, I—what do you want me to do?"

"I want you to testify on Karl's behalf."

There was another silence. Longer this time. "David, I'm not sure I can. Can I have some time to think it over?"

"We don't have much. The arraignment is next Tuesday."

Kristen's voice was so low David had to strain to hear it. "Two days. I'll call in the next two days. Will that be soon enough?"

"It will have to be," David said firmly.

THE SPLINTERED EYE

She thought about Karl West all the next day sitting through Dr. Emmanuel's dictatorial lecture on psychoanalytic concepts of morality, speaking to her classes, walking through the dark, musty halls of Ashe Building where the professors' offices were. During her required counselling hours, she sat at the gray metal desk in the concrete-block-walled room trying to read Jung's *Memories, Dreams and Reflections*, doodling with her marking pencil, unable to concentrate.

A freshman, Darlene Carlman, gilt-haired and red-lipped, clattered in on electric-blue suede clogs. She had been absent frequently. Kristen half-listened to Darlene's excuses, her threats about telling the department head of Kristen's unfairness. "Darlene," Kristen carefully explained, "the psychology department has a mandatory attendance requirement that was thoroughly explained in my first lecture. I have no choice but to drop you from the roll or fail you. It's in your best interest to withdraw before the deadline and retake the course next semester."

"But I've already made out my schedule for September and its neat," Darlene said, scowling.

"I'm really sorry about that," Kristen answered, trying not to sound annoyed. Tearful, Darlene tottered out.

Kristen stared hard at the angular wall. She imagined abstracting the linear configuration formed by the lines of boxes, finding a way to express their texture and form, transforming it to canvas. Then her mind traveled beyond that form toward something she could not quite reach. Puzzled, she scratched her aching head; lost thoughts, she reflected, were like artifacts buried beneath the rubble of centuries, leaving behind dim signs, their exact locations and meaning unknown.

Another student wandered in. Kristen perceived a vague form and refocused. Soretti, Guy, Psych. 101, fair-haired, small and fragile-looking. Kristen turned to greet him. Alcoholic father, suicidal mother whom he visited every month at Chattahouchee State Asylum. Kristen looked up at the floral calendar Scotch-taped to the wall. It was that time. Guy slowly took a paper from his blue spiral notebook and held it out to her shakily, his eyes too-knowing, like Danny's she thought, startled by the sudden, agonizing memory. It was a drawing. "Dr. Emmanuel. I'm taking Social Psych. from him."

Kristen nodded.

"Well, he asked for a self-image." Guy spoke self-consciously.

She looked more closely at the sketch: a modified male stick figure with his hands behind his back.

"What do you think?" Guy asked nervously.

"Looks like you want to take my place at the lectern and, in my opinion, you'll never rival Picasso."

"Why?"

She smiled.

Guy didn't. "Emmanuel thinks I ought to see the campus shrink."

She blinked in amazement. "Christ! Why?"

"Hostility. He thinks the drawing shows an overwhelming amount of repressed hostility and possible homosexual impulses. Do you?" Guy asked fearfully. "My mother is," he pointed to his head, "you know, sick."

Kristen, feeling his tenseness, reached out to pat his shoulder comfortingly. "I think he's been watching too many TV shrinks up too close." Kristen said.

Guy laughed.

He was a damn nice kid, she thought, struggling through a lot of shit to make it. What he didn't need was more crap hurled, either by fate or some psuedo-shrink.

"You don't think I'm crazy?" Guy asked cautiously.

"No more than the rest of us," Kristen laughed.

Guy sighed, obviously relieved. "What should I do?"

"What do you want to do?"

"Tell him where to stick it."

"That might give you some satisfaction. On the other hand he might," the prick, she thought, "flunk you, which would cancel any momentary benefit." She bit the already half-chewed eraser of her yellow pencil. "Why don't I send him a memo about my confidence in your mental stability?"

Guy waved from the door. "Thanks, Teach."

She smiled and waved back.

Kristen felt suddenly elated. The mood continued through the somewhat testy note she wrote to Emmanuel and stuck in his faculty box. But as she gathered her books together, her thoughts shifted back to her own predicament. It could not be as easily resolved as Guy's nor with such dispatch. What was she to do about Karl West and her father? There was no question as to whom she owed the greater loyalty. Nor even of her own inclinations. And what she really wanted to do was to walk away from the situation, to forget it existed. And even if she couldn't, why shouldn't she just say the hell with Karl West? He had brutalized her; left her alone, pregnant. Surely she owed him nothing. And her father everything. Whatever either of them had done. Why then did she feel so guilty?

"I'm babbling," she murmured, hurrying from the Ashe Building into her car. "There's no sense to this. None at all." She turned the key and heard the motor start, flipped on the radio. Loud, pulsing music filled the air. She forced her thoughts to concentrate upon it and managed the drive.

Woodenly, searching the refrigerator for food, she kept her mind riveted on the mechanics. Broiling the lamb chops perfectly, arranging her plate with salad and string beans. "I'm taking good care of myself," she murmured through clenched teeth. She made room on the white provincial dining room table filled with texts and notebooks and ate slowly but determinedly. Then she turned her attention to her assignments, plotting them out, doing each in turn. When she looked up again the moon's bare outline was filling in. Scattered wisps of clouds like sputtering smoke were covered by a darkening sky. Kristen switched on the chandelier and picked up *Memories, Dreams and Reflections*. This time the words concerned consciousness. The essay was late Jung: dark, complex, mystical. She was lost in it; his focus became her own. She dipped back into man's primordial beginnings. These shadows intruding upon the present became more real, gave life some order beyond its own. Kristen sighed at how tactile, palpable it seemed. And then the phantasms of her own brain intruded and she lifted her eyes. When she looked down again, the connection was lost. She pushed the book away, its meaning forgotten.

Flopping on the bed, she glanced at the purring crystal clock on the night table: 11:30. Staring at the nearby telephone, she rolled over and picked up the receiver, dialed New York information. "David Hetherington," she said softly. "Hetherington, H-e-t-h-e-r-i-n-g-t-o-n; no, the residence. Thank you."

Slowly, she dialed. Her fingers trembled, touching the cold disc. She waited for the ringing to stop, half-wishing he would not be home. But when his sleepy, sensual voice came on the phone, she realized she was glad to hear him. "David, it's Kristen Blakely. I'm sorry to call you so late." She paused, waiting for his response, her heart throbbing.

Are you all right?" He sounded surprised. "Nothing has happened?" he murmured softly.

"Yes, quite all right. No, nothing," she said,

noticing how quietly cautious his voice was. In the background Kristen heard a purring feminine voice call out, "Who is it, David?"

She could not hear his muffled reply. Suddenly she became hesitant. "I only wanted to tell you I've decided to come to New York to talk to you about testifying."

"That won't be necessary, Kristen," he answered gently. "I'm coming down to Miami the day after tomorrow. Let me have your number, I'll call you as soon as I get in."

Kristen repeated her telephone number. "But I wanted to ask you—"

He cut her off kindly but firmly. "I really can't talk now," he said, and his voice took on a kind of boyish shyness that made her face redden. "Let me call you when I get to Miami. When will you be home?"

"In the evening," Kristen replied awkwardly. "After six."

"Good." His laugh sounded forced. "We'll talk then." Abruptly, he clicked off.

Kristen lay back on the pillows feeling suddenly foolish, embarrassed. She had been so engrossed in telling him how she felt, she hadn't thought of what he might be doing or with whom. She grimaced. He must think her an absolute dolt. Then she shrugged. Still she wasn't sorry—not for calling him so late nor for telling him her decision. At least now it was made. She felt tired but satisfied and a few moments later, fully clothed, she fell into a deep, dreamless sleep that lasted until morning.

17

She sat on the edge of the rust-colored leather wing chair in David Hetherington's suite at the Dupont Plaza Hotel, directly facing the glass-walled window that overlooked Miami's skyline.

"The case will go on several weeks as I see it," David observed in his rich, vibrant voice. "And I can't be sure yet whether they'll go for the eight-forty-eight, which means indictment on a continuing criminal enterprise and at least ten years with no chance of parole if he's convicted, or let us cop a plea of drug trafficking."

She studied him: lanky, strong-featured, with penetrating hazel eyes and curly brown hair touched with gray, scuffed oxfords propped on the cocktail table in front of the sofa. "But you said Karl maintains he's innocent."

"True," David said thoughtfully, "But I have to figure the odds, and the DEA and customs are involved. This was a big haul and the case is complicated because Karl has a record."

Kristen looked up, surprised.

David continued. "It was a long time ago. The charge was aggravated assault." There was a silence in the room. "But he was on parole for a while and that kind of thing can prejudice a jury or a judge," he mused.

Kristen leaned forward. "I don't think he'll let you plead him guilty, if that's what you're thinking."

"That's exactly what I'm thinking," David said noncommitally. "But you're probably right. Guilt isn't a word in Karl West's vocabulary." David looked at her quizzically. "Karl tells me you're together again."

"David," she interjected gently, "that was only once, weeks ago. I haven't seen or heard from him since. Whatever there was between Karl and me, it's over."

David grimaced. "Then why are you here?"

She didn't answer. Instead she asked, "Why are *you* here?"

David looked away. "We have a lot of ground to cover and not much time."

"I'd like you to answer my question first," Kristen's eyes searched David's face, "and then I'll try to answer yours."

He faced her, tight-lipped. "We flew in the same squadron in the Navy; Karl saved my life. I owe him." Tension showed in his voice.

She nodded. "Karl could be something of a

hero," Kristen recalled with a stab of conscience. "It makes his behavior at other times even harder to understand." She stopped, obviously not wanting to go any further.

"And you," David said gently, "why are you here?"

"I've been asking myself that same question."

"And your answer," he persisted.

With an effort Kristen answered, "I suppose my answer is similar to yours." She paused. "He saved my life once," and then she added more candidly, "but it's really more complex than that. I was addicted to him, I couldn't let him go," she continued slowly, "no matter what he wanted." Kristen choked back tears.

David seemed to sense the depth of her emotions. "Look," he interrupted, "why don't we order some coffee and talk about the case."

Kristen smiled, appreciating his sensitivity to her feelings. "That would be very nice."

David telephoned room service. A few minutes later the waiter appeared and they sat slowly sipping coffee while she regained her composure. "It will be difficult for you to testify," David cautioned. "Especially because of your father. He may very well be called."

She nodded. "I don't think my father would have anything to do with drugs." She pressed David's arm. "Do you?"

"Kristen," he ran his fingers through his hair, "I don't know what to think. I've known your father a long time, but he plays it close to the vest: only tells me what he thinks concerns me, and as you know he doesn't like to get billed for legal advice he didn't solicit."

She laughed. "Scottish heritage."

He grinned in return. "I don't think your father deals drugs, if that was what you meant. But whether he'd frame Karl in retaliation for his seeing you again," he shook his head, "of that answer I'm more unsure."

"Well, I'm not," Kristen said sharply.

"Then let's hope you're right," David responded gently. "It will make my job a lot easier—" he paused, "—and yours."

She nodded.

"Are you ready to see Karl?"

Kristen hesitated. "That's a more difficult question to answer. Ready no, willing yes."

For a while they continued discussing the case. Then David rose. He began to gather papers in his briefcase. "We'd better get started," he said resolutely.

Actually she dreaded seeing him in jail. I don't have to, she told herself, riding in the taxi beside David. I could tell David I feel sick. In fact, I could just tell him the truth. But of course she didn't. Merely ran these excuses like rejected tapes through her mind as the journey continued. Every once in a while she glanced over at David, who remained silent, and wondered what he was thinking. Defending Karl West can't be easy; especially when he was also her father's lawyer. Did her father know? She supposed so. Could he have arranged David's taking Karl's case? Possibly. But David had said he owed Karl his life—that must have been long before either man knew Eben Blakely. Other thoughts played hide and seek in her mind. Rising, falling, swelling, subsiding—causing her to doubt her own conclusions and then to doubt her doubts.

The taxi stopped and let them out at the corner near the jail. Ahead she saw it, an ugly whitewashed stone building among other nondescript dilapidated eyesores. "So this is downtown Miami." She turned to David, who walked at her side.

He shook his head. "Believe it or not. My family and I used to come here on vacations. The streets were safer than any small town you could think of back then. Now they're a center of gunrunning, dope dealing, race riots, and every other kind of mayhem. People up north think of Florida and see visions of sun, sand, and frivolity. But look around you; this is the gateway for most of the cocaine and marijuana entering the United States, and they have the crime rate to prove it."

She looked up and down the street and beyond. A collection of signs, some crudely lettered, some fluorescent, indicated the proclivity of Spanish-speaking customers. Businessmen in three-piece suits, probably lawyers, she thought, and shabbily-dressed men and women intermingled with each other. The more well dressed kept their distance, preferring to walk in the streets rather than pass close by the street people who gathered in bunches at odd places on the sidewalks. "Not much aesthetic value." Kristen forced a smile.

"Aesthetic hell," David said, flushing. "In Miami, bodies compete for space in the morgue and the narco wars here surpass the tourist trade. Come on," he said, taking her arm, propelling her ahead. "There's no use regretting the loss of the past's ambience. We have to live with the present anyway." She nodded, and they mounted the steps to the jail.

In the small airless waiting room into which they were shown, there was a grilled partition separating visitors from prisoners. Waiting for Karl, Kristen's stomach churned. Her face whitened oddly.

"Are you all right?" David leaned toward her, concerned.

"I think so," she murmured. "It's so hot in here."

"Take a deep breath," he advised. "Do you want to go outside for a while?"

Kristen shook her head. "No, I'll stay."

"Good," he said, looking toward an inner door through which Karl West, a bailiff beside him, had just strode.

"Get away from me." West shook off the bailiff's hand.

Kristen's face misted with tears as he sat down before them. In the several moment's silence Kristen and Karl stared at each other. She put her hand up on the wire mesh trying to reach him, to comfort him.

"Move away from the prisoner." A voice rang out on the loud speaker. The policeman in the corner patted the pistol on his hip meaningfully. Startled, Kristen sat back.

"Not exactly your kind of place, princess," Karl said with an ironic smile. She stared at him. His color was heightened, feverish. There were bloodspots near the blue of his eyes and beneath them heavy bruised-looking circles.

"You haven't slept," Kristen said in a strained tone. "You look so tired."

"We don't sleep here," Karl cut in with savage anger. "People don't dare close their eyes that long. You could find a knife in your back or something else up your backside."

David sighed, putting down the pencil he held in his hands. "Look here, West, we're here to help you. Try to keep your enemies straight."

Karl's voice became lower, losing its edge. "Of course, you're right, Hetherington. To tell you the truth, I'm in pretty bad shape." Disjointed words followed. "People stink like cattle here. They put us in cells with broken sinks and toilets that don't flush. Between the sweat and stink the only relief is puking." He looked at Kristen, anguish in his eyes.

"Can't we get him out, David, we have to." Kristen touched David's arm, imploring him.

Hetherington shook his head sadly. "I wish it was that easy, Kristen. I'm going to meet with the

U.S. Customs officer tomorrow. After that I'll be able to understand better what they've got on Karl. Tuesday, we'll try to get the magistrate to set bail and hope the grand jury doesn't come back with the more serious indictment. If they do, the case will be tried in federal court here."

"That's impossible," Karl said; he was becoming intensely emotional again.

Slowly, Hetherington began to speak. "No, West, it's not impossible, and it could get a hell of a lot worse. There's the possibility of criminal conspiracy here."

"If they try that one, her father's going to be implicated," Karl said angrily.

"Maybe, maybe not," Hetherington retorted. "It could be your Uncle Max who will be implicated."

"Don't threaten me, Hetherington. I don't like it."

Kristen was aghast. "David, please," she said. "You're supposed to be helping him."

"I'm going to try," David said decisively. "But I'm going to need cooperation—a lot of it." The lawyer's look was grim as he began to question Karl about the drug bust. Over and over again he hurled the same questions at him with slightly different emphasis until Kristen felt the tension in the room mount unbearably.

"David, he isn't well."

"He isn't as badly off as he could be if the sentence is life, which he could get if he's convicted." He paused and then turned his attention back to the figure behind the partition. "They say they found the stuff in U.S. Postal bags in cargo you were about to unload."

"Sure, I was about to unload it right out in the open." Karl said sarcastically. "Would I have done that, if I knew it was dope?"

"I'd like to be sure of that, West. It could have been a ploy."

"I wasn't born yesterday." Karl glared at him.

"Neither was the DEA," Hetherington snapped back.

Another silence ensued. Then David began the questioning again. His voice gained momentum. The timbre of it startled Kristen. Made her think the policeman would draw his revolver this time. But nothing happened. David's voice became lower, more intense. "I intend to get at the truth, West. If you don't level with me you may end up with a very long jail term. Because of those damned postal bags, the government intends to make an example of you."

"They's just using that as a goddamned excuse." Karl rattled the wire. Kristen's body tensed. She caught sight of real danger.

"Get back, West," the policeman called.

"Fuck off," Karl called back, but he moved back obediently. "And fuck your advice, Hetherington. I'm not guilty, and even if I were, you could make a deal." The thought stuck Kristen that he sounded guilty. His replies to David's questions were inadequate, nonresponsive. His anger obscured the issues. She shook the thought off. Often the innocent seemed guilty, didn't they? Weren't facile answers also a sign of guilt? Perhaps this was how the innocent acted, enraged, striking out because they had been injured. There was no sure answer. One had to have faith. That was the key to real understanding. But how to get it. That was another profound problem. Somehow she would have to will herself to believe in Karl's innocence, or why was she here? Perhaps that was the real answer she would have to puzzle out. Somehow, though, she felt she should be and that helped to still her anxiety at least momentarily.

David broke into her thoughts, his voice commanding attention. "The arraignment is next week, Karl. It's our last chance to fix bail before the grand jury meets. I have to know what the truth is before I choose our strategy for the hearing. It's very important that I have foreknowledge of what you intend to say and what you have really done."

"Maybe I'll just lie like everyone else does." Karl glared at Hetherington.

"There are few liars clever enough to fool a well-prepared attorney or an astute judge," David said wearily.

"Most of them are asses and you know it, Hetherington, especially the ones who work for the government. They can't make it on the outside and that's why they're where they are."

"Karl," David stroked his chin thoughtfully, "smarts don't always count for everything. These people may not impress you, but they have plenty of time to do nothing else than concentrate on convicting you. So don't underestimate them or you may be very sorry. And don't patronize them, they know that little game too."

"The law is a whore," Karl snarled bitterly. "When you're young and don't know better, the world promises justice. Then you lose your teeth learning that justice is only for those who can pay for it. For the rest of us, the law is a whip that laces into you whether you're right or wrong, because your clothes are too dirty or your skin stinks. All the promises were given by a fucking tease who isn't going to deliver, until you fork over the money she wants." Karl jumped to his feet. "And don't you tell me differently, Harvard boy."

Kristen drew her breath in sharply. She stared anxiously at the guard and then back at Karl.

"West, sit the hell down," the policeman yelled, "and don't let your butt get off the chair again or your little visit is over."

"Karl, this isn't doing either of us any good." Hetherington was tight-lipped but decisive. "We can't change the courts or the constitution today. Let's concentrate on getting you out of this mess. You have a record. You've been arrested before."

"When I was a kid."

"You were on parole for years, remember. The charge was aggravated assault, remember." David leaned forward.

"We've already been over that. Damn it, Hetherington. Don't rehash the story of my life.

You believe in the fucking law and its power. Use it. I can't be confined like this." Karl's eyes blazed. "I can't take it."

"I'll do what I can, Karl," David said earnestly.

"I don't mean get me out when my time's up or any crap like that." Karl spit the words out and held up his finger obscenely.

"Okay, Karl, you ought to get an Oscar for that performance." David sighed. "I'll be back later today."

"Just get me out—and soon." Karl's face was a ghastly white under the klieg lights. He motioned to the guard. "Okay, buddy, you've been laying for me. Here's your chance."

Kristen sat for a few more minutes in stunned rigidity as the guard led Karl away. The warmth of the arm David put around her felt comforting, but she wouldn't permit herself to rely on it and twisted herself free. "You must get him out, David, before something happens." Tears welled up in Kristen's eyes.

"Kristen, I just can't get a can opener and spring him. I'm no miracle worker," he said wearily. "Notwithstanding its defects, I believe in our system. It is cumbersome and slow, but I know of no other which is better. Perhaps Karl's arguments about the law have some merit. Still, the alternative to governance by law is anarchy. Karl has a better chance to obtain justice here than anywhere. Of course, power can be used manipulatively, power can corrupt, but it is crudely naive to suppose that by eliminating our courts one will attain utopia. Without law man would not be a carefree primitive unless the world around him also retrogresses to an earlier, more simple civilization. And that is a dubious possibility. Unless that happens, a lawless society will be one in which everyone everywhere will confront chaos. If men object to corrupt laws, they still have to fashion new ones from the old. I prefer to conserve energy but to use electricity rather than to adapt to living as a Neanderthal in darkness."

Kristen stood nervously waiting for the lecture to end. Her stomach constricted as it always did when people strung too many words together and their meaning vanished. She thought, watching him, David is in love with the sound of his own voice. Then she shrugged. So what. It is not the worst of traits. "None of that means anything to me, David, I just want to get Karl out."

"Of course," David laughed apologetically. "It is hard to concentrate on universal objectives when intense personal feelings are involved."

"David," she tried to smile, "that's not why I'm here."

The arraignment took place at ten on Tuesday in Federal Magistrate Scaley's court. Three federal agents and their customs agents were present. Kristen found a seat in front of the courtroom. Her attention fixed upon the figure of Karl West. Around her many people, mostly relatives of other prisoners chattered. Their high-pitched voices hung in the air. David sat beside Karl, who was conservatively dressed in a dark blue business suit. She hardly recognized him. He looked so sensible, she thought. At his long raised bench, the judge smiled thinly at the observers and gave a small speech on procedure. He hardly glanced at the attorneys or the prisoner. Kristen remembered David saying he would soon be up for re-election. Not much of a case to make an impression with. Slowly, she refocused and heard David's plea of not guilty. No one except her seemed to pay attention. People yawned, shuffled their feet, even slept through the words. Outside in the hot, humid hall, the families of other prisoners clutched at people with large tan briefcases, obviously lawyers on whom their future depended. The lawyers for the most part seemed bored, ill at ease. They spoke in muffled, secretive tones which tended to heighten Kristen's fears rather than reassure her. Kristen passed them on the way to the bathroom, only to come back to the courtroom and see others in their place.

Karl's acts were being described by the prosecutor as if he were the announcer of the six o'clock news. Between recesses and breaks, tension and boredom intertwined. She felt herself nodding off. But David's voice kept intruding upon her. She had thought that voice patient and soothing, but now within the dimension of this place it was shrewd, regal. Without anger but intent on an objective, David moved for dismissal. Magistrate Scaley denied the motion. Then the prosecuting attorney offered the government's reasons for denying bail. It was strange, Kristen thought, listening intently. The man who opposed Karl spoke with as much conviction as David Hetherington. To her the two attorneys seemed interchangeable. She almost expected the judge to call time while the sides returned to the combat field, positions reversed. During one recess she saw David speaking animatedly to the government's attorney, his voice without rancor or noticeable dislike. She wondered if away from the courthouse they were friends, perhaps even played golf together—that is, if David played such benign games. No wonder Karl ranted about justice. The scene seemed part of a script from a television serial. It was difficult to tell, however, who the star was. If only one had that information, she mused, the ending would not be so difficult to fathom. Kristen grimaced at her own lack of respect. Was Karl's disillusionment rubbing off?

She looked over at the Federal Magistrate Scaley: his attention seemed to have wandered. His head was bent over, his eyes closed, as if sleep had overtaken his interest. How many similar cases did he hear? Kristen wondered. How many men protesting their innocence and lawyers whose pleas droned on endlessly?

Kristen turned back to Karl. He looked jumpy, restless. I wish it would be over, she thought, and we could go. As if sensing her desire, David tried several times to speed things up. But the judge roused himself and indicated he wanted to hear all pertinent facts. Probably expecting a campaign contribution from the state, she thought bitterly. Even from where she sat, Karl's squirming was noticeable. Several times David put a protective hand on Karl's shoulder, urging him silently to quiet down. Kristen's head pounded. She knew exactly the white-hot feeling which threatened to erupt from Karl and the danger, but then she heard David's determined voice portraying Karl as an adventurous but honest man caught in a bizarre situation. The judge nodded at each point. Gratefully, Kristen breathed a sigh of relief, thinking him to be on their side.

"The unassailable facts," David was saying, "point to this man's innocence and his willingness to be available to prove it."

Kristen tasted relief. Surely, Karl would be released within a few hours. The magistrate would accept David's sane, calm evaluation. She knew that David was not about to put Karl on the stand and chance any wild performance, but then Karl motioned, he pointed in the direction of the stand. She saw David shake his head and lip-read the curses spewing from Karl's mouth.

Magistrate Scaley held up his hand, objecting to the interruption. A split second later, Karl leaped up, shouting, "Let me out of here—this is a goddamned zoo. You fucking animals!" Karl began to roar furiously, like a gorilla, jumping up and down scratching under his arms.

Eveything stopped. The court became dead quiet. People's eyes widened, they stared at the prisoner in amazement. You had only to look at Magistrate Scaley's wary, readable eyes to see his annoyance. Kristen's fears returned. David turned to him politely. His face expressionless, only the rapid flush of his cheeks betrayed any reaction. "My client is quite agitated. However, that is no proof of his guilt, your honor."

The magistrate met his eyes. "I'm going to deny your client bail and bind him over for psychiatric evaluation as well, Mr. Hetherington." Pain shot through Kristen. She looked at Karl and awaited the explosion.

"You fucking bastards," Karl screamed. Bailiffs subdued him and led him away.

Afterwards Kristen and David went to a nearby bar to talk. She ordered a Bloody Mary. "What now?" she asked.

"We wait for the court to reconvene after the shrink's report," David answered, sipping his martini. "I thought he was going to make it, but he blew everything. I'll make an additional motion for dismissal tomorrow, but it will be denied. There is nothing to do but wait."

The blunt hopelessness of this reply jarred Kristen. Waiting was the one thing Karl could not possibly do, and now there was no choice for him but to obey the impossible.

While the psychiatric tests were being run, the grand jury, pressed by Assistant U.S. Attorney

Harrington Young, returned its indictment in Miami's federal courthouse. Karl was charged with operating a "continuing criminal enterprise," the 848 with its mandatory sentence of ten years to life, with no parole. Within days the court-appointed psychiatrist found Karl legally competent and able to stand trial. David Hetherington broke the news to Kristen privately. "What happens next?" she asked grimly.

He shook his head regretfully. "We decide whether to plead him guilty or not guilty."

"Guilty means ten years and no chance of commutation, doesn't it, David?"

"True," he answered decisively, "but it's a heck of a lot shorter than life imprisonment, which he could get if we go to trial and he's convicted."

Kristen listened carefully, trying not to interrupt. Her eyes brimmed with tears. "He'll never go for it," she said, her emotions surging. "I know he won't."

"You're probably right." David ran his hand across his forehead. "But the situation is pretty bad, desperate might be a better word, and since they got the indictment, there's probably a lot Karl hasn't told us. None of it good." David sighed.

"You think he's guilty," Kristen said apprehensively.

"I think he very well might be," David said thoughtfully. "Don't you?"

She looked away. "I don't know what to say or think."

"There's more, Kristen." He spoke gently in

a low, quiet voice; there was something in his manner which nevertheless alarmed her.

"More," she said.

"They've subpoenaed both your father and brother."

Kristen emitted a cry of anguish. David put his arm around her. "I told you it might happen," he said sadly.

She nodded, "I know you did. I just kept telling myself it couldn't."

"They're not on trial, they only have to testify," David assured her.

"For the prosecution," she murmured and put her head down, covering her face with her hands.

"You don't have to do it. I'll release you from your word. You don't have to get on the stand." He looked at her intently.

"David," Kristen said, mustering her strength, "I've already made my decision. This makes it tougher but I'm not about to change my mind." Her amber eyes met his directly.

A soft smile played around his mouth. "You always were an unusual girl, so ethereal-looking and gentle-spirited, but now—" he paused, searching for the right words. "Now you've become an extraordinary woman. So alive and full of character. I really admire you."

Kristen flushed self-consciously. "David, you shouldn't. Even I'm not completely sure of all my motives here." A dark look came over her face. "Testifying just feels right to me." For a moment the inner steel within her flashed. "And withdrawing feels damned wrong. You might say I'm not really being rational, just intuitive."

He nodded knowingly. "Sometimes that's the only thing you can do when you've examined a problem from every angle and one course seems to demand your loyalty as much as another."

She smiled warmly at him. "David, you make me feel so much better." He started to speak and then abruptly changed his mind.

Immediately after the grand jury indictment, Karl was transferred to the Federal Correction Institution. Unless bail was set, he would have to remain there until the trial. Kristen visited him every day. His moods were as changeable as a chameleon. One day he would be boyish and winsome, clinging to her every word as if his world revolved around her; the next he would pace the prisoner's area, a caged animal held captive without recourse. Sometimes he would joke with the guards as if he cared little about where he was and had adjusted to prison life easily and without stress, and at other times he was withdrawn, silent, his hair disheveled, his eyes red and sleepless.

Kristen never knew in what mood she would find him, and the uncertainty made her even more nervous. On the one hand, she wanted to tell him he no longer had the right to control her; in fact, he had never had that right. She had deeded it to him so that he wouldn't leave her. On the other hand, she felt some unnamed tie drawing her back to him. A tie she wanted to sever but somehow couldn't. She watched him intently, trying to ascertain what it was. But the identity still eluded her.

"Kristen." He was speaking now. A rush of excited words. "We're going to do all right here. I can feel it." He looked accusingly at her. "Can't you?"

She sighed. Knowing he wanted, needed her assurances and that she had to give them to him. "Of course, Karl," she said softly. "You'll be out very soon."

He buried his face in his hands. "I have to be. You see that, don't you? I'm not a criminal. I haven't killed anybody. I can understand locking people away for planting bombs or shooting people. But this—" He looked angry now. "The real criminals are hanging out on the streets and they take my freedom away. I'd like to kill the bastards."

Kristen sat silently twisting her handkerchief. She wished the trial was over. Unfortunately, it was about to begin.

18

Kristen and David met at the bottom of the huge gray stone steps leading to the federal courthouse. On a plaque high above them, the figure of a Grecian-garbed woman was etched in stone, her legs outstretched as if to race toward the far end of the panel where a laurel crown was extended by some unknown hand. Hurrying, trying to keep up with David, Kristen made out the word "justice" beneath the woman's legs. The rest of the inscription blurred together in a jumble of unclear letters as they passed under it.

David pushed open the heavy mahogany doors leading inside the building. They walked silently through the densely-packed, smoke-filled corridor. Chatting lawyers in dark suits, carrying bulging briefcases, sweated profusely in the Florida heat. Anxious-looking men in frayed wash-and-wear khakis and the polyester-clad women who inevitably accompanied them hung on the lawyers' every word. Scattered about, their rapid-fire conversations punctuated by sweeping gestures and emotional outbursts, were groups of Spanish-speaking people of all ages, from young children to white-haired grandmotherly types carrying baskets of garlic-scented food as if going to a family picnic. Standing a little apart, heads bowed or slumped in corners with eyes averted, were a few sullen-faced black men who seemed rooted to spots which they had assumed at some early unknown hour.

  David pulled out the notes he carried in his breast pocket and scanned them. "Our courtroom's upstairs," he said matter-of-factly. "We'll have to take the elevator back there." He gestured toward a rear corridor. Kristen, not trusting herself to speak, followed him. She knew David was watching her, gauging her reactions, but she felt too anxious to offer him any reassurance. Her thoughts were riveted on Karl. She wondered about where he was being kept, and the mood in which they would find him.

  "Let's find you a seat," David said quietly at the door of the courtroom. "I'm not sure they'll permit you to stay, but we'll see how it goes." She nodded. "Are you frightened?" David leaned toward her, his manner reassuring.

  "Terrified is probably more accurate." She forced a smile.

  "Just take your time. Remember what we

went over and watch me if you get into trouble," David advised. "You'll have plenty of time to get used to their styles. The prosecution will present its entire case before our turn comes."

"I just wish it was over," Kristen replied quietly.

"I just hope we win," David said emphatically.

She looked at him strangely. "You mean you hope Karl does," Kristen said thoughtfully.

He shrugged. "It's the same thing, isn't it?"

Kristen regarded David searchingly. "Not really."

Walking inside, Kristen looked around. It was a large, gloomy room with the slightly musty odor of the church she had gone to each Sunday long ago. For a moment, she wished herself back in that safe mahogany pew of childhood, seated between her father and mother, but then she shook the feeling off and readied herself for the ordeal ahead.

Turning to her left, she observed the enclave gathered at the prosecutor's table. "The one in tan is Harrington Young, Assistant United States Attorney," David whispered to her. "On either side of him, with the pencils, books, etc. and intent on apple polishing, are his legal lackeys. The group at the far end are U.S. Customs officials; the neatly starched ones dressed in blue are from the Metro Dade Police. Directly across is Warren McAnlis, the head of the DEA Cannabis. Notice his black three-piece suit; it pegs him as a northerner and these southern boys don't like his interference one bit. The rest come from various law enforcement agencies."

"It's an army," Kristen said in amazement. "Isn't that a little heavy for one drug heist?"

David nodded. "That's why I'm on guard." He paused. "It's too heavy for this case. They have to be setting us up."

"Can't we do something?" Kristen asked anxiously.

"Just wait them out until they're ready to show their cards," David observed calmly. "I'd better go up front."

Kristen nodded and scrutinized Harrington Young. He was a short, stocky man with a beaklike nose and pock-marked skin. He sat uncomfortably on the small cane chair that hardly contained his bulk, arranging and rearranging his notes. There was a cold sternness in his manner and demeanor. Kristen shivered as he caught her eye, held it, and with a look of contempt turned away.

Kristen watched David getting settled at the defense table.

"All rise." The high-pitched voice of the clerk cut through her thoughts. She stood up and watched the judge enter the courtroom. "The Honorable Fern Hanley, Judge of the United States District Court, will preside. Be seated." The judge was a woman. Sitting down again, Kristen stared searchingly at her. Small, gray-streaked brown hair, softly rounded features. Kristen breathed a sigh of relief. Perhaps luck would be with them after all.

Karl was led in by two U.S. marshals. He looked tense and haggard and ill at ease in the navy blue suit which she and David had picked out. Once again David moved to set bail and this time the judge relented, agreeing to release Karl to David's custody. Kristen caught David's eye. He nodded and she sighed gratefully. At least Karl wouldn't have to spend another night in jail. That would increase their chances of keeping him calm.

It took several days to impanel a jury. Both the prosecution and the defense quickly used up their peremptory challenges. Finally the twelve were chosen, eight men and four women. Only one black: a high-colored portly man who had on an open-necked frayed white oxford shirt and brown trousers. He owned a small grocery store. Next to him the single bearded man on the jury sat fiddling with rimless glasses which he could never seem to adjust properly. The others seemed an indistinguishable mixture of plain-faced, solid types. Neither old nor young. Kristen watched them for some sign as to their sympathies but could not be sure.

Kristen's head ached with the intensity of it all. Watching Karl drum his fingers on the defense table, squirm in his seat, and become more agitated, her own anxieties grew.

"Are you ready, gentlemen?" the high-pitched, nasal voice of the court clerk inquired.

"Defense ready," David called out.

"Prosecution ready." Young pronounced his words as a jail sentence. He strode toward the jury box ready to make his opening statement.

"Your Honor, Ladies and Gentlemen of the Jury." He paused, scanning each jury member's face. "We charge the defendant Karl I. West with eight forty-eight—continuing criminal activity—and will prove during the course of this trial that he has been a pivotal part of an insidious web of international smugglers."

During the next few days the government pressed for cooperation and Karl repeatedly told them to "go fuck themselves."

"He's innocent," Kristen insisted. "You can't expect him to cooperate."

"Expect has nothing to do with it," David said wearily. "I don't like the way this trial is shaping up. They have more on their minds than smuggling."

"What?" Kristen asked, becoming intensely emotional. "What do they want from him?"

David shook his head. "I don't know yet. But they don't keep asking for cooperation without a reason. There's always a stick in back of the carrot. And I'm waiting for it to strike," he said warily. "My bet is they're looking for bigger fish to fry than Karl and more serious charges."

"Like?" Kristen turned toward him, in her eyes a mute appeal.

"Conspiracy is one possibility." His face creased in a frown. "Another could be tax evasion.

The big questions are: who do they want and what do they know?" Watching Kristen's anguished expression, he stopped abruptly. "Kristen, I'm just doing some educated guessing. None of it means anything concrete, really. But I have to anticipate what may be coming in order to advise Karl."

"But will he listen?"

His voice was flat and had less conviction than formerly. "I wish I could tell you he will, but Karl doesn't take much advice and the chances he'll take mine are certainly small. Nevertheless, I have to try." He shook his head regretfully. "And I guess so do you."

"By the way," he said, changing the subject, "I'm going to keep Karl close to me. Until the trial is over, he'll stay in my suite, and I'd rather you have no contact with him unless I'm present."

Kristen shook her head slowly. "Do you think they might follow him?"

"I'd bet on that," said David. His voice was quiet but his eyes were riveted on Kristen. He decided this was the moment to be blunt. "And I don't want them to implicate you."

"But how could they?" Kristen asked. "I had nothing to do with it."

David gave a dour smile. "I know that, but they don't."

Kristen's mind began to go into a turmoil. She felt fear rising within her. "And my brother and father?"

"Young is playing cat and mouse. Your dad and brother are the 'biggies'; he'll save their testimony until later in the game." In fact, David was right. The government began by parading a fusillade of expert witnesses; the selection included U.S. Customs officials, members of the DEA Cannabis section, agents from Centac. Reports from the Florida Police Force had escalated until they were now calling Karl's capture "the biggest marijuana haul in the last five years."

During the first two weeks, each time court reconvened, there were more witnesses, more testimony, more debates between the sparring attorneys, more rulings from the quietly efficient judge. Kristen heard David rebut rollercoasters of words, turning them round and round, reaching what seemed decisive pinnacles wherein all would be resolved, only to hear them careen downward as Young added piece after piece of further evidence, Kristen's hopes for Karl plummeted downward.

But David was tenacious. As soon as Young pushed aside an idea, grabbed onto an inconsistency, exposed another part of the government's case, David objected and began to climb back up again. Kristen marvelled at his endurance and tenacity.

On and on the trial went: abrupt questions, jarring objections, numbing adjournments, and temporary reprieves as day after day passed, with no end in sight. Finally, she went to David. "I don't think I can take it every day without a break," she said thoughtfully. "Would you mind if I skipped some of the morning sessions and went back to the University? They've been pretty understanding about my missing classes, but my students are complaining."

"That's probably a very good idea," David said, regarding her closely. "This is going to drag on a lot longer than I anticipated. Why don't I brief you each evening on what's occurred and let you know if there's anything that I want you to be in on the next day?" He smiled reassuringly.

"I don't want to cop out," Kristen said slowly. "Just to touch base with the other parts of my life and keep them intact."

"Kristen, you don't have to explain. The fact that you are here is evidence enough of your courage." He looked at her admiringly.

She felt pained. "David, you always see me in the best light. I wish I deserved it."

"And I wish you weren't always so hard on yourself. There's nothing wrong with looking out for yourself. In fact, that is the first step toward being able to effectively help anyone else."

Kristen squeezed his hand appreciatively.

The next day on campus she realized, half in amazement, half in relief, that the current semester was almost over. Tepid spring had slipped into Florida's sweltering summer with hardly a sign, except for a lost ripple of wind. Girls in skin-tight shorts and bikini tops, boys shirtless in cutoff denims, lolled sunbathing, studying under motionless palm trees. The path between the Ferre Library and the Ashe Building of the Graduate School was littered with bodies, suntan lotions, and books. Deadlines for term papers came; exam schedules were posted. Somehow, Kristen managed to do what was necessary for Karl, to pass her courses, and fulfill her obligations to her students. In fact, exam preparations, tedious though they were, calmed her mind, turning her thoughts from the trying, tumultuous trial back into the esoteric lectures and lulling research. In order to keep her thoughts anchored and away from the afternoon hearings, she meticulously outlined her semester's notes, methodically going over and over them. With her consciousness thus narrowed, she became curiously composed, poised, waiting . . . .

And by choice, she saw little of Danny. Once in a while she drifted into Danny's apartment for a cup of jasmine tea or a few words of comfort, but the intimacy between them gradually receded to a memory. During their infrequent meetings, Danny smiled gaily without a word of admonishment, not entreating her to stay, not clinging, allowing Kristen space to make her own decision—to return to or break up their relationship. But at odd moments their eyes were drawn painfully together and their silences swallowed rather than filled the surrounding air. Finally, Kristen could stand the evasions no longer.

"Danny, it's over," she blurted out. "This is so hard to say when you've been so good to me. You don't know how much it has meant. I couldn't have pulled myself together without you."

"A bunch of words, useless garbage. What a futile ending for so much," Danny answered, her eyes filling with tears.

"Thank you," Kristen said, gently reaching out to clasp Danny's hand, "for that feeling, but most of all for your caring, for your tenderness when I had given up hope of ever feeling or finding it."

"We could have made what we had last forever," Danny said.

"No," Kristen said sadly but firmly. "I couldn't."

"That damned honesty of yours," Danny said with a jocular grimace. "It sucks."

"Agreed," Kristen laughed softly, "but I've never been able, at least not for long, to deny my need for it. Will you forgive me?"

Danny gazed at her with a melancholy expression. "No, never, but I will go on loving you."

"And I you," Kristen said gently. "You must believe that."

"I'll try," Danny said, turning away.

"Do you want me to go now?" Kristen asked helplessly.

"Yes." Danny nodded.

Kristen slipped out the front door and stood in the hall for a while staring at nothing. Her head throbbed with pain. "Damn," she murmured, walking away.

When her brother Jamie called late the next evening, she hardly recognized his thin, nervous voice. "I'm coming down to Florida tomorrow, Kristen." There was a pause.

Kristen took a quick, shallow breath, "Will Gayle be with you?"

"Gayle isn't part of my life anymore," he said morosely. "And I guess you know why I'm coming."

"To testify." she said slowly.

He didn't reply, instead saying, "Would you mind if I stayed with you?"

"Jamie, of course not," she said, not knowing whether to be happy or fearful.

"Karl isn't with you, is he?" Jamie asked sharply.

"No, why should he be?" Kristen replied.

"That's a question I'd prefer not to answer," Jamie said curtly, "or comment upon."

He arrived near dinnertime and they went out to The Monks' Cellar, the small restaurant she and Danny had liked so much. But Jamie was silent, distant. He neither rebuked her nor confided in her. Instead the scant conversation was polite but meaningless. Finally Kristen could stand it no longer. "Jamie, we're brother and sister; can't we talk this out?"

"Talk what out, Kristen?" he said bitterly. "The fact that you've implicated us in this mess? The fact that you're testifying against your own brother and father? Do you know what you're doing to our family? To Dad? Dragging him through this slop when he isn't well? Not to mention what you're doing to my life."

"What I'm doing, Jamie, is telling the truth."

"Whose truth and what do you know about it anyway? Truth isn't a half-assed stand you take in defense of some ambiguous mumbo jumbo that vanishes like water into sand and serves no purpose. It's what you do every day. That little bastard comes running to you for protection and you forget your family and all he did. Locking you up in an insane asylum, beating you to pieces time after time. Jesus Christ, when are you going to grow up?" Jamie said wearily.

"I have grown up, Jamie, that's just the point. I'm not willing to let the rest of you think for me anymore," Kristen's voice took on a cutting edge, "or tell me what's wrong or right. I'm aware of everything Karl did. And everything I did. But I don't hate him enough to send him to jail for something he didn't do as retribution. Are you?"

"I'm willing to do whatever I have to to safeguard the members of my family and our name," Jamie said decisively.

Kristen stared at him amazed. Her heart seemed to stop. "Even deceit, even lies?" she said slowly.

"If that were necessary, yes," Jamie snapped back. "And you should be too. Though God knows in this case it isn't necessary."

Kristen shook her head. A thought stirred in her mind. Her father and brother might be guilty. How would she deal with that fact if the trial revealed it? She had to know. "Jamie, is Dad's company responsible?" she asked.

"You'd be able to answer that yourself," Jamie said bitterly, "if you'd ever taken an interest in things or helped out. Where have you been all these years while we worked our tails off? All you've ever done is cost us money and heartache. Now you're trying to destroy everything we've built to satisfy some new commitment you've made to tell the truth. The hell I'm going to give you any answers. You're so smart, figure it out yourself." Jamie's voice was angry and disgusted.

"I guess I'll have to ask Dad then," Kristen said softly.

"I wouldn't do that if I were you." Jamie's face flushed red. "Just because he's always protected you, doesn't mean he's suicidal."

"Then he *is* responsible."

"That's not what I said, but what would you do if he were? Turn him in and let a piece of scum like Karl West go free?"

"If he's innocent," Kristen said slowly.

"Well, he's not." Jamie's eyes bored into her. "And neither are you. Now let's order some coffee, go back to your apartment and try to get some rest. I have to testify tomorrow."

The night passed slowly. Kristen could hear Jamie walking back and forth in the living room, obviously unable to sleep. But she stayed in her room, not wanting to chance the misunderstanding between them growing into something much worse.

"The prosecution calls to the stand James Alan Blakely." Kristen leaned forward so she could watch her brother make his way to the witness chair. Her heart pounded. She was terrified. At what he might say, at what she might learn about Karl and about her father. Yet she was convinced that she had to know. She watched Jamie. Usually he moved with a kind of graceful agility, but today he walked slowly, head bowed. Strain and fatigue showed on his face. His voice was sluggish as he was sworn in.

Young began his questions with the usual inconsequential elicitations. And Jamie answered them in the same monotone sequence as they were asked. The courtroom was slipping into an early morning stupor when Harrington Young's voice took on a cutting edge. "You are acquainted with the accused, Karl West?" He paused.

"Yes, I am," Jamie answered slowly.

"Could you tell us the circumstances under which you met?" Young licked his lips.

"We were introduced at a party by my sister."

"And what was your sister's connection to Mr. West?" Young's eyes hardened.

Jamie shrugged. "She was dating him, I believe—" Young cut him off.

"You mean they were lovers."

Jamie flushed perceptibly. "We didn't discuss their sexual relationship, Mr. Young."

Young retreated momentarily. "Nor do I intend to." Obviously he had remembered that he was interrogating his own witness. "However, the jury needs to be aware of the relationship of the people involved here in order to draw the right conclusions."

"Objection." David Hetherington stood up.

"Sustained," Judge Hanley said.

"Mr. Blakely, will you tell us the circumstances of your last meeting with Karl West." Young's voice rose ominously.

Jamie sought out Kristen among the spectators. His eyes met hers directly. "I refuse to answer on the grounds it may incriminate me."

"You what?" Young uttered the words without thinking.

"I refuse to answer on the grounds it may incriminate me," Jamie repeated.

The U.S. Attorney raised his hands in a gesture of helplessness. "Mr. Blakely, I want you to think carefully about your answers."

Jamie shifted uncomfortably in his seat. "You may be sure I have."

Dead silence filled the courtroom. Judge Hanley broke it. "Mr. Young, get on with your questions."

Young cleared his throat. "What is your business connection to Mr. West?"

David was on his feet again. "Objection. Mr. Young has not established that there is a connection."

"Sustained. Please rephrase your question, Mr. Young," the judge murmured.

Young had no intention of letting go that easily. "Mr. Blakely, is Karl West employed by your company?"

"I refuse to answer on the grounds it may incriminate me."

Young was furious now and barely able to contain it. "I want to remind you, Mr. Blakely, that this court has the power to open an investigation into your company's activities. Are you aware of that fact?" Young asked indignantly.

Jamie met his stare. "I am aware, Mr. Young."

For the next thirty minutes, Young continued to ask Jamie questions and Jamie continued to take the fifth amendment. Finally, Young gave up. "I'm finished with you, Blakely," he said disgustedly. "Your witness, Hetherington."

"No questions," David said matter-of-factly.

"The witness can step down." The court clerk frowned. Kristen shivered. She had learned nothing. Neither who was guilty, nor who was innocent. She shook her head, staring at her brother bewilderedly as he left the stand and walked from the courtroom.

In an abrupt about face, Young, obviously rattled by Jamie's stubborn refusal to cooperate, changed the laconic pace of the trial. Instead of using several days for a single witness, he packed three more witnesses into the afternoon session.

The first, Manuel Ortega, testified that he was Karl West's partner in his new ranch in Santa Marta. "The hell you are!" Karl jumped up, his face glowering. "You goddamned spic!" He slammed the table in front of him. "I wouldn't let you scrub my toilet, much less be my partner."

"Sit down Mr. West," the judge loudly admonished.

The youthful, black-haired impeccably

groomed Spaniard took out his handkerchief and wiped his forehead. Despite the Florida weather, he wore a white business suit with a vest, and already the heat had begun to take its toll. Nevertheless, settling back in his chair, he spoke coolly but decisively as he accused Karl West of having been greedy and unstable. "A seven hundred and fifty pound crop, a landing strip on his ranch," he shook his head. "I told him a few bananas weren't going to confuse either our authorities or his. But he thought he knew it all and that he could market the entire crop without the help of my countrymen. Only an American could be so stupid."

Under cross-examination, Hetherington was able to elicit the fact that Ortega had been promised immunity for appearing. He tried to get the dapper witness to admit that what was behind his cooperation was the wish to get Karl West out of the way so he could take over the ranch, but a smiling Manuel Ortega disagreed. "We have a code of ethics in my country," he said decisively. "We not only espouse it," he paused, looking directly at Karl West, "we live by it."

Even Kristen found his testimony credible. She had to believe the jury did too.

Without a break, the prosecution announced its next witness. A bespectacled thirtyish-looking Floridian named Ted Kantor. He looked more like a shoe salesman than a criminal and he was obviously scared, stumbling over even the introductory questions.

"Would you tell us your connection to Mr.

THE SPLINTERED EYE

West, Mr. Kantor." Harrington Young smiled officiously and gestured toward the witness.

Kantor kept his eyes downcast. "I'm a broker," he said nervously.

"The jury might not understand that term, Mr. Kantor," Young prompted. "Would you explain your occupation?"

"I work on a commission." Kantor paused and fear showed on his face. Although he too had been promised immunity for his testimony in this case, he didn't want to implicate himself in another.

"Yes?" Young prompted.

Kantor cleared his throat. "People who want to make a connection."

"You mean buy dope, don't you," Young said. It was his first antagonistic dig.

Kantor nodded. "Yes, of course, well I get the word out and," he took a shallow breath, "and when my contacts come to town, I show them a piece—"

"A piece," Young repeated coldly.

Kantor hesitated, then shrugged. "A bale from the shipment, so they'll know it's high grade commercial Colombian. Of course," he eyed Karl apprehensively and his voice quivered, "I never knew Mr. West to market any other kind."

"Do you think I'd work with this puny faggot?" Karl yelled out. "This is a goddamned snow job—" he stopped and slapped the table in front of him. "Get on with it, you goddamned fools." He glowered at the judge.

"Sit down, Mr. West," she said curtly. "Mr. Hetherington, if you can't control your client, I will have him forcibly restrained. We'll take a fifteen-minute break now, and when we return I expect the decorum of my courtroom to return with us."

Kristen walked outside, followed shortly by David Hetherington. "Things are going badly, aren't they?" She looked at him searchingly.

He nodded. "But none of it is so devastating that we can't turn it around during cross-examination or our part of the case. Don't let them discourage you, this is their round."

She forced a smile. "It sure is a long one."

He grinned. "The important thing to remember is they're just as tired as we are and the energy drain isn't the only problem. This is costing them plenty of money. Our best move here," he ran his hand through his unruly hair thoughtfully, "is to let them run themselves ragged."

Kristen regarded him levelly. "You never give up, do you?"

"Never," he said decisively as they walked back inside.

Kristen settled back on the bench. She closed her burning eyes and tried to relax. Letting her mind glide to a green, serene place where none of this could touch her. But Harrington Young's voice broke into her meditation, shattering the calm. "Candice Shelton, the prosecution calls Candice Shelton to the stand."

Kristen's eyes opened wide. Dressed in tight

faded denims and a red sweater, Karl West's new lover swiveled her way to the stand. Her testimony was short but hardly sweet.

Twisting a plaid cotton scarf in her hands and sobbing theatrically, she admitted being Karl's half-sister and having been with Karl on several "procuring missons." Yes, she had been with him at the Ireland Inn in Fort Lauderdale. Hadn't they been joined by Mr. Ortega? "He looks very familiar." Candice peered at the dapper ex-witness. And hadn't she and Karl attended parties at the Roundhouse in Tijuana on August 10, 1977, October 3, 1977, and February 12, 1978, where some of the elite of the drug trade underworld plotted multi-million-dollar deals? "Yes, there were lots of famous people there: dazzling parties, lavish food, plenty of champagne. Now it has all come to this." She blew her nose loudly and dabbed dramatically at her eyes.

David Hetherington had only one question. Had she, too, been granted immunity? "Of course," she gestured coquettishly, "or else why the hell would I be here?"

As Candy left the courtroom, she winked and blew a kiss at Karl. In a quicksilver mood change Karl laughed raucously.

By this time the plastic hands of the courtroom clock clicked into the roman numeral five; Kristen and all the other spectators slumped in their seats, weary from the long afternoon of testimony. When the judge announced her intention of adjourning for the night, claps and loud sighs greeted her. Quickly gathering up her things, Kristen made her way to the back of the courtroom, outside and down the steps. Even the humid heavy air was a relief after the stifling courtroom. She breathed it in gladly.

"Wait up," David Hetherington called out in front of the courthouse. She stood in a kind of daze, feeling particularly vulnerable, as if something within her was about to shatter. "Long day." David looked at her sympathetically. "Would you like to go somewhere for dinner?"

Wearily she shook her head. "I don't think I could make it without nodding off."

"These sessions can be brutal," he said slowly. "The best thing to do afterward is to try to forget them completely. Don't even think about what occurred, no less attempt a post-mortem."

"We could go to my place," she said hesitantly. "I'll grill a couple of steaks and make a salad—if that's all right."

"Sounds like just what we need." He smiled, a gentle, warm smile that suddenly made her feel better.

The five o'clock traffic was snarled and bad-tempered. It took them nearly an hour to reach the Grove. Tom Burley, genial and upbeat as usual, took their car in front of the apartment. "Hey, Kris," he laughed. "See the jinx is off dating." She forced a laugh but didn't offer any objections.

"I'm sorry," she murmured to David as they walked back to the elevator.

"Why?" he asked. "I wish we *were* involved."

She handed him the key when they reached the door to her apartment, surprised at her own old-fashioned reaction. In the living room he sprawled out on the black leather recliner, the only masculine piece of furniture in the room, and sighed heavily. "This is perfect; the only thing that could enhance the setting is an ice cold martini."

She flushed self-consciously. "I'm afraid I don't have any hard liquor. Only white wine."

"An admirable substitute," he said a touch whimsically.

She went into the kitchen and brought back two glasses of wine, handing one to him. Then she folded into the armchair nearby, drawing her legs up beneath her. "It does taste good," she murmured, sipping the wine.

"Better than good," he corrected gently. Through dinner the warm glow remained. They never mentioned the trial or Karl West, talking instead about the music, books, and artists they both seemed to agree upon. When they had finished their coffee, he rose, walked over and enfolded her in his arms: not an act of passion, but of warmth, kinship. They stood there quietly, suddenly very much at peace with themselves and the world. Then he turned to her. "I want very much to take you to bed," he said, looking into her eyes.

"I think I want that too," she answered, her

own doubts washed away by his gentleness. She followed him into the frilly bedroom and sat upon the cream-colored, lace-edged quilt while he closed the drapes. A silence fell between them. Then, he sat down beside her, looking with clear, steady eyes into her face.

"Come then," he said gently, unbuttoning her suit jacket and blouse, bending to kiss her breasts, licking her nipples with his warm tongue. She slipped from her skirt and silk panties and lay bare and golden in the lamplight. "You are beautiful," he said simply, "and I've wanted you so much." Swiftly undressing, he lay beside her: tall, lean, glistening copper, as beautiful to her as she to him. And slowly carressing her, stroking her buttocks, her thighs with his gentle, confident hands, he drew her to him until the deepest parts of her lay wet, open to him, and then he entered her as a wave seeking the shore, a wave cleansing the past, rocking her gently, then more furiously, its very undulations creating a rhythm, locking them together in a seaworld of their own. Finally, their cries of pleasure carried them close to rapture. When it was over, he sighed, "I hoped that was how it would be."

They slept for a time and then she felt his cock hardening against her again and sleepily opened her eyes and arms as he bent over her kissing her gently, gently upon the eyes, her cheeks, her hair, her body, and then he took her clitoris in his mouth, sucking it slowly, feathering it with his tongue. And when he finally entered her, her body ached for him and she came over and over until, with a final cry, he flooded her, covering her body so tightly, they were as one.

Later, they showered together, laughing and spraying each other with water. Two children, their passion spent, but the feeling of joy between them deepening, growing.

"I'm ravenous," she said as they toweled each other and set off naked to the kitchen. They raided the refrigerator, grabbing French bread and heaping together a makeshift antipasto from scraps of roast chicken, lettuce, salami, olives, and cheese. They spread it out picnic-style upon the bed and feasted on the food, wine and each other.

"Can I sleep here with you?" he asked. "I don't want to leave."

She hesitated. "Will Karl be all right?"

"Leave that to me," he said firmly.

On entering the courtroom early the next morning, their mellow mood was quickly shattered. In the first row on the aisle, his determined chin jutting out, his piercing brown eyes scanning the room, sat Eben Blakely. Seeing Kristen, he stood up and waved.

"What are you going to do?" David asked, leaning toward her protectively.

Gathering up her courage, Kristen indicated the empty seat next to her father. "Sit down," she said softly but firmly. David led the way down the aisle, stopping to shake Eben's hand. Her father kissed her but said nothing as she slid into the seat beside him.

A few minutes later, the prosecution called him to the stand. With characteristic bluntness, he answered the prosecutor's probing questions. Yes, he was acquainted with Karl West. Knew about his daughter's affair with the man. Yes, he had used his influence to end the affair. And he was quite comfortable with having done so.

Kristen watched her father closely. He was speaking quietly but intently, his eyes riveted on the prosecutor. She found herself holding her breath waiting. Perhaps now she would know the truth about Karl and her father.

"Mr. Blakely, have you in the past or are you now employing Mr. West or his firm, Air Scape?"

The answer came firmly and immediately. "No, I am not."

Kristen gasped. That could not be so. She herself had seen her father's signature on the check Karl had asked her to cash. She shook her head. No one was being completely truthful here. She had always supposed that in the end what had really happened would come out. After all, that was what trials such as this one were about, were they not? Getting final and authorized statements of truth. Ones that you could count on for veracity. But now she was beginning to fear this was not so. That neither she nor anyone else in this courtroom or for that matter any other would be able once and for all to sort out the real facts from the insubstantial fantasies created purposely, in error or through the subtle shadings of each participant's mind. Even when the final verdict was rendered, would not there always be doubts, possibilities, and questions unanswered? A sense of anger rose in her. All that she had hoped to settle here might indeed come to nothing. Too many long-winded words strung together without intrinsic meaning. Words that deceived instead of clarified truth.

"You say, Mr. Blakely, that Karl West is not, nor has ever been given a fee or his services utilized by any company with which you are or have been associated?" broke into her thoughts.

Again her father, his voice now reflecting annoyance, answered. "I believe I answered that question only a few moments ago."

"Objection." David Hetherington raised his pencil in the air. "Counsel is badgering his own witness."

"I don't mind answering again," Eben Blakely said. "Perhaps it is not only we old-timers but those with misleading names like Mr. Young who grow hard of hearing."

Laughter erupted in the courtroom. The judge pounded her gavel. "That will do. Will the witness just answer the question once again," she darted a dark glance at Harrington Young, "and then will the prosecutor get on with it."

Flushing, Young glanced toward the court reporter. "Could you read the question back."

The reporter's sing-song voice read, "You say, Mr. Blakely, that Karl West is not, nor has ever been given a fee or his services utilized by any company with which you are or have been associated?"

"No, he has not," Eben said firmly.

"Mr. Blakely." Young looked intently at the old man. "On or about March 3, 1978, did you meet with Karl West at a cabin in Keene, New Hampshire?"

"I did."

"And," Young asked sharply, "at that time did you give Mr. West six thousand dollars?"

"I did," Eben shrugged.

"Where did that payment come from, Mr. Blakely?"

Eben scratched his head and regarded the prosecutor shrewdly. "From me, son, I already told you that."

Exasperated, Young snapped, "Yes, yes, but where did you get the money?"

Eben took his time answering. "Let me think." He looked across at the seated enclave of law enforcement agents. "I must have suspected our boys in blue would have frowned on my deducting Mr. West as a business expense, so I paid him from my own pocket."

"You're sure of that," Young scowled.

"Quite sure," Eben said decisively.

"And you gave him that much money to bring two associates of yours from New York to New Hampshire for a meeting?" Young asked sarcastically.

"I gave him that money to get the hell out of the country and away from my daughter," Eben said forcefully.

"And you offered him a job as well, didn't you?"

"No, damn it." For a moment Eben's composure seemed to fade and then he regained it. "I certainly did no such thing."

"What exactly did you offer him?" Young wasn't going to give up that easily.

"An introduction to a company located on the northern coast of Colombia."

"Mr. Blakely." Young's face muscles twitched in anticipation. "Are you acquainted with Rafael Emmanuel Castillo?"

There were several moments of silence as Eben looked appraisingly at the lawyer. He obviously sensed a trap, a trap he had every intention of avoiding. "I am," Eben said slowly, his features grimly set and his manner deliberately low-key.

"Would you tell us your relationship to Mr. Castillo?"

"His father and I were old, dear friends. We were in the Merchant Marines together many years ago." He looked sharply at Harrington Young; a faint smile played about his lips. "While you, son, were still in diapers."

Young flushed. Realizing, of course, that the spectators and jury were becoming amused by the cat and mouse game between the prissy, humorless prosecutor and the paternal, forceful ship owner whose quick repartee belied his age. "And it is Mr. Castillo to whom you introduced Karl West?"

"In a manner of speaking, yes. Mr. Castillo's firm needed an air ferrying service and I suggested Mr. West's might fit the bill."

"Did Mr. West leave the United States thereafter?"

"He did."

"Within twenty-four hours?"

"I am not aware of his timetable, but shortly after our conversation."

"On the basis of your somewhat murky recommendation?"

"Objection." David Hetherington stood up.

"Sustained," Judge Hanley said firmly.

"On the basis of your conversation?"

"You would have to ask Mr. West about that," Eben said impatiently.

Young shook his head, fumbling with his notes.

"When did Mr. West return to the States?"

"I'm sure I wouldn't know."

"But he did return," Young said decisively.

Eben's eyes were riveted on Karl West, who shifted uncomfortably in his chair.

"Yes, he returned and stayed with my daughter."

"And how did you find that out?"

Eben paused, still keeping his eyes on Karl. "I can't recall." Karl had begun to sweat profusely. He loosened his tie and ran his hand across his forehead.

"What was your reaction to Mr. West's visit to your daughter?"

"I didn't like it one damn bit." Eben's tone sharpened.

"And didn't your and Mr. Castillo's firm then threaten to terminate Mr. West's contract?"

"I own no firm with Mr. Castillo," Eben said firmly. "And to the best of my knowledge, Mr. West still works for him."

"But you and Mr. Castillo have some financial dealings," Young insisted.

"On a purely personal basis."

Young leaned forward toward the witness. "On a purely personal basis in February of 1978 you loaned Mr. Castillo $50,000?"

"That sounds right," Eben mused.

"And on September 12, 1978, as reported on your federal income tax return, Mr. Castillo paid $178,000 to you?"

"If that's what my return says."

"Are you aware that Mr. Castillo's associates are part of the narcotraficante families and that he himself is at the helm of one of the largest drug empires operating between Colombia and the United States?"

"I am not aware of any such thing."

"Are you aware that Mr. West's company, Air Scape, has been ferrying drugs from Colombia to the United States?"

Eben Blakely pursed his lips and tipped back in his chair, spreading his arms expansively. "I've heard those same rumors myself, young man," he paused, "and I certainly hope you get to the bottom of them. No one wants that more than I do myself," he said, fanning the flame but admitting nothing.

"I have no further questions," Young said wearily.

"No questions," Hetherington said with a smile.

Eben stood up and offered his hand to the judge. "Thank you for your courtesy, Your Honor."

"Quite all right, Mr. Blakely." She smiled despite herself.

"You too, young-Young," Eben chuckled at the prosecutor who reddened and turned away.

Eben insisted that Kristen and David join him for lunch. And at the Biscayne Terrace where they ate he was at his most charming and his most gracious. "I want you both to come home for the Lobster Festival in July," he entreated. Kristen stole a glance at David. She could see he was vaguely uncomfortable, as she was. It was as if her father already knew they had slept together the night before and was planning their future.

Flushing, David answered, "That certainly sounds quite festive."

"It's the summer's grand event for us New Englanders, not quite up to your New York's standard of glamour, but a helluva lot more fun." He smiled at Kristen. "You will come back, won't you?"

"I'll try, Daddy," she said softly. "But right now I want to talk about why I'm testifying."

Her father regarded her levelly. He said feelingly, "The truth is seldom what it seems. I've always lived by my own code. It might not make sense to some but it does to me, and one of the main tenets is to be true to yourself as Shakespeare advised, and then let the rest of the world judge you as it may. I think I've passed on that faith to you, Kristen," he said admiringly. "I can accept its consequences if you can." A soft smile played about his face.

Kristen reached over and took his hand. "I can't do anything else."

Eben covered her golden-tanned hand with his weatherbeaten one. "I figured that. I've felt that way myself too many times not to know the feeling. Now how about one of those gooey desserts you always used to love? They're one of the best antidotes I know for sagging spirits."

She laughed and David joined her. "If you will, Daddy, I will."

"Make that three," David said.

Eben left for the airport as soon as lunch was over, explaining, "The second best antidote for times like these is hard work, and I'm longing to get back to my boats."

When David and Kristen returned to the courtroom, the prosecution put on its most damaging witness: the U.S. Customs officer who had made the original arrest. Christopher Sorling was young, blonde, and squeaky clean. If the government had wanted to advertise the kind of boy who it hoped would grow up and symbolize American law enforcement agents, surely Sorling would have been a perfect choice. He spoke in a soft, respectful voice. But his was eyewitness testimony. He had been the arresting officer.

Young's face creased in a knowing smile as he began to zero in: "Would you tell us the circumstances under which you arrested Karl West?"

"Mr. West had been cleared into Miami International Airport. Following regulations, I boarded the plane to check his cargo."

"Would you tell the jury what you found?" Young looked from one juror's face to the next.

"I showed Mr. West my identification; he objected to my searching his plane, but I explained that I was following procedure. There were quite a few cartons from Castillo Enterprises in which there were petrochemical products. In addition, the aircraft carried numerous U.S. Postal bags."

"And," Young paused dramatically, "what was in those bags?"

Sorling looked slightly embarrassed. "One hundred sixty-two pounds of marijuana."

"What was Mr. West's reaction to this discovery, Mr. Sorling?"

"He said it was news to him."

"And did you think he was telling the truth?"

"Objection," David Hetherington's deep voice cut firmly in. "That calls for conjecture by the witness."

Young smiled like the cat who had eaten the canary. "Quite all right, Hetherington. We withdraw the question." He drew his next words out slowly and carefully. "The government rests."

19

The truth is seldom what it seems. Called to the witness stand as David Hetherington's first witness for the defense, her father's words swirling through her mind, she walked forward slowly. Dressed in a well-cut navy suit and pale blue silk blouse, her long hair swept behind ears on which tiny gold hoops glistened, Kristen gave every appearance of subtle strength and feminine fragility, but her right hand trembled as she held it up.

"Do you swear to tell the truth, the whole truth, and nothing but the truth, so help you God?" the court clerk asked.

Kristen pulled herself erect. "I do," she said softly but firmly.

"What is your full name?" David Hetherington's eyes held a glimmer of amusement as they held hers. Suddenly she felt more at ease.

"Kristen Lee Blakely," she answered.
"Residence?"
"Twenty-five Sixty South Bayshore Drive, Coconut Grove, Florida."
"Are you employed, Ms. Blakely?"
"I am a graduate assistant at the University of Miami, studying for my doctoral degree in psychology."
"What is your marital status?"
"I have never been married."
"Ms. Blakely, would you explain your relationship to Karl West?"

Kristen drew in her breath sharply. "We were lovers," she said quietly. "I lived with Mr. West for more than a year."

"In Florida?"
"No, in New York City."
"And how long ago was that?" David leaned forward.

Suddenly, Kristen felt uncomfortable again. She hated revealing intimate details of her life, especially to those she didn't know or want to. And although it was David Hetherington who asked these first questions, Kristen saw Young seated at the prosecutor's table intently scrutinizing her, a half-sardonic smile on his face. She tried to concentrate on David. "We lived together until March of last year."

"And then you broke off the relationship?" David's voice was gentle.

She bit her lip and answered, "Yes, we did."
"What happened thereafter?"

"I came to Florida to pursue my degree."

"And were you in touch with Mr. West?"

She shook her head. "No, I didn't know where he was."

"But there did come a time when you saw each other again." There was a momentary silence during which Kristen reflected on what she would say.

"Ms. Blakely," Judge Hanley prompted her.

"Yes, Mr. West visited me at my apartment."

David probed gently. "And did he talk about his job?"

Kristen nodded. "He said he was working for one of my father's companies in South America. And," her voice was troubled, "he asked me to cash a check for him."

"Why did he want you to cash it?" David asked.

"He didn't have a local bank account." She tried to stay calm to conceal the agony this was causing her. But despite her efforts her voice shook.

"Could you speak up, Ms. Blakely?" the judge asked.

"He didn't have a local bank account and couldn't get it cashed."

"Ms. Blakely," David Hetherington leaned toward her protectively, "did you notice the signature on the check?"

"Yes." There was a break in her voice. She took a deep breath, trying to steady herself.

"And could you tell us whose signature was on the check?"

Kristen looked directly at him with tear-filled eyes. "My father's."

"You're quite sure?" David asked.

"Quite sure," she said deliberately and carefully.

"Thank you," David said. "No more questions."

Harrington Young stepped forward, paused in front of the mahogany-panelled witness stand, and looked at Kristen with a stern glare. "Ms. Blakely, you've testified that you are a teacher of some sort at the University of Miami?"

"I am a graduate assistant. I teach two introductory courses."

"In psychology?" Young spoke in a voice almost totally free of inflection; only the slight upturn of his lips betrayed his pleasure in interrogating the witness.

"Yes, psychology," Kristen said quietly.

"And you have a great deal of experience in that subject, don't you, Ms. Blakely?" Young pounced. His whole manner was rude and overbearing, that of a relentless detective who wanted to shatter her composure—and her testimony.

"I don't know what you mean—" Kristen stopped, confounded and dismayed.

Young's brows creased. "Well, during February and March of 1978, you were a patient at Brookhaven State Asylum, were you not?"

Before Kristen could collect her thoughts and answer, David was on his feet, shouting "Objection."

Judge Hanley intervened. "Mr. Young, can you establish a rationale for this line of questioning?"

Young said icily, "We're questioning the credibility of this witness."

"I'm going to let her answer," Judge Hanley said.

"Yes," Kristen said quietly. "I was."

"And you left that institution at the instigation of your brother and without a formal discharge from the psychiatrist under whose care you had been placed."

"Yes, that is true," Kristen said carefully and decisively.

"Thank you, Ms. Blakely," Young snapped. "I have no more questions."

"I guess that didn't do much good," Kristen said to David at the break.

"Only God and IBM knows," David said whimsically. "No matter which way you turn in life, there's a huge pile of shit to wade across. And even when you decide to jump, you can't be sure what you'll find on the other side."

"I guess," Kristen said, her voice firmer, "you find what no one else can ever give you." She met his eyes steadily. "Self-respect."

The next defense witness was a bald, stocky-figured man whose short jerky movements as he took his seat seemed faintly familiar to Kristen. His name was Walter Cranston, and as soon as he began speaking, she remembered where she had seen him before. He worked for her father as a boat captain.

"How long were you employed by Mr. Blakely?" David faced him across the witness platform.

"Twenty-two years," Cranston acknowledged curtly.

"And during that period you worked in the Maine boatyard?"

"For most of it. Sometimes when things were slow in the winter, I'd sign on as the first mate for one of Mr. Blakely's friends who had a yacht in the Caribbean, but mostly I'd keep the rigs in shape while they were in dry dock and ready them for the season."

"And while you were in Eben Blakely's employ, you had occasion to contact Karl West."

"That's right." Cranston shook his egg-shaped head, which glistened in the overhead light. "Mr. Blakely asked me to get ahold of West and arrange to bring him to Keene for a meeting."

"Did Mr. West know what the meeting was about?"

"Hell, no. He didn't even know Blakely was behind it. Just that I was chartering his plane."

"And can you tell the court what happened at that meeting?"

"Well, I had to use a little force to get West there, but once he met the boss they seemed to have a meeting of the minds."

"What do you mean, a meeting of the minds?" David asked quietly.

"Well, when we all got to the cabin, Mr.

Blakely asked me to go into the other room. But I couldn't help hearing the conversation."

"Could you tell us what you overheard."

Cranston scratched at his hand. "Mr. Blakely and West talked about her," he pointed to Kristen, "and then Mr. Blakely told West he wanted him to leave the country and take a job with one of his companies in South America."

"You're sure Eben Blakely said one of *his* companies?"

"Yeah, I'm sure," Cranston said decisively.

"And did Mr. West agree?"

"Yes, sir, he did after a while."

"What do you mean, after a while?"

"Well, West didn't want to leave immediately. But Mr. Blakely insisted, and West finally said he would when he heard he'd be getting a twenty-thousand-dollar bonus every three months."

"What happened then?" David said carefully and deliberately.

"I drove West back to his plane and I went back to New York with him. Then I taxied over to Kennedy while he went back to his apartment to get his stuff together. He met me at the airport and I made sure he and the girlfriend he brought with him got off in the right direction."

"In the right direction," David Hetherington repeated.

"I bought their tickets and put them on an Aero America flight to Cali. Then I telegraphed Mr. Castillo to have them picked up."

"Why did you do that?"

A note of doubt crept in. "Those were Mr. Blakely's instructions, and I always follow them to a T or he'd have a fit."

"Thank you, Mr. Cranston."

Harrington Young walked slowly toward the witness box. "Mr. Cranston, you say you worked for Eben Blakely for twenty-two years."

"That's correct."

Young's expression was grim. "But the last few years you actually worked for his son, Jamie, isn't that right?"

"Young Blakely liked to think so."

"Well, it was Mr. Blakely who fired you, was it not?"

Cranston flared. "The lying son-of-a-bitch!"

"Mr. Cranston," Judge Hanley said decisively, "I'm going to ask you to express your opinions without using offensive language."

Cranston slammed a beefy fist on the stand in frustration. "He fired me for his own reasons."

"According to the record," Young interrupted, "he fired you because you were siphoning off money from your accounts."

"That's *his* story!"

"I'm afraid it is," Harrington Young smirked.

David Hetherington stepped forward. "What really happened, Walter?"

Young called out, "Objection."

"Rephrase that, Mr. Hetherington," Judge Hanley said.

"What happened in your opinion, Mr. Cranston?"

"He was siphoning off that money himself and using it to support his nigger girlfriend." Cranston hunched forward accusingly. "And when his father found out there was money missing, little Jamie fingered me. The goddamned liar."

"Mr. Young."

"No further questions," Young shrugged. "We'll let the facts speak for themselves."

Judge Hanley called for a fifteen-minute break, but most of those in the courtroom just stretched. However, when the next defense witness took her seat, even those spectators who had been catnapping or reading copies of *The National Examiner* and other titillating tabloids they shielded from the bailiff's view sat up attentively.

Consuela Castillo was wildly, darkly beautiful with a spectacular mane of blue-black hair and eyes so deeply blue they appeared purple. She wore a white silk jacquard suit cut to expose her perfect cleavage and deep olive skin.

"Mrs. Castillo," David Hetherington began, "you are the wife of Rafael Emmanuel Castillo."

"I am," she answered in a soft, cultured but sexy voice.

"How long have you been married to Mr. Castillo?"

"Twelve years, but we are now separated."

"And you now live in the United States."

"Yes, with my small daughter who is seven. My father, José Indalacio Montoyo, is Minister of Foreign Affairs in Colombia, but my mother is an

American. Because of my husband's influence, my family has decided it best for me to reside here."

"Mrs. Castillo," David inquired gently, "during the time you lived with your husband you became acquainted with Karl West?"

"That is true. When he first arrived. Mr. West stayed with us in our *fincas* in Medellin. My husband was also a former war hero. He had gone to college in the United States and served in the Korean War. So he liked being with Karl. They often went drinking at a place called Kevin's near our residence."

"Were you with them?" David inquired.

"Rarely; in my country wives are sheltered from such evenings," she said quietly.

"But you were made aware of Mr. West's business connection with your husband." David regarded her searchingly.

"My husband and I discussed the fact that Karl West would be adding his small ferrying company to Rafael's fleet of multi-engine aircraft. My husband was building a private air freight complex."

"And your husband used these aircraft in connection with his transporting narcotics?"

"Yes, he did," she answered decisively.

"And was Mr. West aware of this?"

"No, he was not," Consuela shook her head. "My husband was very careful to tell Mr. West only what he wanted him to know, and that was very little. He told Karl he was building up a huge conglomerate in Colombia, which was very believable since Rafael already owned several petrochemical plants, a national radio and television station, a real estate company, an export-import business, and the Banco Americain, and that their major problem was the unreliability of the transport system between Colombia and the States, especially Miami, which was their stateside port of call. He promised Karl that he would eventually run the entire air transport service."

"And during this time did you ever hear Karl West discuss either with your husband or any member of your staff any aspect of the business which would have led you to believe he was part of or even aware of any drug trafficking?"

"Never, and my husband always considered his ignorance a necessity," she insisted firmly.

"Thank you, Mrs. Castillo." Hetherington motioned to Young. "Your witness."

"Mrs. Castillo," Young inquired coolly, "you seem to have gotten to know Mr. West rather well for an employee."

Consucla Castillo appeared flustered for a moment but quickly recovered. "As I explained, he and my husband both had naval military backgrounds, and Mr. West was especially knowledgeable about fixing the aircraft he flew—a trait my husband valued highly."

"Mr. West also flew both you and your husband on personal trips, did he not?" Young's voice rose.

"Yes, that is true."

"And at times he acted as your private pilot?"

"Once in a while on shopping trips."

"In fact," Young stiffened, straightening his shoulders, "on certain of these trips, including one in April of 1978 when you resided at the Pierre Marquez Hotel in Acapulco, Mexico, and in June of that same year when you stayed at the Dorado Beach Hotel in Puerto Rico, you and Mr. West shared the same accommodations?"

The crowd stirred, started, bristled with excitement, and a chorus of twitters grew louder and louder until Judge Hanley banged her gavel. "That will do. Please answer the question, Mrs. Castillo."

"We shared a suite since he acted as my bodyguard." If looks could kill, the one Consuela Castillo gave Harrington Young would certainly have done the job.

His face flushed red. "No more questions," he said, looking away.

"You may step down," the court clerk said matter-of-factly.

When Kristen heard Max West's name called and saw the rather frail old man march forward militarily erect, she could not help but smile. It was as if she already knew him. He wore the same frayed leather jacket Karl had so often described to her and his blue language blasted through the courtroom like a revved-up propeller.

"My nephew is one helluva pilot," he said,

cupping his hand over his left ear. "So why the hell should he take up flying a pile of shit?"

"Mr. West," Judge Hanley admonished.

But whether absolute deafness overcame him or he had something more serious on his mind and was determined not to be disturbed while he communicated it, Max West paid her no attention. David Hetherington held up his hand and said in a loud voice, "Mr. West, would you tell us what crops you raise on your ranch?"

Max drew back offended. "Crops, you say. Son, we raise horses. Pure-bred pasofinos, mustangs, the most beautiful you've ever seen. We do have a field set aside for bananas and such but that's just to suit our own tastes."

"Mr. West." David was dead serious now. "Would you tell us if anywhere on your ranch you raise cocoa plants or marijuana?"

Max's face was brick red. "Young man, I served in World War One as a captain. I'm a forty-year American Legioner. And my nephew," his face was filled with pride, "has more medals, including a Bronze Star, than any officer I've ever seen." The old man's voice became testy. "We're not the kind of Americans who'd fight one war and create the makings of another one."

"Do you raise any kind of raw product to be used in the export of narcotics?" David persisted.

The old man shook his head vehemently. "We sure as hell don't."

"Thank you, Mr. West," David Hetherington said. There was a glint of amusement in his eyes.

"No questions," Harrington Young called out, grimacing.

"I thought not," Max West said sharply. Easing himself out of the chair, he refused David's proferred hand. "No, thank you, boy. I have a little trouble with navigation, but I'm not ready to hand over the ropes yet. I can still handle myself," he looked over at Young, scowling, "and most of the other makeshift men they're sending out today."

"You bet you can, you old card," Karl West called out, laughing.

Judge Hanley banged her gavel lightly but couldn't suppress a smile.

"If the court pleases," David Hetherington said earnestly, "the defense rests."

Since the hour was almost five and everyone was exhausted by the wearing heat and long testimony, Judge Hanley adjourned the session until the following morning, when the sleepy-eyed clerk called, "All rise."

"Are counsels for both parties ready to begin their final arguments?" the judge asked.

"The prosecution is ready," Young said decisively.

"The defense is ready," David Hetherington affirmed.

The closing statements were short and eloquent, and the judge's final charge to the jury was a model of fairness and decorum: "If any of the material facts are at variance with the probability of guilt, it will be your duty to give the defendant the benefit of the doubt. But, it must also be remembered that evidence is not to be discredited because it is circumstantial, for it may often be more reliable than direct evidence. Weigh your decisions carefully and do not be afraid to change your mind when reflecting on the evidence. But once you are sure of the verdict, hold steadfastly to the decision to which your conscience guides you, despite the beliefs and pressures of those around you." The members of the jury rose and filed out, and the biting tension returned.

    The agitation Kristen felt made her mind ache and stirred her memories of the past with all its wounds. She tried to turn her thoughts forward to seize an omen for the present. But the dark, dusty courtroom was almost empty now. As if its very life had ceased.

    She looked at the empty jury box and flicked back her hair with a nervous gesture. In front of the box, Harrington Young, his teeth clamped on an unlighted cigar, stood engrossed in conversation with David Hetherington. They could have been old friends, she mused, watching their heads nodding, the hands gesturing similarly. She shook the thought off. She knew it was a foolish one. After all, the case was almost over now and although surely they weren't friends, the reality was they weren't enemies either. Merely momentary adversaries, each seeing things differently, arguing and rearguing their versions of the truth. Both were bone tired now. It showed in their faces, in the way they leaned back on the wooden panels behind them.

THE SPLINTERED EYE

Kristen tried to remember the faces of the jury members upon whom Karl's future, and in a strange way her own, depended. Except for the black man and the one with the beard, they formed a shadowy collage in which the features and parts of one mingled with the other. During the trial she had often stared at them, the plain-faced women who wore little makeup, and the gray-featured men who mostly wore glasses. Sometimes she had seen them nodding in sympathy, or leaning forward to see a witness better or staring off into space. But they were flimsy impressions. She wished she had concentrated more, tried to ascertain where their sympathies lay so that her present anxiety would have lessened. Instead, she remembered their silence, their lack of voices, even more sphinx-like now that they had been removed from the room.

Only when their uniformed guard, a square-shaped, crew-cut boy with a dull look returned to ask for folders or copies of testimony, was there a vague clue as to what they really thought and which aspect of the case they were considering.

The plastic hands of the courtroom clock clicked loudly each time the minutes advanced and the hours changed. The day inched along. Four hours, then five. The jury was still out. David and Kristen sent out for lunch, then dinner-bland sandwiches and metallic-tasting coffee. A balding clerk with a distant smile flicked on the overhead lights.

"Damn," David Hetherington said, easing into the seat beside her, "jury's out too long."

"Is it a bad sign?" Kristen asked, trembling.

He shook his head wearily. "Hell, I don't really know. If they come back too soon it's usually cut and dried. Guilty. With a tough case, they usually deliberate a while."

"How long a while?" Kristen said slowly.

He shrugged. "I wish I knew."

She reached out and laid her hand comfortingly on his shoulder for a moment. "You did everything you could and more."

"The question really is," David paused, "was it enough?"

They went home that night without knowing.

And the next.

The jury had been considering the case for two days.

Kristen and David sat together at the defense table. They stopped speaking of the case. They talked of small nothings which filled the time and echoed in the empty space of the courtroom. They were too tired and too worried to talk of more important things. And when she saw Karl, he too was unable to speak of what was really on all their minds.

Then on the late afternoon of the third day, the jury sent back a message to the judge: they were hopelessly deadlocked.

Judge Hanley's response was immediate:

"Will Mr. Young and Mr. Hetherington approach the bench."

The two lawyers walked forward.

"Gentlemen," Judge Hanley said indignantly, "we have been through a long and arduous trial. And I find myself in sympathy with the jury. You Mr. Prosecutor," she looked annoyed, "should have brought Mr. West up on trafficking charges and not on Eight-Forty-Eight Continuing Criminal Enterprise, a charge that has seldom been used and which demands the strongest circumstantial or direct evidence. Evidence I don't think you've presented. That leaves you with a possible tax evasion count to prosecute."

Harrington Young shook his head. "I disagree completely."

"That is your prerogative Mr. Young. However, at this point I'm going to strongly suggest to Mr. Hetherington that he move for a severance of the Continuing Criminal Enterprise charge against Mr. West."

"But Your Honor," David Hetherington said wearily, "that was what I moved for back at the beginning. Now we've been through weeks of this miserable trial and my client ought to be acquitted."

Fern Hanley looked tolerantly at David Hetherington. "I know that's what you hoped for, but what's going to happen here if you don't accept this suggestion is I'll be forced to declare a mistrial. The case will be retried and the results are uncertain. I'm going to declare an hour's recess. Why don't you think over what I've said and return here at two o'clock with your answer."

Kristen and David talked about it over coffee at the diner nearby.

"Damn, it isn't a final victory; it's just a way out!" David said disgustedly.

"The trouble with life David," she said gently "is that, unlike books or games, there are no real endings, just pregnant pauses. Victories must begin somewhere and end somewhere to be recognizable. But courage," she patted his shoulder, "that's another story. Courage means not letting the bastards grind you down. And we've done that much."

"Damn right," David smiled weakly. "I'm so fucking tired, I almost forgot."

"Have you thought of what's best for Karl," she continued.

He laughed self-consciously, "I guess that should be a major consideration. Even with my ego needs unsatisfied."

She nodded.

"Okay," David announced. "Let's get it over with. We'd better meet with Karl first."

"I'm ready." Her amber eyes met his directly.

A short while later David Hetherington stood in front of Judge Hanley, "After serious consultation and reflection, I move for severance of the charges of Continuing Criminal Enterprise against Karl I. West."

Within moments the government had made its lackluster objection and the severance was granted.

David sat at the defense table, his head in his

hands. The bailiff passed him a note. He looked up. "Kristen," he said slowly, "Karl wants to see you. He's in the anteroom over there." He pointed to a small room near the judge's chambers.

Kristen got up and walked toward it. Karl West sat quietly at the conference table. Quieter than she had ever before seen him. His tie was loosened because of the heat and at the vee of his shirt opening his hairy chest, the warmth of which Kristen had once so happily nestled in, was visible. Sitting down next to him, Kristen saw that his striking eyes, which most of the time looked out with so much vitality and electricity, were glazed and dull. The strain and fatigue of the past weeks seemed to weigh heavily upon him.

"Kristen," he looked up and smiled wanly at her as if he saw her from a distance. There were several seconds of silence. "Listen," his voice was troubled. "There's so much I wish had never happened."

"I too," she answered, the sadness and emotions within her springing to the surface.

Suddenly he leaned over and put his arms around her. "Kristen, I'd like to make it all up to you—marry you if you still want me to. We could go back to the ranch—"

"Karl," she interrupted him, gently breaking from his embrace. "Karl, don't." She shook her head and felt the tears sting. "It's over." She paused, rising. "We're both free now."

Softly she closed the door and walked back into the mute courtroom. David stood leaning over the defense table carefully sorting out his papers and methodically putting them into the files he had spread in front of him. He seemed completely preoccupied. His face grim, intense. Never had she seen anyone appear so absolutely self-sufficient and so utterly lonely at the same time. "Need a little help?" she asked, smiling.

Startled, he looked up wearily and smiled back. "More than a little."

And in that moment, as their glances met, she saw her reflection in his eyes and knew that his image was mirrored in her own. Whether it was a vision or a mirage she could never be quite sure. For a time they stood there gazing at each other. And then they finished placing the trial papers in his briefcase. Blinking, they went out of the dim, cloistered courtroom into the light.